A WALK WITH THE DEAD

Recent Titles by Sally Spencer from Severn House

THE BUTCHER BEYOND
DANGEROUS GAMES
THE DARK LADY
DEAD ON CUE
DEATH OF A CAVE DWELLER
DEATH OF AN INNOCENT
A DEATH LEFT HANGING
DEATH WATCH
DYING IN THE DARK
A DYING FALL
THE ENEMY WITHIN
FATAL QUEST
THE GOLDEN MILE TO MURDER
A LONG TIME DEAD
MURDER AT SWANN'S LAKE
THE PARADISE JOB
THE RED HERRING
THE SALTON KILLINGS
SINS OF THE FATHERS
STONE KILLER
THE WITCH MAKER

The Monika Paniatowski Mysteries

THE DEAD HAND OF HISTORY
THE RING OF DEATH
ECHOES OF THE DEAD
BACKLASH
LAMBS TO THE SLAUGHTER
A WALK WITH THE DEAD

A WALK WITH THE DEAD

A Monica Paniatowski Mystery

Sally Spencer

severn
House

This first world edition published 2012
in Great Britain and 2013 in the USA by
SEVERN HOUSE PUBLISHERS LTD of
19 Cedar Road, Sutton, Surrey, England, SM2 5DA.
Trade paperback edition first published
in Great Britain and the USA 2013 by
SEVERN HOUSE PUBLISHERS LTD.

British Library Cataloguing in Publication Data

Spencer, Sally.
  A walk with the dead.
  1. Paniatowski, Monika (Fictitious character)–Fiction.
  2. Police–England–Fiction. 3. Murder–Investigation–
  Fiction. 4. Detective and mystery stories.
  I. Title
  823.9'2-dc23

ISBN-13: 978-0-7278-8242-4 (cased)
ISBN-13: 978-1-84751-465-3 (trade paper)

All Severn House titles are printed on acid-free paper.

Severn House Publishers support the Forest Stewardship Council [FSC], the
leading international forest certification organisation. All our titles that are printed
on Greenpeace-approved FSC-certified paper carry the FSC logo.

Typeset by Palimpsest Book Production Ltd.,
Falkirk, Stirlingshire, Scotland.
Printed and bound in Great Britain by
MPG Books Ltd., Bodmin, Cornwall.

'The past is gone forever, and on the journey through the rest of your life, you can't allow the dead to walk beside you and keep spewing their poison into your ears.'

– DCI Monika Paniatowski

PROLOGUE

14th February 1974

He was a practical man – good with his hands. And though, as he reminded himself now, he had made enough mistakes in his life to fill a book, he was determined that this one final act – the leaving of that life behind him – should go without a hitch.

He grinned, with bitter humour, at the words he had inadvertently chosen.

Without a hitch!

Because, ironically, there *would* be a hitch – a hitch was a vital part of the whole process.

At eight thirty on the dot, he heard the shutter on the peephole in the steel door slide open, and knew that the guard would be peering in at him – as if he were a wild animal or a freak. He *knew* this, but he did not see it, because by then he was lying in his bed, feigning sleep.

The shutter clicked again, and he heard the guard's heavy footfalls receding down the corridor.

He was tempted to get out of bed immediately, but he forced himself to wait, since it was always possible that the guard might return and intervene in what he was about to do. And he didn't want any intervention. This wasn't a cry for help – this was a journey into oblivion.

The footfalls stopped for perhaps twenty seconds, then continued again, as the guard checked on another inmate. Stop, continue, stop, continue, as he made his way to the end of the block, and each time, after a pause, the heavy institutional footsteps were growing fainter.

The prisoner waited until he could hear nothing at all, then sprang from his bed. He had already ripped up his shirt and twisted it into a rope, and now it was just a matter of putting it in place. He moved his bed – taking care to make sure it made no noise – until it was under the pipe which ran along the ceiling.

There should have been no gap between the pipe and the ceiling.

Nor had there been, until he had begun – carefully and meticulously – to chip away at the plaster. It had taken him days, and every time that he made a little progress, he had worried that it would be discovered. But it hadn't been, and now, standing on the bed and stripping away the bits of plaster he had used to disguise his work, he was confronted by a groove that was just wide enough to slide the braided shirt through.

That done, he secured it to the pipe with a hitch knot and made a noose at the other end.

It was unfair that he should *have* to do this, he told himself as he worked. He wasn't to blame for his being here – he wasn't to blame *at all*!

He slid the noose over his head, and stepped off the bed. He began to kick – instinctively – and the thought flashed through his mind that this was, after all, a very foolish thing to do, and he should try to get his feet back on the bed again.

Then his brain, already starved of air, shut down – and he stopped thinking at all.

ONE

Had the early-March wedding taken place the year before, the chances were that Monika Paniatowski would probably not have been invited, for though it was true that she knew the parents of both the bride and groom, they were – at best – cordial acquaintances. But a great deal can change in a year, and the previous June, when her old boss had retired to Spain, Monika had been promoted to the rank of detective chief inspector, which, in a provincial, inward-looking town like Whitebridge, made her a person of some consequence – whether she wished it or not.

And this was a wedding which people of some consequence were expected to attend. The groom, Robert Freeman, was the son of Alderman Freeman, and had already made his own mark as a promising young doctor. The bride, Vanessa Freeman (née Clough), managed the soft-furnishings floor of the town's biggest department store, and *her* father was the managing director of one of the local breweries. Add to all that the fact that the reception was being held in the banqueting hall of the Royal Victoria – Whitebridge's poshest hotel – and it was as plain as could be that accepting the invitation was pretty much *de rigueur*.

Even so, Paniatowski had tried to talk her way out of it, and might have succeeded if the *big* boss had not made it perfectly plain that he fully expected her to attend.

Her fate – as far as this wedding was concerned – had been sealed two weeks earlier, in the chief constable's office.

'I've just received an invitation to Robert Freeman's wedding,' George Baxter had said, as he puffed away at his pipe, and filled the area around his large head with light blue smoke. 'It's on the ninth of March.'

'I know. I've been invited too, sir,' Paniatowski had told him. 'It all seems rather rushed, doesn't it?'

'Yes, but I suspect there are good reasons for that,' the chief constable said. He grinned. 'Doctors are very good at handing out advice on how to use contraception responsibly, but they don't necessarily always follow that advice themselves.'

'Ah!' Paniatowski had said. She paused for a moment. 'I think I'll find some excuse for crying off. I don't really know the happy young couple, and weddings can be such a bore.'

'Alderman Freeman has always been very helpful to – and supportive of – the work of the Mid Lancs police,' said the chief constable, as if he hadn't heard her. 'One of us should certainly be there to show our support for him.'

'Well, if you're going . . .'

'I'd be more than willing to go to the wedding if I could, but I can't – which means, of course, that you positively *must* attend.'

Paniatowski had looked at her former lover through suspicious eyes. She both admired and respected Baxter as a policeman, but there were times when (perhaps because of their joint past history) she couldn't help seeing the big ginger-haired man with a yard-brush moustache as no more than a gigantic teddy bear – and it was the teddy bear she was seeing now.

'*Can't* go, or don't *want* to go, sir?' she asked innocently.

'Can't go, Chief Inspector – as you'd know yourself if you ever bothered to read my memos,' the teddy bear said firmly. 'The Home Office wants me to conduct an inquiry over in Yorkshire, starting on the eleventh of March.'

'How convenient for you, sir,' Paniatowski said, not quite under her breath. 'What kind of inquiry will you be conducting?'

'You really *should* read the memos, you know. I'll be investigating the death of one Jeremy Templar, who hanged himself in his cell at HM Dunston Prison last month.'

'And it will be a *full-scale* inquiry, will it?' Paniatowski asked, still not sure whether or not her boss was attempting to pull a fast one over his attending the wedding.

'It depends what you mean by full-scale,' Baxter replied. 'On the one hand, I'll be the only one involved, but on the other, I'll be expected to stay there until I'm satisfied I can write a fair and balanced report.'

'But why do they even need to bring in someone from outside?' Paniatowski persisted.

'I suppose it's because there are special circumstances attached to the suicide. Templar was attacked by the other prisoners several times before he took his own life. I haven't got all the details at my fingertips, but I believe he was scalded in the dining room, beaten up in the showers, and stabbed in the leg while he was exercising in the yard.'

'I assume he was a sex offender, then,' Paniatowski said.

'That's right,' Baxter agreed. 'In most prisons, as you probably know, there's some status attached to being an armed robber – and even more to being a murderer – but if you're inside for a sex offence, then God help you, because a lot of the cons have got kids of their own.'

'Hang about,' said Paniatowski, who'd been doing some rapid calculations, 'you said your inquiry starts on the eleventh, didn't you?'

'Yes.'

'Well, the wedding's on the ninth, so there's really no reason that you can't attend it.'

'I'll need the weekend to travel over to Yorkshire and settle in,' Baxter said, a little uncomfortably.

'Yes, I can quite see how you'll need time to "settle in",' Paniatowski agreed, 'because Yorkshire's completely unfamiliar territory to you, isn't it?' She paused. 'Well, not *completely* unfamiliar,' she amended, 'because you did spend over *twenty years* working for the Yorkshire Constabulary.'

'You're never *quite* insubordinate, are you, Monika?' Baxter asked.

'No, sir,' Paniatowski agreed sweetly. 'Never *quite*.'

And so it had been agreed – or, at least, settled – that she would go to the wedding, as a representative of the Mid Lancs Police, but right up until the last minute, she'd been hoping that work – in the form of a murder – would get in the way of it. Not that she wanted anyone to be murdered, she would mentally add whenever the thought came into her mind, but there would *be* a murder eventually – that was inevitable – and it would suit her if it happened on the morning of the wedding, rather than a couple of days after it.

But there had been no murder, and so here she was – dressed in an appropriate wedding outfit – at the nuptials of two perfectly nice people who she was not particularly interested in.

Still, she told herself as she sipped on her Polish vodka (it had been thoughtful of them, by the way, to have ordered that vodka in especially for her) the whole ritual could have been worse. The church service had been as short as it decently could be, the best man's speech had not been as buttock-clenchingly embarrassing as it might easily have been, the dancing was about to begin, and soon she would be able to slip inconspicuously away.

'You look like you're waiting for a chance to make a bolt for the door,' said a voice.

Paniatowski jumped slightly, startled by the fact that the speaker had found it so easy to read her mind – or, at least, her body language.

'Don't worry, I won't sneak on you to the alderman – because I'm planning on making a similar escape myself,' the voice continued.

The woman responsible for these remarks was probably in her middle twenties, Paniatowski guessed. She had brown curly hair, intelligent green eyes, a nose with a slight – though attractive – tilt, and a wide generous mouth which was now set in a good-natured smile.

'How dare you even suggest that I'm planning to leave soon?' Paniatowski asked, grinning back at her. 'I fully intend to stick with this reception until the bloody bitter end.'

'Liar,' the other woman said. She held out her hand. 'I'm Liz Duffy.'

The chief inspector took the hand. 'Monika Paniatowski,' she said. 'So what makes you one of the privileged few invited to attend the joining together of these two wholesome young people?'

'I'm a quack,' Liz said. 'A junior partner – a *very* junior partner – at the practice where Robert also works. And you?'

Paniatowski's grin widened. 'I'm a civic dignitary.'

'Ah! And what part of civic society are you dignified in?'

'I'm a—'

Liz held up her hand to stop Paniatowski speaking. 'Don't tell me – it'll be much more fun for me to guess. Are you some sort of big wheel in social services department?'

'No.'

'Of course you're not. You're nowhere near self-righteous enough to be working there. Are you a mandarin in the town-planning department, then? No, you don't have the necessary arrogance.' Liz clicked her fingers. 'I've got it – you're a member of the constabulary. I'm right, aren't I?'

'Yes, I'm a bobby,' Paniatowski admitted.

'And since you're important enough to have been invited to this posh do, you must be at least a chief inspector,' Liz speculated.

Paniatowski laughed. 'Right again,' she agreed.

'Which makes you living proof that meritocracy exists – even in darkest Lancashire,' Liz said. 'Though I don't suppose you got where you are now without *something* of a struggle.' She paused. 'What branch are you in?'

'CID.'

'Then we may end up working together, because I've just been appointed assistant to Dr Taylor, the police surgeon.'

'The *acting* police surgeon,' Paniatowski said, more sharply than she'd intended, because although she liked Dr Taylor, she missed her old friend Dr Shastri, who was on an extended sabbatical in India.

'So since I've only been in the area for a while – and you seem positively crammed with local knowledge – why don't you fill me in on who's here?' Liz suggested.

Paniatowski gave her a quick rundown on the assembled guests – the local solicitors and businessmen, the owners of fancy hairdressing salons and assistant town clerks . . .

'So, as you'll appreciate, the *crème de la crème* of Whitebridge society are all gathered together,' she concluded.

'Or perhaps, since this *is* Whitebridge, it might be more accurate to call them the top of the milk?' Liz suggested.

Paniatowski laughed again. She really did like this young doctor, she thought, and talking to Liz was certainly helping to while away the time before she could decently exit.

'Who's the sad-looking girl in the corner?' Liz asked.

Paniatowski followed the direction of her eyes. The girl was indeed in the corner – as far away from the festivities as it was possible to be. She was around thirteen or fourteen, Paniatowski guessed, which made her about as old as her own adopted daughter, Louisa. And Liz was right – she looked thoroughly miserable.

Paniatowski felt a sudden shiver run through her. Ever since the day two months earlier when Louisa had been kidnapped and missing for a few hours, Monika had not been able to look at a girl of her daughter's age without bringing the terrifying experience vividly into the forefront of her mind.

And that was just plain stupid, she told herself every time it happened, because no real harm had been done, and Louisa seemed to have quite got over it.

But even so . . .

'Are you all right?' she heard Liz's voice ask.

'I'm fine,' Paniatowski said. 'I don't know the girl. Why don't we talk about someone else?'

TWO

Jill Harris was sitting in the corner of the banqueting room of the Royal Victoria, feeling thoroughly miserable and angry – though she was not quite sure which of the emotions had the upper hand.

She hated the flounced pink dress her mother had forced her to wear for the occasion.

She hated the fact that being at this stupid wedding meant she was missing out on a Very Important Date.

And worst of all, it broke her heart to see her lovely Auntie Vanessa being dragged through this travesty of a wedding.

Nor were things about to get any better, she realized, as she saw her mother making a beeline for her.

'What's the matter with you *now*?' Mary Harris asked, in a tone which was part concerned, part accusatory. 'Why are you over here in the corner, love, all by yourself?'

'I just felt like being on my own for a bit,' Jill said.

'People will be looking at you,' her mother informed her. 'People will be wondering.'

And that was the trouble with her mum, Jill thought – she spent most of her life worrying about what other people would think.

'These curtains are getting a bit shabby. We'd better buy some new ones, before the neighbours notice.'

'You can't go out dressed like that, Jill. Everybody will think I'm not looking after you properly.'

'Did you hear what I said?' Mary Harris asked sharply.

'Let them wonder,' Jill said.

Mary clicked her tongue disapprovingly. 'You can't go doing that,' she said. 'Look, the bride and groom are having the first dance.'

And so they were, Jill saw. The Mac Williams Quartet, who had been setting up their instruments for the previous fifteen minutes, had finally got their act together, and were playing a sickly sweet tune, to which Vanessa and Robert were gliding smoothly across the floor.

'Don't they look lovely?' Mary asked.

'*She* does,' Jill said, with emphasis.

The dance finished, and, to the sound of thunderous applause, the happy couple returned to their seats at the top table and disappeared behind the three-tiered wedding cake.

Now, as the band struck up its second song, a number of other couples were drifting onto the floor.

'Do you know what would be nice?' Mary asked.

Jill said nothing.

'I asked you if you knew what would be nice!' Mary said.

'How can I?' Jill demanded. 'I'm not a mind reader, Mum – I leave that sort of thing to you.'

'I'm no mind reader – I just know what's right and proper,' Mary Harris said. 'And what would be right and proper at this moment would be you going over to your Uncle Robert and asking him for a dance.'

'I don't have an Uncle Robert,' Jill said stubbornly.

'Yes, you do,' her mother persisted. 'Since half-past eleven this morning, that man at the top table has been your uncle.'

'No, he hasn't!' a voice screamed in Jill's head.

He could *never* be her Uncle Robert, whatever the law and the church said. She positively refused to acknowledge that this man – this *thief* – could ever be part of her family.

And he *was* a thief – he had stolen her lovely Auntie Vanessa right away from her.

Because the simple fact was that before he had appeared on the scene, everything had been going beautifully. Auntie Vanessa had been more like an older sister than an aunt, and looking back on the time they'd spent together, it seemed like a golden age.

She had worshipped Vanessa. She had trusted her. She had even been going to tell Vanessa her Big Secret, because she had known that her auntie would be both sympathetic and supportive.

But she couldn't tell her that secret now.

Not after she had been stolen away.

'If you don't ask him to dance, people will wonder what's the matter with you,' Mary Harris said.

'If *he* wants to dance with *me*, then why doesn't he come across and ask me?' Jill countered.

'You know he won't do that – and you also know why,' Mary said, with an edge to her voice.

'Do I?'

'Yes, you damn well do. He won't ask you because he doesn't know what you'll say. And after the way you've treated him all the while he's been courting your Auntie Vanessa, who can blame him for being cautious?'

'Well, if he won't ask me, and I won't ask him . . .' Jill began.

'It's up to you to make the first move,' Mary interrupted.

'Why is it up to me?'

'Because he's always been perfectly nice to you, and you've always been perfectly horrid to him in return. So if anybody's going to hold out the olive branch, it should be you.'

'And if I don't?' Jill asked.

'If you don't, he'll want nothing more to do with you.'

'Good.'

'And if he doesn't want anything to do with you, Vanessa won't have much to do with you, either.'

'That's not true!' Jill said, agonizingly.

But deep down inside her, she knew it was. Deep down inside, she recognized that Vanessa's first loyalty – for some perverse, twisted reason – now lay with her new husband.

'Go on – ask your Uncle Robert for a dance,' said her mother, sensing that she was faltering.

Jill glanced down at the watch which Vanessa had given her for her twelfth birthday, and realized that, for the moment, at least, she was in a strong negotiating position, and that if she played her cards right, she might just make her Very Important Date after all.

'If I dance with him, can I go home?' she asked.

'Of course you can. We'll all be going home in two or three hours' time,' her mother said, mystified.

'I mean, can I go home straight after the dance?'

'You most certainly can not. Whatever will people think?'

'You can tell them I wasn't feeling well.'

'Then they'll expect me to go home with you and look after you, won't they? And I want to stay.'

'Say Dad's picking me up.'

'Everybody knows that the only reason your dad's not at the wedding is that he's working in Saudi Arabia.'

'Then tell everybody I'm being picked up by a friend of yours.'

'What friend?' Mary Harris asked.

'I don't know,' Jill said, exasperatedly. 'Just invent somebody.'

'And what if people find out?'

Jill sighed. 'Other people aren't half as interested in what we get up to as you seem to think, Mum.'

Mary wavered. 'If I tell a white lie for you, will you promise me you'll be very nice when you're dancing with your Uncle Robert?' she asked.

'I promise you I'll be very nice when I'm dancing with my Uncle Robert,' Jill said earnestly, though she very nearly choked on the penultimate word.

'All right,' her mother agreed reluctantly. 'But I'll be watching you while you're dancing.'

'I'll be the perfect picture of a loving niece,' Jill said.

'But I'll hate it,' she added silently. 'I'll loathe every minute of it.'

Chief Constable George Baxter was in the marital bedroom, packing his small suitcase with the same meticulous attention to detail that he gave to every task which came his way.

Watching him from the fluffy stool at her dressing table, Jo Baxter, his wife, said, 'I thought you told me that you'd be leaving earlier than this.'

'That's what I intended, but I had some paperwork to catch up on at the office,' Baxter replied, folding a pair of underpants and sliding them neatly into a corner of the suitcase.

'So, as it turns out, we could both have gone to Vanessa Clough's wedding after all,' Jo said.

'You're not listening, love – I'm not running late because I've wasted time, I'm running late because I had paperwork that needed doing,' Baxter replied. 'Anyway, you hardly know either the Freemans or Cloughs, so you wouldn't have enjoyed the thing at all, and, speaking for myself, I would have been bored out of my socks.'

'Will there be somebody else at the wedding to represent the police?' Jo asked.

'Yes, there'll be someone there,' Baxter said.

'Who?' asked Jo, sensing he didn't want to tell her who that 'someone' would be.

'A suitably high-ranking officer,' Baxter said, stalling.

'Who?' Jo repeated.

Baxter sighed. 'DCI Paniatowski,' he admitted.

Jo shivered.

'So why were you being so evasive about it?' she asked, with a slight tremble to her voice.

'I'm sorry, love, I should have told you right off that it was DCI Paniatowski, but every time I mention her name, you go weird on me,' Baxter said.

That was true enough, Jo agreed silently. For though she knew her husband's relationship with Monika Paniatowski had been over for some time before she had met him herself, even the mention of Paniatowski's name was sometimes enough to start her feeling insecure.

'Were you the one who wangled her the invitation?' she heard herself ask accusingly.

Baxter sighed. 'No, it wasn't me. I had nothing to do with it.'

'Then why was she invited? Why didn't they invite someone of a higher rank – like Chief Superintendent Potter?'

'Monika knows both families. Maybe that was the reason.'

'*How* well does she know them?'

'I don't know,' Baxter admitted wearily.

'Does she know them better than Tom Potter knows them?'

'Probably not – but Monika's a celebrity, and Tom isn't.'

'A celebrity,' Jo repeated, with disgust.

'That's what she is, whether you like it or not,' Baxter said. 'Since she's taken over from Charlie Woodend, she's solved several murders which were such big news that they were splashed all over the front pages of the papers.'

'*She's* solved them,' Jo said bitterly. 'You don't mention the rest of her team, I notice – it's all down to clever little Monika.'

'Of course it's not, but that's how it's perceived by the general public, and that's why there's a certain cachet to having her at your function. She doesn't like it – I know that for a fact – but she's stuck with it.'

'I'll just *bet* she doesn't like it,' Jo said.

'Perhaps you can see now why I was reluctant to mention her name,' Baxter said. 'The way you react to it, it almost seems as if you think we're having an affair.'

'Having a *second* affair,' Jo corrected him.

'All right, having a second affair,' Baxter conceded. 'Well, we're not.'

'I know you're not.'

And so she did. George was too decent and honourable a man to attempt to reignite the relationship, even if Monika were to prove willing.

'I love you,' Baxter said.

She was sure of that, too. Yet there were times, when they had made love and lay side by side in bed, that she couldn't help feeling that he would rather it was Paniatowski who was beside him.

'Will you be able to slip back home for a few hours, sometime in the week?' she asked.

'I doubt it,' Baxter replied. 'The thing is, love, I never wanted to be given this inquiry in the first place, and the sooner it's over and done with, the sooner I can get back here.'

'Back to running your precious police force,' Jo said – and instantly wished she hadn't.

Baxter looked hurt. 'Back to *you*,' he said.

'I knew that's what you meant, really,' Jo said, smiling in an effort to take the sting out of her previous words.

Baxter closed his case and clicked the fasteners shut.

'Right, I'll be off, then,' he said.

He crossed the bedroom, bent down, and gave Jo a kiss.

It had been a nice kiss, she thought, as she listened to him walk down the stairs – a warm kiss, a loving kiss. But she wondered if there would have been more passion behind it if the person he'd kissed had been Monika Paniatowski.

Jill Harris walked around the far side of the top table and came to a halt next to Robert Freeman's chair. Robert, engaged in conversation with one of the other guests, did not notice her at first, but when he did become of aware of her, he turned and said, 'Is there something I can do for you, Jill?'

He sounded a bit worried, she thought. Maybe he was afraid she would make a scene. Well, it wouldn't be the first time that had happened.

'Would you like to dance with me?' she asked.

Though her new uncle heard the words, he seemed unable to register the meaning.

'What did you say?' he asked.

'A dance. Would you like to dance with me?'

A smile slowly spread across Robert's face. It was a smile of relief, but also of pleasure.

'I'd be more than honoured to dance with you,' he said, standing up and taking her hand.

She might quite get to like this man if he wasn't married to her auntie, Jill thought. But he *was* married to her auntie – and that was unforgivable.

Mac Williams, the leader and saxophone player of the Mac Williams Quartet, stepped up to the microphone.

'It's been both a great pleasure and a great honour for us to play at Vanessa and Robert's wedding,' he said, 'and in anticipation of a rebooking – for their silver wedding celebration – we'd like to give you our own special version of the "Anniversary Waltz".'

Oh God! Paniatowski thought. Haven't I endured enough saccharine for one day?

She looked around for the parents of either the bride or groom, and could see neither pair.

It didn't really matter, she told herself – she would write them both a note apologizing for having to leave without saying goodbye, and thanking them for inviting her to this wonderful wedding.

Sticking close to the walls – to make her exit as discreet as possible – she was already out of the door when the first few chords of the 'Anniversary Waltz' fought their way clear of Mac Williams' golden saxophone.

'Do you know how to waltz?' Robert asked Jill, as he led her over to the centre of the dance floor.

'I'm not sure,' the girl admitted.

'It's not so difficult,' Robert assured her. 'Take my right hand in your left, and put your left hand on my shoulder. Then look down at what I'm doing with my feet, and just do the same yourself, and by the time the song's over, you'll be dancing like a real expert.'

It was all going wrong, Jill thought. He was being much too nice.

They started to dance. Jill was clumsy, but not as clumsy as she might have been, and was beginning to quite enjoy it. Then, as Robert twirled her around, she saw her Auntie Vanessa watching them – an indulgent smile on her face – and something snapped inside.

Jill pressed up tighter against Robert. She was not sure why she was doing it. Perhaps it was to embarrass him. Perhaps it was to hurt the aunt who had betrayed her. Maybe, even, she hoped to stir up trouble between the bride and groom. But whatever her reasons, she moved in on him, her legs touching his, her thin bosom pressed heavily against his lower chest.

'Steady on, little girl,' Robert said jocularly. 'If you're as close to me as that, you'll not be able to see my feet.'

'I'm not a little girl,' Jill said fiercely.

'Of course you're not,' Robert agreed hastily. 'You're a young lady. But I still think you're dancing far too close for both our comfort.'

She was suddenly feeling both hot and ashamed. When she pulled her hand out of his and stepped backwards, she encountered no resistance.

'I'm not feeling very well at all,' she mumbled. 'I need to sit down.'

'Yes, I think that would be a good idea,' said Robert, who was still not entirely clear about what had just happened.

Paniatowski paused to light a cigarette on the steps of the Royal Victoria Hotel, and was surprised to discover that she was feeling guilty about the fact that she had not gone over and talked to the unhappy girl in the pink flounced dress.

'You're an idiot,' she told herself.

Why should she have gone and talked to the girl? She wasn't family. She didn't even know the kid. There must have been at least twenty or thirty people in that banqueting room who were better qualified to deal with the child's misery. And anyway, kids weren't like adults – what looked to them like the end of the world one moment could seem of little consequence a few minutes later.

So she was in the clear, she decided – she absolved herself of all failings, and would banish the sad girl completely from her mind.

And so she did.

But later – when she saw Jill Harris for a second time – all these thoughts would come flooding back to her.

THREE

The village of Dunston was a medium-sized hamlet of stone-built cottages, on the main road from Pickering to Whitby. It had one pub, a post office, a couple of shops, and boasted that it was in the heart of the North Yorkshire Moors. What it did *not* boast about was its penal institution, and the side road which led to HM Prison Dunston was so badly signposted that the first time Baxter had driven through the village, he had missed the turning completely.

He was more successful on his second attempt, and was soon travelling along a narrow asphalt road, with the wild moors on either side of him.

Had any modern government contemplated building a prison in such a beauty spot, he thought as he drove along, there would have been a roar of anger from local conservationists which would have rattled the windows of the Houses of Parliament, two hundred miles away. But the prison had been built in the 1860s, when people had known their God-given place in society – 'the rich man in his castle, the poor man at his gate' – and if the Queen wanted to put a prison in the middle of unspoiled nature, well, they probably supposed that it was *her* unspoiled nature, and nothing to do with them at all.

There was a slight rise in the road, and once he was over it, he had a view of the prison in all its stark majesty.

He could see now that the road did not go beyond the jail, but stopped at its imposing large gates.

'The end of the road,' he mused – and wondered whimsically how many prisoners, about to begin long sentences, had seen the bitter irony of that.

He pulled up at the gatehouse, held his warrant card out of the window, and smiled.

'Chief Constable George Baxter,' he said to the guard. 'I have an appointment to see the governor.'

'He's expecting you,' the guard replied, stony faced.

'Nobody loves an inspector,' Baxter mused, as the gates began to open, and he slowly edged his car forward.

*   *   *

Louisa, who had been building up her cash reserves for some time, had finally decided to build on both Mayfair and Park Lane.

'Are you sure you want to do that, darling?' Paniatowski asked sweetly. 'It is rather putting all your eggs in one basket, and if you should happen to land on either Whitechapel or the Old Kent Road . . .'

'I'll have plenty of cash to pay the rent,' interrupted her daughter, waving a handful of Monopoly money at her, 'whereas if you land on either of my properties, you'll be wiped out. However, since you *are* my dear old mum, I'm willing to offer you a deal.'

Dear old mum! Paniatowski thought. Good God!

But she was edging towards forty, and she supposed that – in Louisa's terms – that *did* make her old.

'What kind of deal are you offering?' she asked, suspiciously.

'Pay me five hundred pounds now, and if you land on Park Lane, I'll let you off the rent,' Louisa told her.

'And what if I land on Mayfair?'

'Insuring against that will cost you a thousand.'

Paniatowski shook her head slowly, in mock disgust. 'I don't know how I ever came to raise such an avaricious girl,' she said. 'Have you absolutely *no* shame, Louisa?'

'What's your answer – yes or no?' her shameless daughter demanded.

Could she ever be happier than this? Paniatowski wondered.

Was anything better than playing a viciously cut-throat game on Saturday night, with the daughter she loved?

'I'm still waiting,' Louisa reminded her.

'Hang your offers, you bloated capitalist,' Paniatowski said. 'I'll take my chances.'

'Then roll the dice,' Louisa suggested.

The phone rang in the hallway.

'I'll have to answer that,' Paniatowski said.

'Go ahead, Mum,' her daughter agreed. 'But it'll be a reprieve, rather than a rescue.'

The caller was a woman.

'My name's Mary Harris,' she said. 'You don't know me, but I saw you at my sister's wedding reception this afternoon.'

'Yes?' Paniatowski replied, puzzled as to what might come next.

'Did you happen to notice my daughter, Jill? She was sitting in the corner, on her own.'

'Pink flounced dress?' Paniatowski asked.

'That's right. The thing is, you see, she's gone missing.'

Paniatowski felt her stomach turn over.

'What do you mean, Mrs Harris – missing?'

'Well, she left the reception a couple of hours before I did. I know I shouldn't have let her go on her own, but it was still light outside, and we only live walking distance from the Royal Vic, so I didn't see that any harm could come to her.'

'But now you think you might have been wrong about that?' Paniatowski asked cautiously.

'I don't know,' Mary Harris said, obviously almost in tears.

'Take a deep breath, and tell me exactly what's made you so worried,' Paniatowski continued.

There was the sound of air being gulped in at the other end of the line, then Mrs Harris said, 'She wasn't here when I got home.'

'She might just have gone out to see some of her friends,' Paniatowski suggested.

'Not in her Miss Selfridge top,' the other woman moaned.

'What do you mean?'

'She bought this top from Miss Selfridge's. She saved up for it, and it's her pride and joy.'

'She looked pretty miserable at the reception, so she probably put it on to cheer herself up.'

'She wouldn't do that, would she? Not when our Vanessa wasn't there to see it!' Mary Harris said exasperatedly.

'I don't think I'm quite following you.'

'She only wears it when she goes out with her Auntie Vanessa, but Vanessa's not there to see it – she's already set off on her honeymoon.'

'Come on, Mum, I'm getting bored waiting for you,' Louisa called from the living room.

Paniatowski covered the phone mouthpiece. 'Won't be a minute, love,' she promised.

Then, removing her hand again, she said, 'If you're worried, you should report all this to your local police station, Mrs Harris.'

'I've already done that. The sergeant I spoke to told me it's far too early to report her as missing, and that I should wait until after her bedtime before calling again.'

'And that is probably the best thing to do.'

'But it'll be too late by then,' Mrs Harris sobbed. 'I just know

that it will be too late. So if you could just come round . . . if you
could see for yourself . . .'

Paniatowski sighed. 'You'd better give me the address,' she said.

Louisa looked up expectantly when Monika returned to the living
room, then, reading the expression on her mother's face, her own
face flooded with disappointment.

'You have to go out,' she said – and it was more of a statement
than a question.

'I'm sorry, love,' Paniatowski said contritely. 'A girl's gone missing.'

'Like I did,' Louisa said.

'Like you did,' Paniatowski agreed.

'But I was back home again – safe and sound – within a couple
of hours,' Louisa pointed out.

'I know you were, but it doesn't always work out like that,'
Paniatowski told her.

'Couldn't somebody else deal with it?' Louisa asked hopefully.

'No, love, it has to be me,' Paniatowski said.

Because nobody else would be *prepared* to deal with it after the
girl had been gone for such a short time, she thought – nobody else
would be willing to give up the comfort of their home on a Saturday
night for what was probably a wild goose chase. But she *had* to
go, because she knew exactly how Mrs Harris must be feeling – and
no one should ever have to feel like that.

And besides, she admitted reluctantly, if she'd talked to the girl
at the wedding reception, this might never have happened.

'Call up some of your mates, and ask them if they'd like to come
round,' she suggested to her daughter. 'You can take anything you
want from the fridge, and if you've pigged out and eaten all the ice
cream, I promise I won't say a word when I get back.'

'All my friends will have made their plans for the evening by
now,' Louisa said despondently.

Of course they would have, Paniatowski agreed silently.

'Then I'll ring your Uncle Colin, and ask him to drop round,'
she said, with a hint of desperation in her voice.

'He'll already be out chasing girls,' Louisa told her.

Paniatowski smiled. 'You don't miss much, do you?' she asked.

Because her daughter was quite right – DI Colin Beresford, after
years of seemingly showing no interest in women, had suddenly,
for no apparent reason, become what in Whitebridge they called 'a
bit of a lad'.

Louisa's eyes narrowed. 'This isn't an *official* investigation, is it, Mum?' she asked.

'What makes you say that?' Paniatowski wondered.

'I couldn't hear what you were saying on the phone, but I could hear the *way* you said it, and it didn't sound to me like you were talking to one of your bobbies. So my guess is that you were speaking to the mother of this girl.'

She *really* didn't miss much, Paniatowski thought.

'So if it's not an official investigation, there's no reason why I can't tag along with you,' Louisa added.

'That's out of the question,' Paniatowski said automatically.

'*Why* is it out of the question?'

'It would probably upset you.'

'Because the mother will be upset?'

'Yes.'

'Do you think I've never seen anybody upset before? Do you think I've not noticed how upset *you* are, when you're investigating some horrible murder.'

'That's not the same,' Paniatowski said.

'No, not *exactly* the same,' Louisa conceded. 'But I really want to see how you work, Mum.'

'And why is that?'

'Because it'll make it easier for me to accept it when you don't come home at night.'

'I've offered to get a transfer if you wanted me to,' Paniatowski said defensively.

'I *don't* want you to get a transfer. You love your job, and I'm proud of you for doing it – I just want a better idea of what it's like.'

Her daughter was growing up, and the older she got, the harder it would be to shield her completely from the work she did, Paniatowski thought. So maybe it wouldn't be such a bad idea to have her along on the edges of an investigation which, in all probability, would have a happy outcome.

'If you start to get upset, you must tell me, and we'll leave immediately,' she said sternly.

Louisa grinned. 'I'll just go to the loo, then I'll be ready,' she said, rushing towards the stairs.

Paniatowski stepped into the hallway to get her coat, and while she was there, she couldn't resist the temptation to look in the hall mirror in order to discover just how much of a 'dear old mum' she'd actually become.

The face that looked back at her was not half bad, she decided. The blonde hair was still naturally wavy, and if there were any white hairs, they didn't actually show yet. The eyes were still blue and lively and interested. The central European nose – which she had once desperately wished was smaller – had not suddenly shrunk down to standard Whitebridge size, but she had got used to it over the years, and anyway, she knew from the glances she got that most men found it attractive. Her lips were still full, her chin was still firm . . .

'Don't be so vain, Mum,' Louisa called, from halfway down the stairs.

'It's nothing to do with vanity – I'm conducting a facial assessment,' Paniatowski replied.

'Yeah, right,' Louisa said sceptically.

Paniatowski turned – *almost* reluctantly – away from the mirror.

Pulling men would still be no problem for her, if that was what she wanted, she told herself. But she didn't want to pull any man at that moment, and – slightly worryingly – she was not sure she would ever want to pull one again.

There were three of them at this initial meeting – the governor, the chief officer and Baxter. The governor was sitting behind his desk. Baxter and the chief officer were in armchairs which were positioned so that they could see both each other and the man in charge of the prison.

Baxter made a quick assessment of the governor, whose name was Wilton. He was probably in his late fifties, the chief constable guessed. He had an indecisive chin, and had tried – unsuccessfully – to camouflage his bald spot by brushing the longer strands of his thinning grey hair over it. And it was obvious that though he felt an obligation to stick to his chosen career path in the prison service, he would actually have been much happier just pottering about in his back garden.

The governor's chief officer – a man called Jeffries – was a different case entirely. He was around forty and unashamedly bald. He had sharp, intelligent eyes and a hard body. When he'd shaken hands with Baxter, the shake had been perhaps a little firmer than it needed to be, but that – the chief constable thought – was because he was making a point.

'We are, of course, willing to give your investigation our full cooperation, Chief Constable,' the governor said, 'and if we are in any way at fault over what happened, I'd be most grateful if you'd draw our attention to it.'

If you're in any way at fault for what happened, then you're already in deep shit, Baxter thought.

But aloud, all he said was, 'I'd like to ask a few preliminary questions, just so I can get things clear in my mind.'

'Please feel free to do so,' the governor invited.

'Let's start with the fact that Templar was *able* to hang himself,' Baxter suggested. 'Couldn't the pipe which ran across his cell have been boxed in, thus making that impossible?'

The governor glanced at his chief officer for guidance.

'Yes, the pipe could have been boxed in,' Jeffries said.

'Then why wasn't it?'

'I think it comes down to the question of money, doesn't it, sir?' Jeffries asked the governor.

'Exactly,' Wilton agreed gratefully. 'We simply don't have the funds to do most of the things we'd like to do. The toilet block is a disgrace and the kitchen facilities are positively medieval, but whenever we put in a request for more money, we're told there's none available.'

Baxter nodded his head, understandingly. 'Yes, I know what that's like – we have similar problems in the Mid Lancs Constabulary,' he said. 'Second question – what system do you use for monitoring the prisoners' mental state?'

'I'm not sure I know what you mean,' the governor confessed.

'I assume that Templar was exhibiting signs of depression before he hanged himself. Were you made aware of that, Mr Wilton, and if you were, what action did you take?'

Wilton glanced across at his chief officer again.

'Most of the men in here don't like being in prison, so most of them are depressed for some of the time,' Jeffries said. 'I dare say most of them even feel suicidal once in a while. Those of us on the other side of the bars sometimes feel that way, too. But if every time one of the cons was feeling a bit down in the mouth we reported the fact to the governor, he'd have no time to carry out any of his pressing and important duties. And let's be honest – even though they might *think* about it, most cons *don't* hang themselves, do they?'

'No,' Baxter agreed, 'but Jeremy Templar did.'

'That was regrettable,' the governor said.

The conversation was all going a little too cosily, Baxter decided. It was time to stir up the murky waters, and see what bobbed to the surface.

'Was Templar alone in his cell when he topped himself?' he asked.

'Yes.'

'And why was that? Was it because of the nature of his crime?'

'That was indeed the reason,' the governor said. 'The other prisoners hate sex offenders, and if we'd put him in a cell with any of them, we couldn't have guaranteed his safety.'

'We couldn't have guaranteed his safety,' Baxter repeated. 'It seems to me that in terms of guaranteeing his safety *in general*, you did a pretty poor job.'

'Now, look here—' the governor said, flushing.

'How many times was he attacked?' Baxter interrupted. 'Was it three? Or was it four?'

'It was four,' said Chief Officer Jeffries, who, unlike his boss, still seemed to be completely in control of himself.

'It's all very well for people like you to come in from the outside and start criticizing us,' the governor said, turning almost scarlet now, 'but without a completely separate wing for sex offenders – *which we don't have* – there's only so much we can do.'

'You could, at least, have punished Templar's attackers,' Baxter said. 'Have you?'

Chief Officer Jefferies' eyes flashed the governor a warning that he should calm down before he said any more, but the governor, like all weak men who find themselves trapped in a corner, chose to ignore it.

'No, we haven't punished them,' Wilton said, 'because we have no idea who they are.'

'Then shouldn't you have made it your business to find out?' Baxter asked. 'I shouldn't imagine that would be too hard.'

'Do you have any idea of how a prison actually works, Chief Constable?' the governor demanded. 'Do you really think that the staff are in total control for twenty-four hours a day?'

'I certainly think they're *paid* to be in total control for twenty-four hours a day,' Baxter said.

'We keep a large number of convicted men – many of whom are

violent – within these walls while they serve out their sentences,' the governor explained. 'In general, we manage to curb most of their worst excesses, but we can't watch them all the time, and when we are not watching them, they play by their own rules. That's how it's been since the very first prison was opened centuries ago – and that's how it will *always* be.'

'You must get heartily sick of people like me coming here and acting as if they know everything already – when in fact there are holes in their knowledge you could drive a double-decker bus through,' Baxter said, suddenly shifting gear again. 'I'd like to apologize for being so arrogant, and I promise you that I'll be much more circumspect from now on.'

'That's quite all right,' the governor said, taking out his handkerchief and mopping his brow. 'We all make mistakes once in a while.'

The governor believed in the volte-face because he *wanted* to believe in it, Baxter thought, but it was plain from the expression on the chief officer's face that Jeffries wasn't fooled at all.

Mrs Harris must have been watching from the lounge window for Paniatowski's arrival, and she flung the front door open before the chief inspector had even had time to ring the bell.

'It was very good of you to come,' she babbled. 'I don't know what I'd have done if . . .' She paused, noticing Louisa standing there. 'Is she . . .?'

'She's my daughter,' Paniatowski said. 'If you don't want her to come into the house, she can stay in the car.'

Being offered a choice in the matter seemed only to add to Mrs Harris' confusion.

'I don't know what to . . .' she began. 'I mean, it'd be a bit odd – and what will the neighbours think if they see your daughter sitting all by herself in the car, while you're in the house.' She pulled herself up sharply. 'What's the matter with me? How can I still be worrying about the neighbours when my Jill is missing?' She brushed a strand of hair out of her eyes. 'Come inside, the both of you.'

She led them into a lounge, which was full of contemporary – and very conventional – furniture, and Paniatowski would not have been the least surprised if Mary Harris had confessed that she'd bought the whole lot from a single stand at the most recent Ideal Homes' Exhibition.

'I've rung all Jill's friends,' she said. 'Every single one of them. Nobody knows where she is.'

'And can you think of anywhere else she might be? Could she have gone out to visit relatives, for example?'

'All her relatives were at the reception.'

'Does Jill have a boyfriend?' Paniatowski asked.

'She's only thirteen!' Mrs Harris said, almost scandalized.

'Children grow up quicker these days,' Paniatowski replied, and, not wishing to abandon this possible avenue of inquiry, however eager Mrs Harris seemed to dismiss it herself, she added, 'Have you noticed if Jill has suddenly started taking an interest in make-up?'

Mrs Harris shook her head. 'No, she hasn't. It's quite the reverse, in fact. I bought her some as part of her Christmas present – nothing too grown-up, just what all the other respectable girls seem to be wearing – and it's still in the box on her dressing table.'

'Perhaps I'd better take a quick look at her bedroom, in case there's some clue there as to where she's gone,' Paniatowski suggested. 'That would be all right, wouldn't it?'

'I suppose so,' the other woman agreed.

'Can I see it, too?' Louisa asked.

'Why would you want to see it?' Paniatowski wondered.

Louisa sighed. 'Because I'm a kid, just like Jill,' she said, in a tone which hinted that she considered it a pretty stupid question to ask. 'Things in the bedroom might look different to me from the way that they'll look to old people.'

'Would you mind?' Paniatowski asked Mrs Harris.

'No, no,' the other woman said. 'I don't mind anything if it will help me find out where Jill is.'

Mrs Harris led them up the stairs. 'That's her room,' she said, pointing to a door which had a hand-painted notice pinned to it.

Louisa had one of those, too, Paniatowski thought. Hers said optimistically:

TODAY IS THE FIRST DAY OF THE REST OF YOUR LIFE.

Jill's sign was rather different. The brush strokes were angry, and it read:

IT REALLY DOESN'T MATTER WHAT OTHER PEOPLE THINK.

'Kids have some funny ideas, don't they?' Mrs Harris asked, seeing Paniatowski had noticed the sign. 'I mean, you can't go through life ignoring other people's opinions, now can you?'

Paniatowski opened the door and looked around the room. It was quite like Louisa's bedroom – the same sort of furniture, the three-quarters sized desk, the bright rug on the floor. And yet there seemed to be something significant missing – and she couldn't quite put her finger on what it was.

'Where are Jill's fluffy toys?' Louisa asked.

'She's too old to be buying fluffy toys,' Mrs Harris said dismissively. And then, realising she might have caused offence to this nice little girl, she quickly added, 'Of course, there's absolutely nothing *wrong* with buying fluffy toys. It's perfectly normal.'

'I didn't mean *new* fluffy toys,' Louisa said, speaking slowly and patiently, as though she accepted that she was talking to someone who was not quite on her level. 'I meant her *old* fluffy toys – the ones that she's had with her ever since she was a little girl.'

That was it! Paniatowski thought. That was *exactly* what was missing!

'She threw all those kinds of things out a few months ago,' Mrs Harris said. 'She said she was too old for them. She's becoming a bit of a tomboy, if truth be told. I don't know what people must make of her.'

'I wouldn't worry about it if I were you. It's just a phase all young girls go through, and Louisa was just the same,' Paniatowski said, knowing that her daughter wouldn't openly contradict her, but sure that if she looked into Louisa's eyes, she would see an expression which only just fell short of anger.

Having found nothing in Jill's room to indicate where she might be, they trooped downstairs again.

'I'll get a message to all foot patrols and crime cars to be on the lookout for your daughter,' Paniatowski promised.

'Is that all?' Mrs Harris asked.

'Yes. What else were you expecting me to do?'

'Well, I'd have thought that you'd have organized a massive search or something.'

'I can't do that quite yet,' Paniatowski said firmly.

Nor could she. There was too little manpower to cover all the Saturday night crime in Whitebridge as it was, and to pull men off their normal duties in order to search for a girl who might not even be missing would be like issuing the local criminals with a free pass. Besides, it was already dark now, and she knew from experience that night searches were pointless.

'Jill will probably come home when she gets hungry or tired,'
she told Mrs Harris. 'And even if she doesn't, you shouldn't automatically start suspecting there's something wrong, because I've
known of cases in which girls have been missing for *two or three*
days, and have turned up again completely unharmed.'

But not many, she added, as a silent rider to herself. Not even
close to half of them.

'If you could just . . .' Mrs Harris pleaded.

'I'm sorry, that really *is* all I can do for the moment,' Paniatowski
said, opening the door and ushering Louisa outside. 'Ask one of
your neighbours to sit with you, Mrs Harris. You'll find that will
help.'

But it won't help that much, she thought, as she set off down the
garden path, holding her daughter's hand firmly in her own.

The governor, who had calmed down considerably after Baxter's
apology, reached into his desk drawer and produced an unopened
bottle of malt whisky and three glasses with all the aplomb of a
conjurer.

'I've been saving this for a special occasion,' he said, as he
unscrewed the top, 'and I think we can all agree that having a
distinguished visitor *makes* it a special occasion.'

He poured two generous glasses, but as he was about to pour the
third, Chief Officer Jeffries said,' Not for me, thank you, sir.'

'But I thought you enjoyed the odd tipple,' the governor said,
looking a little hurt.

'And so I do, sir,' the chief officer agreed. 'More than enjoy it
– but I've given it up for Lent.'

'Ah, yes, you're quite right, it is Lent,' the governor said. He
hesitated for a second, then added, 'You won't be offended if we
indulge ourselves, will you, Mr Jeffries?'

'Of course not, sir,' the chief officer replied. 'Every man should
be guided by his own conscience in this, as in every other matter.'

It was an excellent malt, and while the two non-abstainers
savoured it, one of them – the governor – talked volubly about
football, the weather and his golfing handicap. Baxter, for his part,
made the odd comment, but spent most of the time wondering about
when, exactly, he should drop his next bombshell.

The glasses were finally drained – the last few precious drops
slipping down as easily as the first.

'Another one, Chief Constable?' the governor asked.

Baxter shook his head. 'No, thank you, I think it's about time I settled into my accommodation.'

'Ah yes, of course,' the governor agreed. 'We've booked a room at the pub in Dunston village. It's not exactly luxury, but it's the best available, and I'm sure you'll find it pleasant enough.'

'I probably *would* find it pleasant enough – but I won't actually be needing it,' Baxter said, opening his mental bomb hatch.

'Won't be needing it?' the governor repeated, mystified.

'No,' Baxter said, 'I think it would be better all round if I lodged here instead.'

'In the prison!'

'That's right. I rather embarrassed myself earlier by showing a complete ignorance of what goes on here, and since I'd rather not make the same mistake twice, it's pretty obvious that I need a crash course in what makes it tick.'

'Even so . . .'

'And where better to learn about prison life than in the prison itself?'

The governor had not even suspected the bombshell until it had actually exploded. But Chief Officer Jeffries had, Baxter thought. In fact, he was willing to bet that Jeffries had been waiting for the bang since the apology which had made his boss feel so much more relaxed.

'The thing is, we don't really have the facilities for accommodating people here, do we, Mr Jeffries?' the governor asked.

But Jeffries was not about to play that game – not when he could see the battle had already been lost.

'We could give you one of the camp beds that the lads sometimes use between shifts,' the chief officer said. 'Would that suit you?'

'It would suit me perfectly,' Baxter said.

'But don't you think that would be a little lacking in . . . in . . .' the governor gabbled.

'In home comforts?' Baxter supplied.

'Well, yes.'

'I get my home comforts at home – which is where I intend to return as soon as I possibly can. Give me a camp bed, and an office you're not using at the moment, and I'll be as happy as a pig in shit.'

'Very well,' the governor said defeatedly. He turned to his chief officer. 'Could you arrange that, Mr Jeffries?'

'Certainly, sir,' Jeffries replied, in a crisp, sergeant-major-like voice.

'I've never – ever – in my entire life, been a *tomboy*,' Louisa said resentfully, as her mother pulled the MGA away from the curb.

'I know you haven't,' Paniatowski agreed.

'Then why did you say it?'

'It made Mrs Harris feel a little better – because if a terrific girl like you had been a tomboy, then there was nothing abnormal about her daughter, Jill, being one, too.'

But Louisa was not about to be bought off with flattery.

'You wanted to make her feel better, so you deliberately told her a *lie*!' she said accusingly.

'A white lie, perhaps,' Paniatowski conceded. 'But you will admit, it was all in a good cause.'

'The rules have changed, then, have they?' Louisa asked, unyielding.

'What rules?'

'You told me there was never *any* excuse for telling a lie.'

'I lied about that,' Paniatowski confessed, laughing awkwardly. Then, to change the subject, she added, 'So did you learn anything from Jill's room, Chief Inspector Louisa?'

'Don't patronize me, Mum,' Louisa said sharply.

'Sorry!' Paniatowski replied – and meant it. 'Well, *did* you learn anything from Jill's room?'

'I learned she has a very big secret,' Louisa said.

'And what is it?'

Louisa snorted. 'If I knew that, it wouldn't be much of a secret at all, now would it, Mum?'

'All right,' Paniatowski said. 'What was it that you *saw* that told you Jill had a big secret?'

'It wasn't anything I actually saw,' Louisa admitted. 'It was just a feeling I had,' she rubbed her stomach with her right hand, 'down here.'

Paniatowski smiled. A gut feeling! Louisa might not be biologically her child, but she was still a chip off the old block.

FOUR

The first thing Baxter noticed when he woke up that Sunday morning was just how stiff he felt.

'You must be getting old, George,' he told himself. 'There was a time when you could have spent the night sleeping on bricks, and still sprung to your feet like a randy young ferret.'

But he wasn't feeling like a randy young ferret that morning – or even, if he was honest with himself, like a middle-aged ferret that had reluctantly put its years of sexual conquest behind it – and for some moments Baxter merely lay there, calculating which way of getting out of bed would afford him minimum discomfort.

He settled on swinging his legs off the bed first, and as he stood up, he tried not to wince as his body sent out shooting pains in protest.

Once on his feet, he looked down and examined the thing he had been sleeping on. It could not be claimed in all fairness that it *wasn't* actually a camp bed, he decided – it did, after all, have the necessary parts – but if someone had told him that Alexander the Great had bought it as flood-damaged stock from Noah's Ark, he would have had no difficulty in believing it.

It was unlikely that there weren't better camp beds available in the prison, he thought as he stretched to relieve his aches, which probably meant that giving him this particular one had been a deliberate tactic, designed to change his mind about spending his nights in the prison.

Well, if that *had* been the tactic, it had backfired, because he was now more determined than ever to stay exactly where he was.

He crossed his temporary office/bedroom, and opened the door. He was not surprised to see Chief Officer Jeffries standing in the corridor outside. In fact, he would have been surprised if the man *hadn't* been there.

'Good morning, Mr Baxter,' Jeffries said. 'I hope you had a good night's sleep.'

'I slept like a log,' Baxter lied. 'Do you just happen to be passing, Chief Officer Jeffries, or have you been standing out here waiting for me?'

'I've been waiting for you,' Jeffries said. 'I'm here to escort you down to breakfast.'

'An important man like you shouldn't have to hang around in corridors as if he was a mere errand boy,' Baxter prodded, to see what reaction he'd get.

'I haven't been here long,' Jeffries replied, stony faced. 'Shall we go down to breakfast now?'

'Is it a good breakfast?' Baxter asked.

'It's an excellent breakfast.'

'Sausages, bacon, fried eggs, fried bread – the works?'

'The works.'

Baxter pretended to consider it.

'It's certainly a tempting offer,' he said finally, 'but my doctor's told me that if I don't stay off the fried food, I'm heading for an early grave. So, on balance, I think I'll skip breakfast and take a look around the prison.'

'You don't *have* to have the full works, if you don't want to,' Jeffries pointed out. 'You could just settle for cornflakes.'

'To tell you the truth, I'm not at all hungry.'

Jeffries frowned. 'You are *expected* in the canteen.'

'I dare say I am,' Baxter agreed, 'but I've always found that you learn more by going to the places where you're *not* expected. Let's go and take a look at the main wing, shall we?'

'If you insist, Mr Baxter,' Jeffries said, in a tight voice.

'I do insist, my old son,' Baxter said. He patted the other man on the shoulder. 'And by the way, since I'm here in an official capacity, I'd prefer it if you addressed me as Chief Constable.'

'I'll try to remember that,' Jeffries replied, not even attempting to sound convincing.

A heavy grey sky hung depressingly over the Whitebridge police headquarters car park, and in the car park itself stood two dozen police officers who had had other plans for that Sunday morning.

The plans had been as varied as the officers were themselves. Some had been expecting to take the field in the fiercely contested Sunday football league. Others had made promises to their kids that they'd take them out for the day – or sworn to their wives that they'd finally get around to repapering the back bedroom. A few of the single men had been anticipating a fairly heavy lunchtime drinking session, and a handful of the more devout had even intended to put on their best suits and go to church. Now – as a result of early morning phone calls – all those plans had turned to ashes, and the men stood around stamping their feet to ward off the cold, and waiting to be told what to do next.

DCI Paniatowski and Chief Superintendent Tom Potter stood side by side at the far end of the car park, waiting for the police transit vans to emerge from the garage.

'Assuming that the little lass decided to sleep rough last night, she'll have woken a bit stiff this morning, but she's young, and it shouldn't have done her any permanent harm,' Potter said.

Yes, assuming Jill *had* slept rough the previous night, that was probably the case, Paniatowski thought.

But there was another possibility – one never spoken of at the start of this kind of search, but hanging over the whole operation like a thick choking black cloud – that she hadn't noticed the cold (or anything else for that matter) because she was already dead.

'The men I've called in will be reinforced by firemen, relatives and neighbours, so we should have a search party of close to a hundred,' the superintendent continued. 'Now, the only question is what the search's focus should be. Where do you think we should be looking, Chief Inspector?'

He didn't really need an answer, Paniatowski thought – he knew as well as she did where to search – but he was drawing her into the process as a professional courtesy, and she appreciated that.

'The old mills are a good starting point, sir,' she suggested.

And so they were. The mills had thrived when cotton was king in Lancashire, but had been abandoned for years. They were now so easy to gain access to that it was commonplace for bodies to be discovered in one or another of them, and though most of the dead eventually turned out to be tramps who had died of natural causes, Paniatowski herself had been involved in three investigations in which mills had either been the actual location of murders or the places where the victims were dumped.

'Where else should we be looking?' Potter asked.

'The river bank,' Paniatowski replied, remembering her first case as a DCI, in which a severed hand had turned up on the bank. 'Also the canal tow path. Essentially, anywhere that members of the general public *could* go if they chose to – but usually don't.'

The chief superintendent nodded his agreement. 'This is clearly a job for the uniformed branch, so I won't be requiring your assistance during the actual search,' he said, 'but I would like you and your team standing by, in case there's a negative outcome.'

Or to put it another way, Paniatowski thought, in case the unhappy girl – who she had last seen wearing a flounced pink dress – turned up dead.

'I've already notified my team, sir,' she said aloud. 'In fact, I've arranged to meet them at lunchtime.

The superintendent smiled. 'And that meeting will be taking place in the public bar of the Drum and Monkey, will it?'

Paniatowski grinned. 'That's right. It's where we seem to do our best thinking, sir.'

'So I've heard,' the superintendent told her.

The main wing of Dunston Prison was connected to the administrative block by a short tunnel, which had heavy steel doors at either end. The wing was four storeys high, rectangular in shape, and had a central patio. Internal walkways ran around the top three stories, and a suicide net had been stretched over the entire patio at second-floor level.

Baxter and Chief Officer Jeffries arrived in the wing just as the prisoners from the third floor were slopping out, and they stood in the patio, watching a stream of men clanking down the metal stairs and gingerly carrying their buckets towards the toilet block.

'Just look at it,' Jefferies said, as the prisoners passed by them. 'What a waste of officer manpower. We're highly trained personnel, you know. And what do we end up doing, for at least an hour a day? We end up standing and watching the prisoners slopping out!'

Baxter nodded, but said nothing.

'The problem isn't that this prison was built in the time of Queen Victoria – which it was,' Jeffries continued. 'It's the fact that we're keeping these men under conditions that even the Victorians would never have tolerated.'

'Is that right?' Baxter asked neutrally.

'It is,' Jeffries confirmed. 'The Victorian idea of punishment was that when you locked a man away, you really locked him away. He wasn't allowed to fraternize with the other prisoners. He was in his cell for most of the day, and even when he was given exercise time, wasn't permitted to talk to the other prisoners. The only people he did get to talk to were the guards and the prison chaplain.'

'And you approve of that system, do you?' Baxter asked.

'Of course I don't approve of it,' Jeffries said. 'It was inhuman.'
He paused. 'Mind you, under that system, they never had trouble
with prison gangs, like we do these days.' Another pause. 'But the
point I was trying to make was that each of these cells was designed
to hold one man – and that, remember, was in Victorian times, when
conditions for most people were a lot rougher than they are now.'

'I imagine they were,' Baxter said.

'So we have cells which the Victorians considered were just about
good enough for *one* prisoner, and we're putting two or even three
men in them now, because we don't have any choice in the matter.
And if one of those men has the shits in the middle of the night, the
others have to live with the stink until morning slopping out time.'

'I know what you're doing,' Baxter said quietly.

'Do you?' Jeffries asked, with a hint of aggression in his voice.
'Then why don't you explain to me exactly what that is.'

'You're trying to show me what strain you're all under – the
prisoners as well as the guards. You hope that by doing that, you'll
get me to make allowances for the fact that things don't always go
as they should do.'

'And will you?' Jeffries asked.

'I'm not some academic who's just stepped out of his ivory tower
and expects everything beyond that tower to be perfect,' Baxter said.
'I live in the real world. I run a police force that operates within a
flawed system, and I accept that certain corners have to be cut and
certain regulations ignored in order to make that system work. So
sometimes, when I see there are things not being done exactly by
the book, I deliberately look the other way.'

'That's a sensible attitude,' Jeffries said.

'But there are principles I have to stick by, and actions that I
can't ignore,' Baxter continued. 'I will not tolerate my officers taking
bribes, intimidating witnesses or doing favours for their mates, for
example, and if they cross any of those lines, there are no second
chances – they're out of the force and probably in gaol.'

'That's all very interesting, but I'm much more interested in
finding out how you'll apply these "principles" of yours to this
prison,' Jeffries said.

'Oh, that's very simple,' Baxter told him. 'If there's nothing your
men could have done to prevent Jeremy Templar's suicide, they're
in the clear, and if there was something they could have done, then
they're not.'

'We've already explained that there weren't the funds to box in all the pipes,' Jeffries said.

'And I accept that,' Baxter countered. 'I also accept that if a man really wants to kill himself, he'll eventually find a way, however careful those around him are.'

'In that case, I don't see why you're here at all,' Jeffries said.

'Don't you?' Baxter asked. 'Then perhaps I'd better explain it to you. Templar committed suicide because he found life intolerable, and the reason he found life intolerable was because of the attacks on him by other prisoners. So the real question is – could your men have prevented those attacks?'

'I don't think that *is* the real question,' Jeffries said.

'Then what is?'

'The real question is not whether they could have prevented those *four* attacks – it's how many more attacks on him there *might have* been if my lads hadn't been doing the best they could in nearly impossible circumstances. And we'll never know the answer to that – because if something didn't happen, you can't prove it was ever going to.'

He had a point, Baxter admitted. And maybe he was right – maybe his men, rather than being *inefficient*, had been as efficient as was possible in the circumstances. But at this stage of the inquiry, it was far too early to reach any such conclusion.

'Who fills in the time sheets?' he asked the chief officer.

'What do you mean by time sheets?' Jeffries replied evasively.

'I mean the sheets on which you keep a record of which officer is on duty at which particular time.'

'That would be me – or one of the junior officers working under my supervision,' Jeffries admitted.

'I'd like to see all the ones relating to the times Jeremy Templar was attacked,' Baxter said.

'I don't really see the point of that,' Jeffries replied.

'You will – if you really put your mind to it,' Baxter promised him.

There was no sign on the corner table in the public bar of the Drum and Monkey to say that it was reserved, but then there didn't need to be. The regular customers got vicarious pleasure from seeing DCI Paniatowski and her team in deep and urgent discussion on – say – a Tuesday night, and then reading about her making an arrest in the evening newspaper on Wednesday. They knew she wasn't *their* bobby – that she was nobody's bobby but her own – but occasionally, when they gently pointed non-regulars to another table, they could not help feeling a little pride over the fact they were, in some small way, contributing to the investigation.

The whole team was at the table that Sunday lunchtime, and Paniatowski looked at them all with the fondness of a mother hen who knows she has raised some very fine chicks.

There was DI Colin Beresford, whom she had worked with since he had been a young detective constable, and she had been a sergeant. A big, solid man in his early thirties, he was her best friend, and though he had almost gone off the rails in their last investigation, she would trust him with her life.

There was fresh-faced and film-star-handsome DC Jack Crane, who she sometimes thought of as barely out of nappies, while fully acknowledging the fact that she would not be in the least surprised if she ended up working for him.

And there was DS Kate Meadows, the newest member of the team, and her bagman. Kate was still something of a mystery. She had a sex life that Paniatowski couldn't even begin to comprehend, but was gradually learning to accept. She had the cavalier investigative style of someone who was working for her own amusement, rather than because she needed the money. And she had an expensive taste in clothes that she should never have been able to indulge on a DS's salary. A mystery then – but a bloody fine bobby, for all that.

Paniatowski became aware of the fact that the rest of the team were watching her, and waiting for her to speak,

'I don't want to put a jinx on the search by assuming it will end with what Superintendent Potter chooses to call a "negative result",' she said, 'but we have to accept the fact that Jill's been missing for over eighteen hours.' She paused to take a deep breath. 'That means that the prospects don't look good, and if things do turn out badly, we need to be ready.'

'I've already informed the divisional commanders that we may be drawing on them for manpower,' Beresford said.

Paniatowski nodded. 'Good. If the worst does come to the worst, I'll want your lads to trace Jill's movements from the time she left the wedding.' She took a drag on her cigarette. 'Kate, your job will be to go to Jill's school, and find out what you can about the parts of her life that her mother probably has no idea of. And before you ask,' she continued, turning to Crane, 'the reason I'm sending Sergeant Meadows is because most of the information she'll gather will probably come from the girls.'

'I don't quite follow, boss,' Crane admitted.

'It's not your fault, but you have an effect on girls of a certain age,' Paniatowski said. 'They quite lose their heads when they're talking to you. And don't deny it – because I've seen it happen.'

Crane grinned sheepishly. 'I wasn't about to deny it, boss,' he admitted. 'I'm cursed with good looks.'

'And burdened with humility,' Paniatowski said dryly. 'Sergeant Meadows, on the other hand, comes across to teenage girls as an older sister. Admittedly, it's a slightly *dangerous* older sister – the one they'd like to copy if only they had the nerve . . .' She paused. 'I've got that about right, haven't I, Kate?'

'If you say so, boss,' Meadows replied.

'And because that's how they see her, they'll tell her things they'd never dream of telling the rest of us,' Paniatowski continued. 'That leaves you, Jack. You can stick with me, and carry my bag.'

'Fine,' Crane said, doing his best to hide his disappointment.

'That's about as far as we can go for the moment,' Paniatowski said, rounding things up. 'Any questions?'

Meadows shook her head, and Crane said, 'It all seems clear enough.'

'Will you two excuse us for a minute?' Beresford asked, looking first at the sergeant and then at the detective constable.

He'd posed it as a question, but both Meadows and Crane knew it was nothing of the kind, and they immediately stood up and walked over to the bar.

'I hope you're not looking for advice on your ever-more-complicated love life, because I never discuss sex on a Sunday,' Paniatowski said, with an uneasy grin.

She knew what he was going to say, Beresford thought – and she didn't want to hear it.

'Are you sure you want this case, Monika?' he asked, anyway.

Paniatowski's forced grin froze, and then melted completely away.

'Firstly, we don't know yet if it *will be* a case,' she said. 'And secondly, if it does turn out to be a case, why *wouldn't* I want it?'

'It's less than two months since your Louisa was abducted,'

Beresford said. 'Do you remember what sort of state you were in when that happened?'

'Of course I remember. How can you ever think I'd forget it? Now can we change the subject, please?'

'We were in the pub in Bellingsworth village when you got the call that she'd gone missing, and—' Beresford continued steadfastly.

'I know where we bloody were,' Paniatowski interrupted him.

'—and when you came back to the table, you were trembling – and as white as a sheet. You tried to find your car keys in your handbag, and you couldn't even manage something as simple as that, so in the end I drove you back to Whitebridge myself.'

'Are you enjoying dredging all this up?' Paniatowski asked. She shook her head. 'I'm sorry, that wasn't fair.'

Beresford said nothing.

Ten seconds ticked slowly by before Paniatowski continued, 'Yes, I was in a state. I admit that. Louisa's my only child, for God's sake! How would you have expected me to react?'

'Exactly as you did,' Beresford said. 'And you're not *so far* from that state now. So do you really think that you're strong enough to handle an investigation which is bound to remind you of that terrible night?'

'I'm strong enough,' Paniatowski said.

'I'm sure that the deputy chief constable would be more than willing to hand the investigation – if there is one – over to some other chief inspector,' Beresford told her.

'I'm strong enough,' Paniatowski repeated, firmly.

FIVE

Sunday drifted lazily on, as Sundays invariably and inevitably did. The pubs closed at two in the afternoon, the drinkers wandered home, and by half-past two, the centre of Whitebridge – and the suburbs that clung to it like dependent limpets – were almost deserted. Once inside their own houses, the Sunday drinkers tucked into their traditional Sunday lunch of roast beef, Yorkshire pudding and three veg, and then settled down in front of their television sets, soon falling asleep while watching old films they'd already seen half a dozen times before.

It was only on the edges of the town – in the industrial wasteland – that there was any sign of activity. There, teams of searchers, usually led or supervised by a police officer, checked out decaying mills and rotting warehouses, dilapidated scrap yards and dubious used-car establishments.

The searchers had started the day in somewhat high spirits. They were doing something for their community – they were acting together – and they felt good about it. They knew, of course, that their search might end in tragedy, yet they could not actually bring themselves to believe that it would.

By three o'clock, the mood had changed. The searchers were tired and hungry, but more than that, they were beginning to tell themselves that they were on a pointless mission – that if Jill Harris was safe and well, they would have found her by then.

At four o'clock, when darkness was beginning to fall and the search was finally called off, they felt a mixture of relief and disappointment – and began to prepare themselves for the inevitable.

It was just after six o'clock when Elaine Hardy and Eddie James began walking – gloved hand in gloved hand – through the Corporation Park.

The winter and early spring were difficult times for young lovers, Elaine reflected as they walked. At least, they were difficult times if you had a mother like hers – one who refused to accept the fact that by the time you were seventeen you'd stopped being a girl and become a woman, with all the natural urges that went with womanhood.

She envied the young Americans she had seen in films at the Odeon. They were able to 'make out' any time they felt like it, because they all had big flashy automobiles, with plenty of room on the ample back seat for a spot of nooky. If you were a teenager in Whitebridge, on the other hand, then all you had was a sodding push bike, and however randy you were feeling, having sex on the crossbar was just about impossible.

And so she and Eddie – who would one day be her husband, and the father of her children – were forced to practice *their* 'making out' in isolated bus shelters and on wooden park benches. And in winter, that could be bloody cold!

As they passed the bandstand, she caught her boyfriend glancing speculatively at the bushes, so she knew what was about to come next.

'Do you fancy a quick tumble?' asked Eddie, always the romantic.

'It's a bit chilly for that sort of thing,' Elaine said dubiously.

'It's warmer than it was last Friday – and we did it then,' Eddie pointed out, with impeccable logic.

'It doesn't feel warmer to me,' Elaine said. 'Have you got a rubber Johnny on you?'

'I don't think so,' Eddie said dubiously.

'Well then . . .'

'I'm joking with you,' Eddie said, grinning. 'Of course I've got one. It's right there in my wallet. I always carry one – 'cos I never know when you'll start making your insatiable demands on me.'

'Now, don't go pretending that it's always me who's wanting to have it,' Elaine said. 'You're the one who keeps saying you can't have too much of a good thing.'

'So what do you think?' asked Eddie, who was getting tired of the debate. 'Are you up for a quick one or not?'

'As long as it *is* a quick one,' Elaine said. She grinned, impishly. 'But not *too* quick, or you'll leave me unsatisfied.'

'As if I'd do that,' Eddie replied.

They looked around, to make sure no one was watching them, then quickly headed for the bushes.

Eddie stripped off his overcoat and laid it on the ground. Then he ran his hands over the lining, to make sure he hadn't placed it on any roots.

'There you go, my princess,' he said grandly.

Elaine lay down on the coat, raised her backside slightly, and pulled down her knickers.

'And don't be too rough with me this time,' she warned.

Eddie grinned in the darkness. 'It'll be as smooth as silk,' he promised. 'You'll hardly know I'm touching you.'

'There's no need to go to extremes,' Elaine told him.

As Eddie began the foreplay, which he read about in the book his older brother had lent him, Elaine closed her eyes. She wasn't quite sure *why* she always did that at this point, except that was what they did in the films, so she supposed it was no more than standard procedure.

She felt her excitement growing, and when Eddie entered her, she groaned loudly.

'Shush!' Eddie whispered urgently.

He was right, she thought. Make too much noise, and you were likely to attract the attention of some passer-by.

And then where would they be?

Up before the magistrate, more than likely, with her mother glaring at her from the public gallery!

'Do me, do me,' she groaned – though quietly.

She was really into it now, and with her eyes still closed, she groped around for Eddie's hand.

The hand seemed very cold, she thought, as her fingers found his – cold, and rather lifeless.

And then she realized that it wasn't Eddie's hand she was holding, and she let out a loud scream – not caring *who* heard.

By the time Paniatowski reached the park, temporary floodlights had been set up, and now the bushes were an island of illumination, floating in the middle of a sea of darkness.

Beresford was already there, gazing down intently at the body, as if he thought that by doing that, he would somehow miraculously bring her back to life.

'Is that the girl who you saw at the wedding reception, Monika?' the inspector asked, when he noticed that his boss had arrived.

Paniatowski looked down at the body, which was lying half hidden under one of the bushes.

The girl looked so tiny, she thought. So helpless!

'Yes, that's Jill Harris,' she said mournfully. And then, more crisply, she added, 'Who found her?'

'A lad called Eddie James,' Beresford said. 'He *claims* he was just taking a short cut through the bushes, but when he turned round to leave, I noticed there were grass and dirt stains on the back of his overcoat, so you can draw your own conclusions.'

'There's no chance he was involved in the murder, is there?'

'In my opinion, none at all. He's just a poor innocent soul who happened to stumble on a murder victim, and then did the responsible thing and called the police. There's nothing that he – or the girl he wasn't with – can tell us that we can't see for ourselves.'

'Do we know the cause of death?'

'The doctor hasn't arrived to examine her yet, but there's bruising all around the throat, so it seems more than likely that she was choked.'

Paniatowski looked at the girl again. Jill's coat was open, and under it she was wearing her prized Miss Selfridge top, just as her mother had said she would be. And it *was* a nice top, so it was hardly surprising that a young girl like her had been so proud of it. In fact, in some ways, it was *too* nice a top.

'Do you think this is what the girl was wearing when she left home on Saturday afternoon?' asked Beresford, whose mind seemed to be running along similar lines to his boss'.

'Yes, I'm almost certain it was,' Paniatowski replied.

'It seems a bit posh for a Saturday afternoon stroll in the park.'

Yes, it did, especially when Jill had known her Auntie Vanessa would not be there to see it.

Paniatowski wondered if there was anything more she could have done after she'd been to Jill's room and finished interviewing her mother. And that, she recognized, was just a short step from wondering if she could have done anything to prevent the murder.

But it was pointless thinking like that, she told herself, because you can't protect everybody, all the time – however much you might want to.

She lit up a cigarette. 'How long do you think the poor child has been dead?' she asked.

'Well, she looks like she's coming out of rigor, so my guess would be she was killed some time on Saturday evening,' Beresford replied.

Paniatowski took a deep drag on her cigarette.

Smoking, according to the subtle messages hidden deep inside the adverts, was an almost magical process, which both soothed the body and made the world seem a slightly better place, she thought – but when you were looking down on the face of death, there was no magic to be found anywhere.

The chances were that even as she was talking to the mother – and trying to give the poor woman some hope – the girl herself had already been lying here. The chances were . . .

'It's not too late, you know,' she heard Beresford say in a gentle voice.

'Too late for what?' she asked.

'Too late to ask for this case to be assigned to another DCI.'

But it *was* too late, Paniatowski told herself. It had already been too late to shrug off the responsibility for Jill Harris when she'd sneaked out of the wedding reception.

'I told you at lunchtime, in the pub, that however this turned out I could handle it,' she said.

'Yes, you did,' Beresford agreed. 'But now that you've seen the girl for yourself . . .'

'There's not much more that we can accomplish in the dark,' Paniatowski interrupted him. 'Here's what I'd like you to do, Colin. First of all, make sure that all non-essential officers are moved back well away from the crime scene . . .'

'I still think that . . .'

'. . . and then I want the park locked, and uniformed officers posted all around the perimeter. Make sure there's at least a dozen of them on duty throughout the night, and if anybody from upstairs starts bitching about how much that's going to cost in overtime, just refer them to me.'

'I'll see to it, boss,' Beresford said, giving up on his attempt to change her mind. 'Should I also arrange for somebody to inform the mother?'

'No,' Paniatowski said. 'I'll do that myself.'

'I'd make sure that whoever was sent was well trained and sympathetic,' Beresford said.

'I know you would, Colin – but it has to be me.'

'All right,' Beresford said dubiously. 'In that case, I'll see you in the Drum in, say, an hour.'

Paniatowski forced herself to take another look at the dead girl, and then thought about the other girl – the one who would be waiting for her back home.

'No, after I've told Mrs Harris the bad news, I think I'll make an early night of it,' she said.

SIX

It was still dark when Paniatowski left home, but by the time she reached police headquarters, the sun was shining weakly down on the sheen of frost that covered the pavements.

By six thirty-two she was at her desk – a cigarette in her left hand, a cup of strong black coffee conveniently close to her right – and had started to make phone calls to people who were still snugly wrapped up in a cocoon of sleep.

Roger Hardcastle, the producer of Northern Television News was her first victim.

'I'd like to book a spot for a police spokesman on the nine a.m. news bulletin, Roger,' she said.

'Is it a murder?'

'Yes, you can get the details from the police press office.'

'Will it be you who's putting in an appearance?'

'I doubt it. I'll probably send DI Beresford.'

'Pity,' Hardcastle mused. 'Colin Beresford's a nice enough lad, but you look much better on television.'

'It's not entertainment were talking about here, Roger – it's *murder*,' Paniatowski said.

'Sorry,' Hardcastle replied, sounding slightly shamefaced, 'but when you've been in the news business for as long as I have, it's sometimes hard to tell the difference.'

Her next call was to the editor of a local evening paper.

'I want the story on the front page,' she told him, 'and I want it emphasized that while we always appreciate help from the general public, we *really* need it this time.'

'Understood.'

'What time does your first edition come out?'

'Usually around two o'clock in the afternoon.'

'If you make it midday, I'll owe you one.'

'We can't possibly have it ready by midday,' the editor protested.

'The girl was *thirteen*,' Paniatowski pointed out. 'Thirteen!'

'All right, all right, I'll do my best,' the editor promised.

It was as she hung up the phone that she noticed the slight tremble in her hand.

'You're just tired,' she told herself.

Of course it was just tiredness. It couldn't be anything else, for while it was true that the murder victim this time was a girl of around the same age as Louisa – and a girl, moreover, who she might have talked to at the wedding reception but hadn't – this was still a case just like any other.

Ideally, the subject of an interrogation should be tired and hungry, and the two prison officers who had just come off the night shift, and were now sitting across from George Baxter, fitted the bill perfectly.

Their names were Higgins and Fellows, and they were in their mid-thirties. They both wore their hair short, though Higgins' hair was blond and Fellows' was brown. Fellows looked the more intelligent of the two, but also the more cautious.

'You were on duty the morning Templar was beaten up in the shower, weren't you?' Baxter asked.

'That's right,' Fellows agreed.

Several seconds' silence followed the admission, then Baxter said, 'I'd appreciate it if you'd tell me exactly what happened.'

'The shower block has ten showers, and the procedure is to take the prisoners there in batches of twenty,' Higgins said. 'What's supposed to happen is that ten of them stand in the corridor, while the other ten take their showers. Then the ten that have showered take their turn at waiting in the corridor, while the other ten get *their* showers.'

'The thing is, that assumes all ten showers are working properly,' Fellows added.

'And sometimes they're not?' Baxter asked.

'At best, there's never more than five or six of them in working order,' Fellows said. 'That means there has to be five prisoners in the showers, and fifteen waiting outside.'

'And there are only two officers supervising them?'

'That's right.'

'Isn't that rather a high ratio of prisoners to officers?' Baxter wondered. 'What if they decided to attack you?'

'They wouldn't dare,' Higgins said.

'Why not? What would stop them?'

'The thought of having their fingers broken,' Higgins smirked.

'Shut up, Tony!' Fellows warned him.

'So if any prisoner attacked any officer, the governor would have his fingers broken?' Baxter asked.

'Yeah, right – like this governor of ours would have the balls to do that!' Higgins said contemptuously.

'I told you to shut up,' Fellows said.

'So if you're not talking about the governor, you must be talking about the chief officer,' Baxter said.

'Mr Jeffries wouldn't even think of doing that,' Fellows said, obviously furious at his colleague for putting him in this position.

'Then who would?' Baxter pressed.

Fellows sighed. 'There are a few hotheads in this place, but most of the prisoners just want a quiet life,' he said. 'And that means that the last thing they need is for an officer to be assaulted while going about his duties.'

'So the prisoners who want a quiet life break the fingers of anyone who steps out of line?' Baxter asked.

'No,' Fellows replied. 'As long as everybody knows they'd do it if they had to, there's no need for any violence.'

'But there *is* violence,' Baxter pointed out. 'Violence was done to Jeremy Templar.'

'They didn't hurt him because he stepped out of line,' Higgins said. 'They hurt him because he was a sick bastard.'

'Which brings us neatly back to that morning in the showers,' Baxter said. 'What happened?'

'I was in the shower block, and Officer Higgins was supervising the prisoners in the corridor,' Fellows said. 'Then Officer Higgins came into the showers, and asked me to help him deal with a situation that had developed.'

'What kind of situation?'

'Two of the men waiting in line had got into a fight, and he needed help separating them. I stepped out into the corridor and dealt with the matter. When I returned to the showers, Templar was lying on the floor of the stall. He'd been beaten up.'

'And there were only four or five men who could have been responsible for the attack, weren't there?'

'Yes.'

'Did you question them?'

'Yes.'

'And?'

'And they all denied having anything to do with it.'

'What did Templar have to say about it?'

'Templar knew better than to say *anything*,' Higgins said, with another sneer.

'Our hands were tied,' Fellows added. 'You can't charge five men with an attack when only one of them might be responsible, and since Templar refused to help us . . .'

'I'd like to see the report you wrote on the attack,' Baxter said.

'You'll have to ask Mr Jeffries for it – but it won't tell you anything we haven't already said,' Fellows said.

'I'd also like to see the other report.'

'What other report?'

'The one on the incident that occurred outside the shower block – the one that Officer Higgins called you out of the showers to deal with.'

'Ah, well, you see, I'm not sure there is one,' Fellows said uneasily.

'What do you mean – you're not sure?'

'In comparison to what happened to Templar, that was no more than a scuffle, and we may have forgotten to write it up.'

'But it did happen, did it?'

'Yes, of course it happened.'

There were only two possible explanations of the incident, Baxter thought. The first was that there had been no fight in the corridor, and the two officers had invented it to excuse the fact that they'd failed to protect Templar.

The second was that there *had* been a fight, and that it had been carefully orchestrated to distract Higgins' and Fellows' attentions while someone in the showers laid into the pervert.

Both explanations had their merits, and it was impossible – for the moment – to decide which one of them was the truth.

'Thank you, gentlemen,' he said. 'You've been very helpful.'

And he couldn't miss the look of relief on Fellows' face that the interrogation was over.

Fairfield High School for Girls was about as posh as schools got in Whitebridge. It was situated on the edge of the town, in an old neo-Gothic mansion, and such had been the demand in the previous

few years for the kind of 'superior education' it claimed to offer,
that several modern annexes had been grafted onto the original
building.

Looking at the gothic part of Fairfield from the road, Kate
Meadows thought back to her own school days.

She recalled vividly the countless occasions on which she had
been hauled into her headmistress' study, a stuffy overbearing room
which smelled of leather and spinsterhood. She had only to close
her eyes to see the headmistress, Miss Harvey, a woman in late
middle age, who had worn heavy tweed costumes, kept her grey
hair rigidly in place with a complex network of pins and grips, and
looked at the world through heavy-framed glasses.

'So you're here again, Katherine.'

'Yes, Miss Harvey.'

And then one of the obligatory lectures would begin. They were
long, rambling lectures, full of disapproving adjectives and adverbs
that were framed within rhetorical questions.

The only relief from the stream of condemnations came when
Miss Harvey broke off to point to one of the numerous photographs
of 'old girls' that adorned her wall.

'That's Lucinda Hubbard. She's only a few years older than you,
but she's already a junior partner in a most prestigious firm of
accountants.'

Good for her – the smug-looking cow!

'And that's Miranda Bonneville. She's a junior lecturer in St
Hilda's College, Oxford now, and I wouldn't be the least surprised
if she is offered a chair by the time she is forty.'

And she was more than welcome to plop her big fat academic
arse on it, because Kate didn't want it!

'I really would have thought, Katherine, that these girls would
serve as an inspiration to you.'

'They do, Miss Harvey.'

'Well, I must say, that's certainly not apparent from either your
work or your attitude.'

But they had inspired her – though not in a way the headmistress
would have hoped.

'Look at me now, Miss Harvey,' she said to the empty air. 'A
common-or-garden police sergeant, rubbing shoulders with all sorts
of riff-raff. Ain't that just grand?'

*   *   *

It seemed somehow wrong to be entering the morgue without Dr Shastri standing there at the door to greet her, Paniatowski thought, and she found herself hoping that the beautiful and delicate doctor would soon get bored of exploring her exotic roots and return to dank, chilly Whitebridge.

It was the new doctor – wasn't her name Liz Duffy? – who was conducting the post-mortem, and as the attendant showed Paniatowski and Crane into the dissecting room, she looked up from her work and said, 'Good God, Jack Crane! What are you doing here?'

'You know each other, do you?' Paniatowski asked.

'Know each other?' Dr Duffy repeated. 'I should say we do! Jack and I were at—'

'At school together,' Crane interrupted hastily and – it seemed to Paniatowski – rather shakily. 'As a matter of fact, our families lived on the same street, didn't they, Liz?'

'Er . . . yes . . . er . . . they did,' Duffy said, and though she was wearing a surgical mask, Paniatowski could still read the puzzlement in her eyes. 'But I still don't know what you're—'

'I'm a detective constable now,' Crane said, interrupting her again. 'I bet that shocks you, doesn't it? You probably always imagined I'd end up as a bricklayer or a window cleaner.'

'Well, I certainly never thought you'd end up as a policeman,' Liz Duffy said, in evident confusion.

'Anyway, we're not here to chat about old times,' Crane said. 'We've come to find out what you can tell us about the body, haven't we, boss?'

'Yes, we have,' Paniatowski replied.

But she was thinking, What's just been going on?

Dr Duffy straightened up and said, 'They say you should never carry out a post-mortem on someone you've known in life, and I believe them, because this morning I've found out for myself that it's bad enough if the cadaver is only someone you've simply *seen*.' She paused. 'You do know we have both seen this girl before, don't you, Monika? She was at the wedding reception.'

'Yes, I did know that,' Paniatowski agreed. 'What can you tell us about her, Doc?'

'Death was by manual strangulation,' Dr Duffy said. 'There's a bruise on her cheek, so I'm assuming that the killer first knocked her down, and then, when she was on the ground, strangled her – but

I could be wrong about that. There are bruises on her ankles, too, and they were probably caused during the struggle.'

'So she was strangled from the front?'

'That's correct. The pattern of contusions around her windpipe confirms that absolutely.'

'Would the killer in this case have to have been a very strong man?' Paniatowski asked.

The doctor shrugged. 'Strangulation always requires a certain degree of physical force, but the victim was probably dazed by the blow to her face, and anyway, she's only a slip of a girl, so he didn't need to be *particularly* strong.'

She'd been a slip of a girl – and so was Louisa, Paniatowski thought.

'Was there any evidence of sexual assault?' she asked.

'Not from the night she was murdered,' the doctor told her.

'But from earlier?'

'She has love bites on her shoulder and her chest, but they are at least several days old. I suppose, given her age, those love bites qualify as sexual assault, but there's no old bruising to suggest that she resisted in any way.'

'And you're certain the killer didn't do anything of that nature.'

'Completely.'

'Was she a virgin?'

'Yes.'

'Did the killer take anything away with him?'

'You mean like a lock of her hair? Or a finger?'

'Exactly.'

'No, nothing like that.' Duffy paused before speaking again. 'Please don't think I'm being insensitive by using the term, Monika, but it was what some of my colleagues would call a "clean kill".'

Paniatowski frowned. There were cases on record of other clean kills, but they were few and far between – and largely unsolved. On the whole, this kind of predator wanted to defile his victim in some way – either by raping her or taking part of her body as a souvenir.

'When did Jill die?' Paniatowski asked.

'I'll be able to give you a more accurate estimate when I've run more tests, but at the moment, I'd say it was some time between five and seven o'clock on Saturday night,' the doctor told her.

From the point of view of possible witnesses, that was just about the worst time she could have died, Paniatowski thought. In the afternoon, the park was full of parents pushing prams and lads playing football. In the evening, it was inhabited by people walking their dogs, and young couples – like Eddie and his girl – in search of a little privacy. But between five and seven, most people had gone home for their tea, and the park was largely deserted.

'Is there anything else you can tell us?' she asked.

'I know what you're hoping for, Monika, but I'm afraid there was no skin under her fingernails,' Dr Duffy said. 'The attack seems to have been sudden and unexpected, and by the time she realized what was happening, she had probably already begun to lose consciousness.'

'Thanks, Doc,' Paniatowski said. 'If you come up with anything else, you'll let us know immediately, won't you?'

'Of course,' Duffy agreed. She turned to Crane. 'Nice to see you again, Jack, even under such grisly circumstances,' she said.

And Paniatowski could have sworn she saw a mischievous twinkle in the doctor's eyes.

SEVEN

Mrs Garner, the headmistress of the Fairfield School, wore a pale jacket and skirt which had only recently gone out of fashion, had half-moon glasses perched on her nose, and allowed her blonde hair to fall freely to her shoulders. It was obvious that she considered herself a very modern headmistress, and her office, too, reflected that modernity, with its Scandinavian desk – on one side of which the sergeant was currently sitting – its Paul Klee prints, and its clean, functional lines.

But it was all only skin deep, Meadows decided. She had seen through the disguise, and knew that lurking underneath it was the tweed-encased soul that made her another Miss Harvey.

Yes, the two women were *both* petty tyrants, and both wore a cloak of snobbery to disguise their social insecurity, Meadows thought. And having reached this assessment, she sat back and waited for the inevitable to happen.

'Speaking strictly, as an individual, I would be more than willing to cooperate fully with your investigation, Sergeant Meadows,' Mrs Garner said, in a serious, self-important voice, 'but alas I do not have the freedom that is granted to ordinary people. My first duty is to this school, and, having stated my position, I think there's really no more to say.'

The headmistress clasped her hands in front of her, and looked first at Meadows and then at the door.

'You can't ignore the death, you know,' the sergeant said, staying firmly where she was. 'For its own mental health, the school needs to grieve the loss of one of its own.'

Mrs Garner snorted at her presumption in offering advice. 'We are all, of course, greatly distressed to hear that Jane has been murdered . . .' she began.

'Jill,' Meadows told her. 'The poor girl's name was Jill.'

'That Jill was murdered,' the headmistress corrected herself, though her tone suggested that if she *had* been wrong, it was probably Meadows' fault. 'But as distressed as we are, Sergeant, I'm afraid we cannot allow you to turn this school upside down in order to pursue your inquiry.'

'*We?*' Meadows said, looking around the room as if expecting to see someone else. 'Oh, I see, you're using the royal "we", are you?'

'I am quite convinced that Jill's death had nothing to do with anyone in this school, and that you would be making much better use of your time looking in the centre of Whitebridge for the tramp or drunkard – or whoever it was – who mindlessly killed her,' Mrs Garner said, ignoring the comment.

'Yes, you might well be convinced of that, but you see, you're not an expert in murder – and *we* are,' Meadows said. 'And *we* think it would be useful to talk to Jill's friends in the place where they spent most of their time together. We'll have to get the parents' permission first, of course, but I'm sure *they'll* be more than willing to cooperate.'

'You may choose to speak to the girls in their own homes – I can do nothing about that – but I will not allow you to speak to them within the confines of my school,' the headmistress said firmly. 'On the other hand, if you wish to speak to any of my staff . . .'

'Yes?'

'I will give my permission for that – but only after school has finished for the day, and only in my presence.'

It was time to crank up the pressure a little, Meadows decided. She contemplated going for the jugular straight away, but then – perhaps out of a sense of pity – she decided to give Mrs Garner one more chance to do the decent thing.

'I understand that you have the reputation of your school to consider, and that you don't want it associated with a horrendous crime like murder,' she said, 'but it already *is* associated with it, and the best thing you can do for its reputation would be to help us find the killer.'

'The best thing I could do for my school is to see that it returns to normal as quickly as possible,' the headmistress countered. 'We have GCE examinations in June, and though that might seem a long way away to a police officer who probably cannot see the value of an academic education, I can assure you that in our little community, three months is a very short time indeed.'

Well, she'd tried being reasonable, and it hadn't worked, Meadows told herself.

'You do realize that this means I'll have to go over your head, don't you?' she asked.

'Over my head!' the headmistress repeated, outraged.

'That's right.'

'Over my head to *whom*?'

'I'm going to have to contact the chairman of your school governors.'

Mrs Garner's outrage melted away, and though she probably rarely saw the humour in anything, she laughed now.

'Please feel free to do just that, Sergeant Meadows,' she said, 'but I can assure you that Lord Briargate has complete confidence in the way I manage this school, and will back me to the hilt.'

'You may well be right,' Meadows conceded.

'I *am* right.'

'But then again, Pinky may decide to back *me* to the hilt, since we're such old mates.'

'Pinky? Old mates?' the headmistress repeated.

'That's right,' Meadows said airily. 'Pinky and I go back a long way.'

The headmistress laughed again, even more scornfully this time.

'Of course you do,' she said disbelievingly. 'I expect he's an "old mate" of *all* the detective sergeants in Whitebridge.'

'No, I don't think that's the case at all,' Meadows said seriously. 'Or at least, if they are his mates, I don't think I've ever met any of them at one of his weekend house parties.'

'You surely don't expect me to believe . . .' Mrs Garner began.

'Funnily enough, I'd been meaning to give him a ring even before you decided to be so bloody uncooperative,' Meadows interrupted her.

'I will not tolerate that sort of crude language in *my* school,' the headmistress hissed.

'The thing is,' Meadows continued, unconcerned, 'the poor old bugger's been rather worried about Jess's health, and you know what it's like when one of the family gets ill – you really appreciate a shoulder from outside to cry on.'

'This has all been one big bluff from the start, hasn't it?' Mrs Garner crowed triumphantly. 'You don't know Lord Briargate at all!'

'What makes you think that?'

'His lordship's wife's name is Lady Elizabeth! And his children are Rachael and Charles.'

'So?' Meadows asked blankly.

'He has no close relations called Jess.'

'I never said she was a relative, I said she was a member of the family,' Meadows pointed out.

'You're making no sense,' Mrs Garner told her.

'Jess is Pinky's gun dog,' Meadows explained. 'She's a lovely little black Labrador, and she's had a liver infection.' A sudden puzzled look came to her face. 'Surely he *must* have told you about it. He tells everyone.'

'No, I don't remember him mentioning it,' the headmistress said with increasing uncertainty.

'I should imagine he'll be quite cross when I tell him how you've been obstructing me, but if I was you, I shouldn't worry about that too much,' Meadows said cheerfully. 'As you know yourself, he rarely holds a grudge.' She frowned. 'Although, when he *does* . . .'

'There's no need to bother Lord Briargate,' Mrs Garner said. 'I'm sure we can reach an understanding that will satisfy both of us.'

'I'm sure we can,' Meadows agreed.

'Perhaps I could put you in touch with my head of pastoral care, and if she has no objection, you could talk to some of the girls.'

'That would suit me perfectly,' Meadows agreed.

'Then if you'd like to wait in the outer office . . .' Mrs Garner said, turning back to her paperwork.

It was a dismissal – a minor victory on Mrs Garner's part – but Meadows did not mind, because she had achieved her objective, and as she left the office she found herself wondering if Lord Briargate – whom she had never met – really did have a Labrador called Jess.

'That was rather strange, wasn't it, Jack?' Paniatowski asked, as she and Crane walked back across the morgue car park towards the MGA.

'What was rather strange?' Crane asked, unconvincingly.

'The little exchange that I just witnessed between you and the new police doctor – you know, the one in which she kept trying to say something and you kept shutting her up before she had the chance.'

'You're right, I was trying to shut her up, but I was afraid she'd start telling you about some of the embarrassing things I did when I was a kid.'

'You're lying to me,' Paniatowski told him.

'Yes, I am,' Crane admitted.

They had reached the car, and were staring at each other across the red bonnet.

'Don't ever lie to me again, Jack,' Paniatowski said, with an edge to her voice. 'Don't even have a reason to *want* to lie to me.'

'Sorry, boss,' Crane muttered. He lowered his head gazed down at the bonnet for a few seconds, then lifted it again, and said, 'There's something I need to tell you, boss – something we need to talk through.'

'I'm listening.'

'Not now. Not when we're in the middle of a case. I'd rather leave it until after we've caught the killer. Could we do that, please?'

Paniatowski turned the idea over in her mind.

'Does what we need to talk about have anything to do with Liz Duffy?' she asked, finally.

'Not really,' Crane said. 'Or, at least, if it does have anything to do with her, it's only very indirectly,' he amended, in the interest of accuracy.

'Well, that's as clear as mud,' Paniatowski said.

Crane waved his hands helplessly. 'Liz is . . . well, I suppose she's just what you might call the final catalyst.'

'In what?'

'That's what I'd rather not say at the moment.'

'Will this thing that you're holding back on – whatever it is – have any impact on the investigation?'

'No, boss, I swear it won't.'

'I don't like mysteries,' Paniatowski said.

'Then you shouldn't be a detective, boss,' Crane said, sensing her wavering and risking a joke.

A smile flickered across Paniatowski's face. 'I *will* wait – but you'd better be right about it not affecting the case.'

'Cross my heart and hope to die,' Crane said.

'Well, if you're wrong, you'll certainly *wish* you were dead,' Paniatowski said dryly.

George Baxter looked down at his notes he'd taken during the four interviews he'd conducted that morning, and decided that while he had made *some* progress, he hadn't made nearly enough.

He'd certainly established a pattern of sorts. The second, third and fourth pair of officers had all claimed – just as Fellows and Higgins had done before them – that when Templar had been attacked, they'd been dealing with a disturbance elsewhere.

So *had* the prisoners who wanted to hurt Templar orchestrated the whole thing?

Or had the officers invented the disturbances – or had them invented *for them* by Chief Officer Jeffries – to cover their own inefficiency?

He needed a break from work, he told himself, and since there was a news bulletin on the radio, he might as well find out what was happening beyond the walls of this closed, claustrophobic prison.

He switched his transistor radio on.

'Sport,' said the announcer. 'Despite the best efforts of its manager, Tommy Docherty, Manchester United looks increasingly likely to be relegated to the second division at the end of the season. A spokesman for the club . . .'

Baxter sighed. After years of hearing United fans mock Whitebridge Rovers' efforts to climb out of the second division, he should be taking pleasure from the fact that they would now be getting a taste of the unpleasant medicine themselves, he thought, but he doubted he could take pleasure in anything at that moment. He was less than forty-eight hours into his inquiry, and he was already heartily sick of it.

'The closing headlines,' the news reader said. 'Police in Lancashire are investigating the death of a girl found strangled in Whitebridge Corporation Park. The girl has been identified as Jill Harris, and she was thirteen years old. The officer in charge of the investigation, DCI Monika Paniatowski, has urged all members of the public who feel they may have some information to come forward, and . . .'

'Thirteen years old! Monika Paniatowski!' Baxter exclaimed.

He reached for the phone and quickly dialled a Whitebridge number.

'Jesus, who've I got working for me?' he asked himself. 'Imbeciles?'

Mrs Pierce, who was head of pastoral care at Fairfield High School, was dressed like a frump, but had the keen eyes of a brain surgeon.

'If you asked me about Jill only a couple of months ago, I'd have had very little to tell you,' she admitted to Meadows. 'What I suppose

I would have said is that she was quiet, industrious and a little
boring – and I'd probably have put that down to that mother of
hers.' She paused. 'Have you met Mrs Harris?'

'No,' Meadows said, 'I haven't.'

'Count yourself lucky,' Mrs Pierce said. 'The woman's a monster.
Not an evil monster, you understand – not even a malicious monster
– but a true monster, nevertheless.'

'Tell me about her,' Meadows suggested.

'Mrs Harris' one aim in life is to fit in,' Mrs Pierce said. 'She'd
do anything to conform. She's a bit of a prude, but if you told her
that everyone who was anybody was planning to strip off naked,
cover themselves in paint, and run around the Boulevard, she'd be
off to the ironmongers to buy a tin of Emerald Green before you
could turn around.'

Meadows laughed. 'You said that everything changed, as far as
Jill was concerned, a couple of months ago,' she reminded Mrs Pierce.

'Yes, it did. Jill was suddenly in trouble. Not in the classroom
– she was still as good as gold there – but in the playground.'

'What kind of trouble?'

'Girls of her age can be so vicious that they'd make Adolf Hitler
seem like Tiddles the Cat, but most of their viciousness is purely
verbal. Having said that, of course, you should realize that verbal
violence can often be more wounding than the physical kind.'

'But you're saying that Jill went beyond the purely verbal stage?'

'Indeed she did. She had not one, but several fights – and with
several other girls.'

'And what were the fights about?'

'That's the *really* interesting thing. *If* girls have fights – and as
I've said, that's very rare – they're always very keen to shift the
blame on to the person they've had the fight with. They'll say the
other girl said nasty things about their parents, or stole from them,
or copied their homework.'

'But in the case of Jill . . .?'

'In the case of Jill's fights, neither of the participants was prepared
to say a damn thing. They'd just sit there in absolute silence. To be
honest with you, I found that an unnerving experience, because
normally I can get girls to open up to me – whether they want to
or not.'

'I'm sure you can,' Meadows said. 'What's your theory on why
the fights started?'

'How do you know I even have a theory?' Mrs Pierce asked.

Meadows grinned. 'I think you're the kind of woman who'll *always* have a theory.'

Mrs Pierce smiled. 'Yes, I suppose that is an occupational hazard,' she agreed. 'I did have a theory at first, but, as events turned out, it didn't quite stand up to investigation.'

'I'd still like to hear it.'

'We had a new girl join us at the start of the spring term – a quiet, pretty, very timid little thing called Tilly Roberts. She and Jill became firm friends almost at once, and the fights started soon afterwards.'

'So your theory is that the new girl was being bullied, and that Jill was defending her,' Meadows guessed.

'Exactly,' Mrs Pierce agreed. 'But then the friendship broke up – that happens with girls, they're joined at the hip one day, and scarcely noticing each other's existence the next. The friendship broke up – but the fights continued.'

'So perhaps Jill had just acquired a taste for fighting,' Meadows suggested.

'I'd be open to that idea if Jill had been a boy,' Mrs Pierce said, 'but girls are not like that. Perhaps that comes from giving dolls to little girls, and guns to little boys.'

'I'd like to talk to the girls who Jill got into fights with, and also to this Tilly Roberts,' Meadows said. 'Do you want me to ring around the parents and get their permission, or will you do it?'

'I'll do it,' Mrs Pierce said. 'The parents have confidence in me.' She paused for a moment. 'And even after talking to you for only a few minutes, I have confidence in you, Sergeant Meadows.'

'Thank you,' Meadows said.

'How are things going in Yorkshire, sir?' Fred Comminger, the assistant chief constable, asked the man on the other end of the line.

'You assigned the murder of that young girl to DCI Paniatowski,' Baxter said angrily. 'What the hell were you thinking of?'

'It seemed a perfectly sensible decision to take,' Comminger replied. 'DCI Paniatowski isn't involved in any other major investigation at the moment, and she'd expressed an interest in the case even before the body was discovered.'

'You are aware that her own daughter was kidnapped not two months ago, aren't you?' Baxter asked.

'Well, yes, but as I understand it, she was only missing for a couple of hours, and no real harm was done.'

'There speaks a man who hasn't got any kids of his own,' Baxter said witheringly.

'And neither have you, sir,' his deputy countered, rankled.

No, he hadn't, Baxter agreed silently, but he knew Monika well – which was more than Comminger seemed to.

'I'm not at all sure DCI Paniatowski is up to handling this particular case at this particular moment,' he said aloud.

'So you're telling me to take her off the investigation, are you?' Comminger asked.

'No!' Baxter said, and was surprised at the note of what could almost have been panic in his own voice.

She couldn't be taken off the case like that – not so brutally! If that happened, she would never forgive him.

'I'll come back to Whitebridge and talk to her. Then I'll make my own assessment of the situation,' he heard himself say.

'You'll come all the way back to Whitebridge?' Comminger asked, with evident surprise.

'I'm not on the other side of the world, you know. The drive won't take me much more than two hours.'

'And it'll be another two hours back to Dunston.'

'I'm more than willing to sacrifice four hours of my own time for the good of the force,' Baxter said. 'And that's what this is all about you know – the good of the force.'

'I'm sure it is, sir,' Comminger said, unconvincingly.

'I want each case investigated by the officer who is most suited to investigate it,' Baxter continued, 'and I'm not sure that DCI Paniatowski – because of her recent experience – is the best person in this instance.'

'I know what you mean, sir,' Comminger said. 'It's certainly a challenging case in which emotions will be running high, and if DCI Paniatowski fails to get a result, it certainly wouldn't do much for her reputation.'

He knows what Monika and I used to be to each other – or, at least, what she was to me – Baxter thought, and whatever I say, he thinks that's what's driving me.

'I'm more concerned about putting a dangerous man behind bars than I am about protecting DCI Paniatowski's reputation,' he said.

'Of course you are, sir,' Comminger agreed.

'And since I won't decide whether or not she should stay on the case until after I've talked to her, I'd be grateful if you didn't even hint, before I get there, that there's a possibility she might be replaced,' Baxter said.

'Whatever you say, sir – you're the boss,' Comminger replied.

And there was something in his tone that implied that his respect for the chief constable had gone into a nosedive over the previous few minutes.

EIGHT

'Where's young Jack?' asked Beresford, glancing across the pub table at the seat that should have been occupied by DC Crane.

'He asked me if he could have half an hour off,' Paniatowski replied. 'He said he had some personal business to attend to.'

'Personal business,' Beresford repeated, with mild disgust. 'Doesn't he realize we're in the middle of a murder inquiry?'

Paniatowski grinned. 'You've gone from being the playboy of Whitebridge to a grumpy old man in less than a month, Colin,' she said. 'Surely that has to be some kind of record?'

'I just think he should be here,' Beresford said.

'And he will be,' Paniatowski promised. 'What have your lads out on the street come up with?'

'There were several sightings of Jill Harris between the Royal Vic and her home – which is about half a mile away from the hotel – but that's hardly surprising, because the dress she was wearing would have made her rather conspicuous, wouldn't it?' Beresford said.

'It would have made her stand out like a sore thumb,' Paniatowski agreed, remembering the flounced pink horror.

'A couple of the neighbours remember seeing her leave her house again, about half an hour after she got home, and their description of what she was wearing matches the clothes she was found in,' Beresford continued. 'However, from the point at which she passed the end of her street, we lose the trail.'

'Maybe we'll get more witnesses as a result of the television appeal,' Paniatowski said hopefully. 'How did that go, by the way?'

'I believe that, on the whole, it went rather well,' Beresford replied. 'I think I made all my points clearly, and that anyone who saw the broadcast will know what sort of information we need.'

'Not that that will stop the odd nutter ringing up to claim he saw Jill being abducted by a space ship,' Meadows said.

'No, there are always a few nutters,' Beresford agreed.

'The problem is that anyone who saw her is likely to have seen her *before* she entered the park,' Paniatowski said. 'What we really need is witnesses who were *in* the park – and the chances are, they don't even exist.'

'Maybe we'll get lucky,' Beresford said, encouragingly.

Maybe they would, Paniatowski agreed silently – but somehow this didn't feel like a lucky case.

It was as Dr Liz Duffy was crossing the morgue car park that she noticed the handsome young man standing next to her vehicle.

'Why, it's Detective Constable John Crane, isn't it?' she asked.

Crane grinned. 'Sorry to have put you in such a difficult position earlier,' he said.

'That's all right,' Liz told him, 'once I got used to it, it was rather fun. But I must admit that I am interested in finding out *why* it was necessary to drop me into the middle of a pantomime without even a script to work from.'

'You were about to say that we'd been up at Oxford together.'

'Well, we were, weren't we?' Liz Duffy smiled. 'Or have I simply imagined it all?'

'No, you didn't imagine it,' Crane said, 'but nobody I work with knows I went to university.'

'Nobody?' Liz Duffy repeated sceptically.

'Well, Sergeant Meadows knows – but she's a special case.'

'What makes her special?'

'She's just weird,' Crane said. He paused. 'You'd have to meet her to understand what I'm talking about.'

'So Monika has no idea that you're really Jack Crane, MA (Oxon)?'

'No, and Inspector Beresford doesn't know, either.'

'Why are you making such a big secret of it?'

'Monika was educated at the local secondary modern, and Inspector Beresford went to a comprehensive school. God alone knows what exotic course Sergeant Meadows followed before she finally turned up in Whitebridge – but like I said, she's weird.'

'If that was an explanation of why you're being so mysterious, it wasn't a very good one,' Liz Duffy said.

'There's still a lot of prejudice against a university education in the force,' Crane explained. 'As it stands, I'm being judged on my merits, but if people knew I was a "university boy", they wouldn't take me seriously.'

'Not even Monika Paniatowski?'

'She'd take me seriously now, because I've worked with her for a while – but I'm not sure even *she* would have done at the beginning.'

'You should come clean, you know, Jack,' Liz Duffy said. 'Living a lie – even a relatively harmless one like that – can have a very destructive effect on your personality. Believe me, I know.'

'*You* know?'

'As a doctor, I've seen it with my own eyes – on so many occasions.'

'I've been meaning to confess to the boss, and I will – very soon,' Crane said. 'But in the meantime, I'd be grateful if you didn't say anything.'

'You can rely on me,' Liz Duffy told him.

'Thank you.'

A silence fell between them – that awkward sort of silence which comes when two people who haven't seen each other for years have finished the business in hand, and don't know what to say next.

'So what have you been doing since the days when we'd go punting up and down the Isis, with me doing all the work and you sitting back and stuffing yourself with strawberries and cream?'

'I did *some* of the work,' Liz Duffy said, in mock rebuke. 'And I never *stuffed* myself with strawberries and cream, because, even back then, I had to watch my figure.'

The conversation sounded all wrong, Crane thought. Liz had described what had gone on in the morgue as a pantomime, but what was happening now was more like a play – a bad, hastily written drama about two Oxford graduates who had just happened to meet up again after several years. And perhaps the reason they were behaving in that way was because playing a part was so much less painful than playing themselves.

'Seriously, what *have* you been doing?' he asked, in an attempt to break away from the role that his psyche had imposed on him.

Liz Duffy shrugged. 'I've been doing pretty much what you'd have expected me to do. I qualified as a doctor, I worked in a hospital for a while, then I went into general practice. It's all been quite exciting – in its way – but compared to your career path, it seems very dull and predictable.'

'I'm sure nothing you ever did could be dull,' Crane said.

Was he slipping back into playing a role, he asked himself.

No, he was sure he wasn't. This was Jack Crane speaking – and when he'd said Liz could never be dull, he'd meant it.

'Are you married?' Liz asked.

'No. Are you?'

'Sadly not,' Liz told him. She took a deep breath. 'Would you like to come round to my flat one night – for dinner? I promise you, I'm a much better cook than I used to be.'

'I'd like it very much,' Crane said.

'Then let's set a definite date for it. What about tomorrow night, for example?'

'I'm not sure,' Crane told her.

'I'm being too pushy, aren't I?' Liz Duffy asked. 'It's always been a failing of mine.'

'No, it's not that,' Crane protested. 'It's just that I'm part of a murder investigation, and my time's not really my own.'

'You could surely squeeze in an hour or so to slip round for a drink, couldn't you?' Liz asked hopefully.

'I'm not even sure of that,' Crane admitted.

'Well, how about we make the arrangement purely tentative?' Liz suggested. 'I'll be at home, and if you can manage to come round, we'll have that drink. If not, we can postpone it to another night, when you have your killer safely behind bars.'

'That seems a bit unfair on you,' Crane said dubiously.

'I'll be at home whether you come or not,' Liz Duffy said. 'Being so new to the area, I don't have much of a social life.'

'I'll try to make it if I possibly can,' Crane promised.

'I know you will,' Liz Duffy said.

Since Beresford and Paniatowski were not facing the door of the public bar, they didn't see Crane come in. Meadows, on the other hand, had a clear view of his entrance, and, noticing an obvious spring in his step, wondered what had caused it.

'Ah, DC Crane!' Beresford said, when Crane reached the table. 'How good of you to find the time to drop in and talk to us.'

Crane's *joie de vivre* drained away.

'The boss said it would be all right—' he began.

'Sit down, Jack,' Paniatowski interrupted him. 'We were considering the possibility that the reason Jill went to the park was to meet a boyfriend. What do you think?'

'She obviously *had* a boyfriend,' Crane said, taking his seat.

'You can't put love bites on your *own* neck. And what other reason could a young teenager have for going to the park on Saturday *but* to meet her boyfriend? Besides, she was wearing her favourite top – the one she only usually wore when she was out with her Auntie Vanessa.'

'Then we're all agreed,' Paniatowski said. 'She went to the park because she had a date with a boyfriend who her mother knew nothing about – and having met her mother, I can quite see why Jill might want to keep him a secret. But did she actually *see* that boyfriend?'

'And if she did, did he kill her?' Beresford added.

'And if he *did* kill her, *why* did he kill her?' Meadows said.

'It could have been through jealousy,' Crane suggested. 'Perhaps he found out she was seeing another boy.'

'I don't think that's likely,' Paniatowski said.

'You don't think *what's* likely?' Meadows asked.

'I don't think it's likely that she'd have *two* boyfriends. In fact, after seeing her for myself at her aunt's reception, I'm surprised she even had one – though all the evidence clearly indicates that she did.'

'If we assume for the moment that there's only one boyfriend, and that he didn't kill her, why hasn't he come forward?' Beresford asked.

'He might not even know she's dead yet,' Meadows said.

'That's rather unlikely, isn't it?'

'She attended a girl's school,' Meadows pointed out. 'If the boyfriend's school is at the other end of town – and if he's not the kind to read the newspaper or listen to the radio – then it's more than possible that he hasn't heard yet.'

'And even if he has heard, he might be frightened to come forward,' Crane said.

'I don't think the boyfriend did it,' Paniatowski said decisively. 'Dr Duffy called it a "clean kill". I don't like the term – and neither does she, as a matter of fact – but I do know what she means by it. Jill's murder seems to me to have been a rather cold – almost clinical – one, and I can't see it being carried out by a schoolboy.'

'If we could only find the boyfriend in question, we'd be able to rule out all kinds of possibilities,' Beresford said.

'I'll have his name for you by the end of the afternoon,' Kate Meadows told the team.

'And how do you propose to do that?' Beresford wondered.

'I'm interviewing a number of girls from Jill's school this afternoon. They'll tell me who he is.'

'You seem very confident that you'll be able to get them to talk,' Beresford said.

'I am,' Meadows replied.

The first thing that Paniatowski noticed as she crossed the pub car park was the big blue Jaguar – and the second thing was the big ginger man, who was towering over her little MGA.

'I thought you were investigating that prison suicide in Yorkshire, sir,' she said.

'I was,' Baxter replied. 'Or, to be more accurate, I am. But I felt the need to talk to you about your investigation.'

'I don't like having people looking over my shoulder when I'm working on a case,' Paniatowski told him. 'And with respect, sir, you should know that better than anyone.'

'The question is, after what happened to Louisa, should you be on the case at all?' Baxter said.

'I can handle it,' Paniatowski said.

'Are you seriously trying to tell me that you're not finding it a tremendous strain?'

'Well, of course I find it a bloody strain. I find all my cases a strain. Murder's a straining business.'

'But this one is particularly hard on you – and you know it.'

Paniatowski sighed. 'Yes, I do know it,' she admitted.

'So why not hand it on to someone else?'

'I couldn't do that, even if I wanted to.'

'Why not?'

'Because of Louisa.'

'Ah, now I see it,' Baxter said. 'So you're looking for someone to vent your anger on for what happened to your daughter, are you? You can't punish the man who took Louisa, and this killer is standing in as a sort of substitute.'

'It's not that at all,' Paniatowski said, shaking her head.

'Then what is it?'

'Louisa was very shaken just after the abduction, but she's got to the point now where she can tell herself that the whole incident was just one of the things – like falling off a swing or getting lost in the woods – that can happen when you're growing up, and that while it

might have been very frightening at the time, it's of no real importance in the general scheme of things.'

'That's a very sensible attitude, and I'm glad she's been able to
adopt it,' Baxter said.

'But if I walk away from this case, that will be a signal to her
that I couldn't handle it. And it won't take her long to realize *why*
I couldn't handle it. And suddenly, because it's still so important to
me, the abduction will start to be important to her again.'

'She'd have to make the connection first,' Baxter pointed out.
'And how likely do you think that is?'

'It's very likely,' Paniatowski said firmly. 'She's got Bob Rutter's
genes – and that means she's a very smart girl. She might not see
the link immediately, but she *will* see it – and when she does, her
whole world will collapse around her.'

'You could lie to her about your reasons for withdrawing from
the case,' Baxter suggested.

'I could,' Paniatowski agreed, 'but she wouldn't believe me.'

'I see your problem and, believe me, I really do sympathize with
you,' Baxter said, 'but I'm the chief constable, and I have to look
beyond Louisa's needs to those of the wider community.'

'And what exactly does that mean?'

'It means you're so emotionally involved that I'm not sure you
can lead this investigation effectively. It means that a killer may get
away because you're not up to the job. It means that you could
damage the reputation of the Mid Lancs Constabulary and your own
reputation. And I'm not sure I can run the risk of any of those things
happening.'

'It's *because* I'm emotionally involved that I'm the best person
for the job,' Paniatowski argued desperately. 'There's nobody in the
force who wants to catch this killer more than I do. There's nobody
who'll be prepared to pull out as many stops as I will.'

'It's not your *commitment* that I'm casting doubts on . . .' Baxter
began.

'Give me four days to get a result, George,' Paniatowski pleaded.
'That's all I'm asking – just four days!'

Baxter hesitated for perhaps half a minute, then he looked down
at his watch.

'You have exactly seventy-two hours to make an arrest, Detective
Chief Inspector Paniatowski – and your time starts right now,' he
said.

She could have hugged him – hugged so hard that she'd have half squeezed the life out of even his massive frame – but instead, she just said, 'Thank you, sir. I really appreciate it.'

'Don't thank me until we both know I've made the right decision,' Baxter told her.

Then he turned, and walked quickly back to his Jaguar.

As he drove away, he didn't wave goodbye. In fact, he didn't even glance in her direction.

And that was perhaps a good thing, because after all the effort she'd put into persuading him to keep her on the case, she was exhausted, and anyone looking at her at that moment would have seen a lone and uncertain figure.

Jo Baxter stepped out of the jewellery shop in the centre of Whitebridge clutching a small box in her hand. The box contained a pair of rather expensive cufflinks that she had just bought for her husband to welcome him home after he had completed his investigation in Yorkshire.

As she walked along the street, she wondered just how long George was likely to be away.

'I'm planning on it being a week,' he'd told her, 'but if I hit resistance, it could be much longer than that.'

'But if it is any longer, you will come home at the weekends, won't you?' she'd asked.

'Prisons don't close down at the weekends – and it was over a weekend that Jeremy Templar hanged himself.'

'Which means that you *won't* be coming home?'

'The more time I put into the investigation, the sooner it will be over.'

And she knew that was true, she told herself now, but even though her husband had been gone for less than two days, she already missed him.

Before she met George, it had always been a mystery to her why no one had ever wanted to marry her. She was a good-looking woman – not stunning, but certainly pretty enough. She was competent, she was loyal, and she'd known that she could be very loving if only she were given the chance.

George had given her that chance. She had grabbed it with both hands, and been deliriously happy at first. Then they had moved to Lancashire, and she had met Monika Paniatowski at some police function or other – and it had been like looking into a very unflattering and disturbing mirror.

She pushed the thought of Paniatowski to one side, in order to concentrate her mind on what kind of feast she would prepare for George's homecoming – and that was when she saw the big blue Jag stopped at the traffic lights.

She increased her pace, hoping to catch up to her husband before the lights changed, but she didn't quite make it.

A warm glow filled her as she watched the car go up the street and disappear round the corner. George must have had a breakthrough in the inquiry, and wrapped it up in record time. And when she got home, he would be waiting for her. There would be no victory dinner, because she wouldn't have had time to prepare it. But at least she had the cufflinks.

And then it occurred to her that if George *was* going home, he was heading in the wrong direction.

NINE

Mrs Pierce's pastoral-care office was decorated in soothing pastel shades. There was a large cork notice board running the whole length of one wall, and on it Mrs Pierce had placed examples of painting and writing.

'Whenever I have to deal with a girl with problems, I always make sure that I put some of her work on display,' she explained to Meadows. 'It makes her feel that she's at least achieved something. It's only a small step towards building her confidence up, of course, but it is *a* step.'

'I can see how it would be,' Meadows agreed.

'Before we start the interviews, we need to talk about how they'll be structured. Growing girls – growing minds – need to feel enveloped in a structure. It's like a tightrope walker's safety harness to them – it encourages them to take steps they'd otherwise feel quite nervous about.' Mrs Pierce walked over to her desk. 'My first thought was you should sit at the desk, and I should stand some distance from it, but now I think it would be better if I was sitting beside you, so that I can offer the girls face-to-face guidance, should they need it. Would that be all right?'

'Certainly,' said Meadows, who had already worked out that she would be playing the game by Mrs Pierce's rules or not at all.

'You will ask the questions, but it must be clear to the girls that I am *inviting* you to ask them. And you must not tell them either to stand up or sit down. That's my job – part of the structure again.'

'Understood,' Meadows said. 'Could I ask a question now?'

'Of course.'

'There are two chairs on "our" side of the desk, but only one on the other side. Does that mean there won't be any parents present at the interviews?'

'Yes, that's what it means,' Mrs Pierce agreed. 'But you mustn't think their absence is an indication that they don't care about their children.'

'Then what does it indicate?'

'That they think I'll make a much better job of defending their little angels than they could possibly do themselves.'

'And are they right?'

Mrs Pierce smiled. 'Undoubtedly,' she said. 'As I see it, we have a duty to seek justice for the dead – poor little Jill Harris – but that shouldn't make us overlook our duty to protect the living.'

'Is that another way of saying that if I start to push too hard – or you don't like the direction the questions are going in – you'll cut me off cold?' Meadows guessed.

'Absolutely,' Mrs Pierce said. 'I'm so glad you understand.' She paused for a moment. 'By the way – and on an entirely different subject – did I ever mention the fact that, in my time, I've taught the daughters of some of the highest-ranking policemen in Whitebridge?' She smiled. 'And that, for some reason, they all seem to think that I'm wonderful.'

'I'm sure they do,' Meadows said, smiling back. 'And I'm also sure that if you made any complaints to them about my conduct during the interviews, they'd take them very seriously indeed.'

'I'd like to think so,' Mrs Pierce said. 'Not that it will be necessary to make any complaints, will it, Kate?'

'Of course not,' Meadows agreed. 'You do know, don't you,' she continued, 'that you'd make a much better job of running this school than Mrs Garner does?'

'I don't want to run Fairfield High,' Mrs Pierce said. 'I like the job that I've got.'

'I can see that. But it's still not an answer to my question.'

'I'm not interested in having Mrs Garner's job,' Mrs Pierce said firmly.

'I'm sure you're not,' Meadows replied. 'But if you ever *do* decide you want it, then God help her. Shall we see the first girl now?'

'Yes, I think that would probably be a good idea,' Mrs Pierce agreed.

Baxter had only just arrived back at Dunston Prison when the phone call came through from Whitebridge.

'You were in town at lunchtime,' said the accusing voice on the other end of the line.

'Yes, I was,' Baxter admitted.

'But you didn't bother to come and see me.'

'There simply wasn't time for that, sweetheart.'

'So what *was there* time for?'

'I was there on police business, Jo.'

'Business that couldn't have been done over the phone?'

'Yes.'

'So it was important?'

Baxter sighed. 'Yes.'

'There's only one important bit of police business going on Whitebridge at the moment, and that's the murder of that young girl.'

'There's a lot of important police business going on – it's just that you don't know about it,' Baxter said. He paused. 'But you're right, in a way. The visit was connected to Jill Harris' death.'

'And your very good friend Monika is in charge of that investigation, isn't she, George?'

'DCI Paniatowski's in charge of it, yes.'

'So you could find the time to go and see her, but you couldn't find the time to come and see me?'

'She's been through a great deal, recently,' Baxter said. 'Her own daughter went missing, and I was not sure she'd be able to handle . . .'

He stopped talking – because there was really no point in going on after Jo had hung up.

The first girl that Meadows and Mrs Pierce interviewed was large for her age, overweight, and wore crumpled stockings and a sulky expression.

Meadows knew the sort. There'd been a similar bully at her own school, and after enduring her taunts for more than a term, she'd decided to take matters – and clumps of the other girl's hair – into her own hands. The bullying had stopped after that.

But the problem with most bullies, she thought, was that they were not just physical cowards but also moral ones – and they'd rather set their own grandmothers alight than admit that they'd done anything wrong.

'Please take a seat, Antonia,' Mrs Pierce said, indicating the chair in front of the desk.

The girl sat down.

'Antonia was the first girl – though by no means the last – to get into a fight with Jill,' the head of pastoral care said to Meadows. 'Would you like to ask her about it?'

'Yes, please,' Meadows said. She turned the girl, hiding her dislike with the widest smile she could muster. 'What was the fight about, Antonia?'

'It wasn't my fault,' the girl muttered.

'Now we've discussed this before, haven't we, Antonia?' Mrs Pierce said sternly. 'And if you remember, we reached the conclusion that, to a certain extent, a fight is the fault of everybody who takes part in it. Isn't that right?'

'Yes, Miss,' Antonia agreed sullenly.

'So what was it about?' Meadows asked.

'I don't want to talk about it.'

'You didn't want to talk about it with me, either, and I let you get away with it,' Mrs Pierce said. 'But Miss Meadows is from the police, and not only should you *want* to talk about it – because it might help her to catch whoever killed Jill – but you *have* to talk about it.'

'She said my mum was a cow,' Antonia volunteered, reluctantly.

'Why did she say it?'

'I don't know.'

'You hadn't had a disagreement earlier?'

'No.'

'So she just walked up to you in the playground, and said your mum was a cow?'

'Yes.'

'I don't believe you,' Meadows said.

'I don't care,' Antonia told her. 'And I don't care that Jill Harris got killed, either. She deserved to be killed, because she was a . . . a . . .'

'A what?' Meadows asked.

'Nothing,' Antonia said. She turned hopefully to Mrs Pierce. 'Can I go now, Miss?'

'Yes, you can go for the present,' Mrs Pierce said, 'but don't imagine, Antonia, that after your terrible outburst about Jill, we won't be having another little talk later.'

The girl climbed to her feet and stomped out of the door.

'I try to find the good in all my charges, but sometimes it's an uphill struggle,' Mrs Pierce said philosophically.

'Jill was a what?' Meadows asked.

Mrs Pierce shrugged. 'A bitch? A tart? Who knows? But whatever

Fat Antonia thought about her, it certainly wasn't something she was prepared to say in front of me.'

Mrs Pierce had described Tilly Roberts as a pretty little thing, and that was exactly what she was, Meadows thought. She had an oval face and delicate features, and with them went an air of appealing vulnerability that would ensure that, when she got older, men would be fighting each other for the right to protect her.

'You made friends with Jill Harris almost as soon as you got to this school, didn't you, Tilly?' Meadows asked.

'Yes.'

'But then – suddenly – you stopped being friends?'

'Yes.'

Strictly speaking, she was telling the truth, Meadows decided – but it was a *half truth* at best.

'Did you stop being friends *altogether* – or just in school?' she asked, taking a stab in the dark.

'Just in school,' Tilly admitted.

'And why was that?'

'We just did.'

'We'd like the truth, please, Tilly,' Mrs Pierce said firmly.

Tilly's lower lip began to tremble.

'It was easier,' she said.

'Easier?'

'I thought if we weren't friends in school, then Jill wouldn't have to get into fights any more.'

'Why *did* she get into fights?' Meadows asked. 'Did she do it to protect you? Were you being bullied?'

'Yes . . . no . . . not exactly,' Tilly said. She bit her lip. 'Some of the other girls didn't like us being friends.'

'Was that because they wanted you to be *their* friend, instead of hers?'

'No.'

'Then why?'

Meadows had been expecting tears for some time, and now they came in a flood.

'I was too late,' the girl sobbed. 'I . . . I was t-too late, and it's all my f-fault.'

'What was it that you were too late for?' Meadows asked urgently. 'And why was it all your fault?'

'I think that's quite enough for the moment,' Mrs Pierce said decisively. 'Go to the nurse's office, Tilly. Tell her that I said she should let you lie down until you're feeling better. Have you got that?'

The girl nodded.

'Y-y-yes, Miss.'

'Off you go then.'

Another couple of minutes, Meadows thought. Just two more minutes and I'd have found out all I needed to know.

But she was starting to suspect that she knew most of it already.

Jane White was quite a pretty girl, who had kind eyes but looked as if she could be easily led – and as she walked into the room, she was clearly upset.

If there was any weak link in the chain that held together the conspiracy of silence, she was it, Meadows decided.

'Miss Meadows would like you to tell her why you got into a fight with Jill Harris, Jane,' Mrs Pierce said.

'She called my mum a cow,' Jane said woodenly.

'She seems to have spent half her time in school telling other girls that their mums were cows,' Meadows said.

'She did,' Jane agreed – but her heart was not in it.

'Tilly told us that the reason she stopped being friends with Jill was so the fights would stop. Why do you think she said that?'

'I don't know.'

'You see, there's no reason why the two of them not being friends any more would stop Jill being rude about other girls' mothers, is there?'

'No.'

'So I don't think the fights were about rudeness at all.'

'They were.'

She was about to start crying any second, Meadows thought, and when she did, Mrs Pierce would call an end to the interview.

'You need to ask the *right* question!' screamed a voice somewhere at the back of her mind. 'Ask the right question, and she'll give you everything you want!'

And with a certain flash of insight, she realized what that right question was.

'Are you sorry that Jill's dead?' she asked Jane.

'Yes,' the girl replied, as tears started to appear in her eyes.

'Why are you sorry?'

'Because . . . because we were all so horrible to her.'

It wasn't a logical connection, Meadows thought – but it was a perfectly understandable one.

'Horrible?' she repeated.

'Yes,' Jane confirmed, and started to sob in earnest.

Meadows looked anxiously at Mrs Pierce, who nodded to signal that she could go on for just a *little* longer.

'What made you decide to be horrible to her?' Meadows asked.

'We . . . we caught her kissing Tilly.'

'On the lips?'

'Yes. And Antonia said . . . Antonia said it was disgusting, and we had to make them stop.'

'So why did you tell all those lies about the reason for the fights?' Meadows asked.

'Because . . . because Miss is here.'

'Why should that stop you?'

Even through Jane's tears, Meadows could see the look of amazement in her eyes that anyone should need to ask such a stupid question.

'We couldn't say anything because teachers don't know about things like that,' Jane said.

TEN

When Dolly Turner's lover called her (how she adored that term – *lover* – it was so sophisticated, so grown-up!) he suggested that they meet in the park as normal, but Dolly herself was far from happy about that.

'There was a murder there, only a couple of nights ago,' she protested. 'It was a girl – just like me.'

'I'm sure she wasn't *at all* like you, you little sexpot,' Tony – the lover – replied.

Dolly felt a warm glow flush through her entire body. If one of the boys she knew at school had called her a sexpot, it would have meant nothing to her, because they were no more than pimply youths, and didn't know what they were talking about anyway. But when Tony – a man of the world – used those words, it was like being crowned the May Queen.

Even so, she still didn't like the idea of going to the park.

'The bobbies will be there,' she said weakly.

'The police *were* there – there were all over the place yesterday – but they're not there now,' Tony said, with a firmness in his voice which she sometimes found a little intimidating.

'What if the murderer comes back?' Dolly asked.

Tony laughed. 'What if the murderer comes back?' he repeated. 'You are a silly little sexpot. Whoever he is, he'll be long gone, won't he?'

'I don't know.'

'Look,' Tony continued, more seriously, 'we both know why the park is the best place for us to meet, don't we?'

'Do we?'

'Of course we do – and it's the best place for us to meet *because* . . .'

He paused again, for her to complete the lesson that he had taught her.

'Because it's safe,' she said reluctantly.

'Exactly!'

'But it wasn't safe for Jill Harris.'

'I'm not talking about Jill Harris – I'm saying it's safe for *us*.'

'A pub would be safe.'

'No, it wouldn't. People would soon notice us in a pub. Besides –' Tony laughed again – 'I'd get into big trouble for taking a girl of your age into licensed premises.'

'I want to go to a pub,' Dolly said stubbornly.

'Well, you can't,' Tony replied, and now he sounded more like her father than her lover. Another pause. 'Look, I know this is difficult for you . . .'

'It is.'

'But it's not exactly easy for me, either. So if we were to both decide that, *because* it's so difficult, we probably shouldn't . . .'

'No,' she gasped, cutting him off before he said something he would find it hard to go back on.

'So we'll meet in the park – usual time, usual place?' he asked, with a hint of satisfaction in his voice.

'Yes,' she agreed, defeatedly.

It was early evening. The quick-drink-after-work brigade had already gone home, and the out-for-the-night boozers had not yet arrived, so the team had the public bar of the Drum and Monkey almost to themselves.

It was Colin Beresford who had everybody's attention at that moment.

'I'm afraid it was just as we thought it might be,' he said, opening his briefcase and laying the results of the detective constables' search on the table. 'It was a nice day on Saturday, and there were a fair number of people in the park in the early afternoon. But by the time Jill got there, it was pretty much deserted.'

'When did Tilly Roberts get to the park, Kate?' Paniatowski asked her sergeant.

'At about a quarter to five,' Meadows answered.

'And did she see anybody?'

'Not a soul. She spent about five minutes looking round for Jill – because Jill had promised she'd be there if she could get away from the wedding – and then she went home.'

'Have you drawn up a list of possible suspects, Colin?' Paniatowski asked.

'Yes, I have,' the inspector confirmed, 'but I'd be lying if I said I was happy with it.'

'Why's that?'

'Because given the actual details of the crime – no torture, no sexual assault – it's a pretty *thin* list. If Jill *had* been mutilated or interfered with, we could have pulled in at least a dozen men who've shown a tendency towards that sort of thing, even if they haven't actually gone over the edge before. As it is, I've only come up with three or four names, and I've been scraping the bottom of the barrel a bit to find even that many.'

'Maybe the murder had nothing at all to do with the killer's own sick sexual fantasy,' Jack Crane suggested. 'Maybe he killed her simply because he hated her.'

'Hated her?' Beresford repeated. 'But she was just a kid!'

'*You* think of her as a kid,' Crane said, 'but perhaps when the killer looked at her, he didn't see a kid at all – he saw a lesbian.'

'In other words, he hated her not for *who* she was, but for *what* she was,' Paniatowski said, with quickening interest.

'That's right, boss.' Crane turned to Meadows. 'Jill and Tilly had met in the park on other occasions, hadn't they, Sarge?'

'Two or three times.'

'And they probably did more than just hold hands when they were there, didn't they?'

'Tilly's very sketchy on the details, but the love bites on Jill had to come from somewhere, so I think we can assume that that's the case.'

'So say our killer sees them on one of those occasions. He's shocked and horrified by what they're doing. He regards it as an abomination.'

'Why doesn't he say something to them about it, then and there?' Paniatowski asked.

'I don't know,' Crane admitted. 'Perhaps he's *too* shocked to do or say anything. Perhaps he doesn't quite appreciate what he's seen at the time, but thinking about it later, the full implications hit him.'

'Or maybe he *wants* to kill her then and there, but since there are so many people around, he decides it would be wiser to hold off,' Meadows said.

'So he's got her marked down as his target, and the first real opportunity he gets is last Saturday afternoon?' Paniatowski asked.

'Or possibly he had no intention of killing her *until* he saw her in the park again,' Crane said.

'It's Bill Horrocks!' Beresford said excitedly. 'It's bloody Bill Horrocks.'

'Who's Bill Horrocks?' Meadows asked.

'I should have thought of him before,' Beresford said, ignoring the sergeant and directing his remarks to Paniatowski, 'but until young Jack came up with his lesbian-hating idea, he didn't fit the profile!'

'Easy, Colin,' Paniatowski cautioned. 'I admit he's starting to look like a good prospect . . .'

'It has to be him.'

'. . . but we don't want to go putting all our eggs in one basket, so while we'll certainly pull him in for questioning, we'll pull in the men already on your list, as well.'

'It has to be Billy Horrocks,' Beresford said firmly.

Dolly liked the sex. It could be uncomfortable – and sometimes even quite painful – but she was sure she liked it. What she *didn't* like – what depressed her – was the time straight after it, when Tony had taken the thing off his thing, thrown it into the bushes, and was pulling his trousers back up.

She wasn't quite sure *why* it depressed her. Perhaps it was because Tony didn't really seem to be any more. Or perhaps because she sensed that he wished *she* wasn't.

'That was nice, wasn't it?' she said tentatively.

Tony brushed some dirt off his suit. 'Could you get off my coat now, Dolly?' he asked.

She stood up, feeling thoroughly miserable. Tony picked up the coat, shook it, then slipped it on.

'You did like it, didn't you?' she asked desperately. 'I did everything you wanted me to.'

'You were great,' he said.

But there was no conviction behind his words – no real warmth.

Her lover clicked on his lighter, and examined his wrist watch in its naked flame.

'Right, I'd better be off,' he said. 'I'll give you a ring when we can meet again.'

'Couldn't you walk me to the end of the park?' Dolly asked.

'You're a big girl now – you don't need me to hold your hand,' Tony said, irritated.

No, I don't *need* you to hold my hand, but I *want* you to, she thought.

'What if the murderer's still about?' she asked, almost in tears.

'I've told you, he'll be long gone.'

'It wouldn't take you five minutes.'

Tony sighed. 'Somebody might see us. Besides, I've got another appointment.'

'You mean, you have to go home,' Dolly said bitterly.

'You've known right from the start about my domestic situation,' Tony countered.

'You what?'

'You've known that I was married.'

'Yes, but . . .'

'But nothing! This is the way it has to be – at least for the present.'

'At least for the present,' she repeated.

He put his hands on her shoulders and kissed her forehead.

'One day, we'll be together all the time, but that day hasn't come yet,' he said softly. 'You will wait, won't you?'

'Yes,' she agreed, 'I'll wait.'

He removed his hands. 'Right then, as I said, I'd better be getting off,' he told her.

And then he walked rapidly through the bushes, heading for the path which led to the south gate.

Dolly shivered, partly because it was cold in the park, but partly because she had an uneasy feeling that she was being watched.

George Baxter – a whisky in one hand, his pipe in the other – was sitting in his room at Dunston Prison, feeling personally and professionally miserable.

It hadn't been a good day, he told himself. In fact, it had been a perfectly awful day.

He had rung Jo twice and she'd hung up on him both times, which – he admitted – was perfectly understandable when you looked at things from her perspective. But he had a perspective, too. He had a police force to run, a marriage to prop up and a suicide to investigate – and it was all bloody hard work.

He forced himself to focus on his investigation. The crucial question of whether or not the prison authorities had been negligent was still unanswered. And it was likely to *remain* unanswered, because though he couldn't say definitely that everyone he'd interviewed had deliberately blindsided him, he strongly suspected that was just what they *had* done.

He'd been far too orthodox in his approach to the whole inquiry, he decided. It was time he started talking to a few officers who didn't have a vested interest in what conclusions the investigation drew. And it was time, too, that he started questioning someone from the *other side* of the bars.

Louisa, already wearing her pyjamas and dressing gown, met Paniatowski at the front door.

'How did it go today, Mum?' she asked, with a barely suppressed gleam of excitement in her eyes.

Paniatowski placed her briefcase on the hall table and bent down. 'A hug would be nice – if you could spare one,' she said.

'Oh, sorry, Mum,' Louisa replied, flinging her arms around her mother. But it was a very short embrace, and when she broke away again, she said, 'So how *did* it go today?'

'It was a day like any other day,' Paniatowski said, putting her hand on her daughter's shoulder and guiding her into the living room. 'We made some progress, and we've had some setbacks.'

'Tell me about the progress then,' Louisa said, jumping into one of the armchairs.

Paniatowski sat down opposite her. 'You know I can't do that, Louisa,' she said.

'Why not?' her daughter demanded. 'I went with you to Jill's house, didn't I? Doesn't that make me almost part of the team?'

Paniatowski frowned. It had been a mistake taking Louisa with her on an investigation – she saw that now – but at the time she hadn't even known it *would be* an investigation.

'For goodness' sake, don't look so severe and disapproving, Mum,' Louisa said.

'Sorry,' Paniatowski replied. She smiled. 'I can't tell you anything about the case. You know that yourself.' And then, to mitigate the severity a little, she added lightly, 'You'll have to be at least a detective sergeant before I can go into any kind of detail.'

'And how long will that take me?' Louisa asked, in a serious voice. 'Ten years?'

It had been a long day – most of them were – and Paniatowski wondered if she'd really heard Louisa say what she thought she'd heard her say.

'Are you telling me you want to a police officer when you grow up?' she asked, expecting, despite the look on the girl's face, that Louisa would laugh and say of course she didn't.

'Yes, I do.'

'But why?'

'Wouldn't you like me to follow in your footsteps?'

'Yes . . . no . . . I don't know,' Paniatowski said, confused. She took a deep breath. 'There's nothing wrong with being a police officer . . .'

'Of course there isn't – or you wouldn't be one.'

'But with all the advantages you've had . . .'

'So you're saying I should only join the force if I really can't do anything else?'

'No, but a bright girl like you . . .'

'Aren't *you* bright?'

'I suppose so, but . . .'

'Well, there you are, then.'

Paniatowski was delighted to see her daughter could stand up for herself in an argument, and rather distressed that she should have chosen this *particular* argument to demonstrate the talent. She had never given much thought to what Louisa might do when she grew up, because that time was still so far away. But it wasn't actually *that* far away, she suddenly realized. In fact, it was just around the corner.

'I want you to do whatever will make you happiest,' she said.

'Really?' Louisa asked sceptically.

'Really,' Paniatowski said. 'Of course, I'd be very proud of you if you ended up as a brain surgeon or an architect – but I'd be equally proud of you if you worked in a shop, as long as that's what you wanted.'

'And you'd also be proud of me if I became a police officer,' Louisa said relentlessly.

'And I'd also be proud of you if you became a police officer,' Paniatowski agreed, biting on the bullet. 'I just don't want you joining the force because of me. You understand that, don't you?'

Louisa gave a half nod – which might have signalled understanding, or might not – then said, 'I was right, wasn't I?'

'Right about what?' Paniatowski asked, mystified.

'About what I said in Jill's bedroom – that she was hiding a very important secret.'

As she was signing the adoption papers, Paniatowski had promised herself she would never lie to Louisa, and that promise held firm now. And anyway, there would have been no point in lying, because the girl would have seen right through her.

'Yes, Jill had a secret,' she admitted.

Louisa grinned. 'See?' she said. 'I've already got the makings of an excellent detective.'

There were lights running along the path to the north gate of the park, but Dolly was still some distance from that path, and was picking her way through the bushes in semi-darkness.

Twice, she thought she heard a bush close to her move, as if somebody was hiding behind it.

'It's nothing but the wind rustling through the leaves,' she told herself desperately, ignoring the fact that there *was* no wind to speak of.

She wanted to run towards the lights. But she knew that would be a mistake, because if she lost her footing, she would fall on her face, and once she was on the ground . . .

Fighting her ever-increasing fear, she forced herself to put one foot before the other and test the ground before entrusting her full weight to it.

The path was no more than a dozen yards away, she thought – she was going to be all right!

And perhaps the prospect of reaching the path was enough to encourage her to abandon her caution a little, because suddenly her left leg buckled slightly under her, and she stumbled forward.

She stumbled – but by some miracle, she didn't fall. She came to a halt, took a deep breath, and concentrated on re-establishing her equilibrium.

'Only ten yards,' she mumbled to herself. 'Ten yards at the most.'

And it was at that very moment that she felt the hands locking around her throat.

Her attacker was standing right behind her, his rubbery fingers pressing down hard against her soft skin.

She began to choke, and dark spots were already starting to appear before her eyes.

In a panicked attempt to break free, she twisted first to the left, and then to the right, but the attacker had his body pressed closely against hers, and breaking free was simply impossible.

She tried to scream – but she couldn't.

More through desperation than planning, she lifted her right leg and kicked backwards. She felt the heel of her shoe make contact with something hard – maybe the man's knee – and suddenly the hands had gone from her throat and she could hear the sound of a body falling to the ground.

Now she was free to scream. And scream she did. It was a harsh, rough terrified scream, which seemed to fill the whole park.

She was conscious of her attacker moving, and knew she should run away, but her legs seemed frozen to the spot.

She screamed again – even louder this time – and heard the sound of feet, crashing through the undergrowth in the distance.

'Tony!' she sobbed. 'Help me, Tony.'

Behind her, she heard a scurrying noise and the whoosh of branches being knocked roughly aside.

Her attacker was leaving, she thought. She was going to live!

The crashing grew louder, and suddenly Tony was by her side.

'What the bloody hell's happened?' he demanded.

'I was attacked,' she croaked. 'The murderer . . .'

'Are you sure you're not just making this up?' Tony asked suspiciously.

She could not believe he had said that.

'The murderer,' she repeated. 'He . . . he was here.'

'I mean, how do I know you're not just pretending – to punish me for not escorting you out of the park?' Tony asked.

'My throat,' she gasped. 'Look at my throat.'

He flicked on his lighter, and held it so close to her neck that she could feel the heat.

'Jesus!' he said, 'you really were attacked!'

'Yes . . . I . . .'

'We need to think,' Tony interrupted. 'There's a taxi rank at the end of the park. I'll give you some money, and walk most of the way to it with you. I promise I won't let you out of my sight until you're safely inside the cab. But you mustn't tell the taxi driver what happened. You mustn't tell *anybody* what happened.'

'But we have to let the police know,' Dolly protested.

'I don't think that's a very good idea,' Tony told her. 'If we go to the police, they'll want to know what we were both doing in the park. And that could be rather tricky, couldn't it?'

'Somebody tried to kill me!' Dolly moaned.

'Yes, I know that, but they didn't succeed, so there's no real harm done,' Tony said. 'Those bruises look nasty, but if you say you've got a sore throat and wear a scarf, they'll be gone in a day or two.'

'Somebody tried to kill me,' Dolly repeated – because there didn't really seem to be anything else to say.

'Look, I was keeping this a secret until the next time I saw you, but since you're so upset, I suppose I'd better tell you now,' Tony said. 'It's your birthday next week, isn't it?'

'Yes.'

'Well, I've arranged a special treat to celebrate it – a slap-up meal in a really posh restaurant.'

She was confused. Everything was *so* confusing.

'A really posh restaurant?' she said. 'But you told me we couldn't even go in a *pub* together.'

'Ah, yes, that is what I told you, and it's quite true,' Tony said awkwardly. 'But . . .'

'But what?'

'But . . . err . . . I was only talking about Whitebridge when I said that. This posh restaurant's in Accrington, where nobody knows us.'

'But wouldn't they think . . .'

'You can pretend you're my daughter while we're in the restaurant – you wouldn't mind that, would you? – but later, when we're in the park . . .' Tony pulled himself up suddenly, as he realized what he was saying. 'No, not in the park . . . of course not in the park . . . somewhere nice . . . maybe down by the river, maybe out on the moors.' He paused to take a breath. 'Later, after all that pretending in the restaurant, we'll go somewhere nice, and you'll be my little sexpot, just like you always are. You'd like that, wouldn't you?'

'Yes,' she said – because she *would* like it.

'Only, if we go to the police, that can't happen, can it?' Tony asked. 'There'll be no posh restaurant and no little trip out to some-where nice – because I'll be in gaol. So I think it's best we forget the police. Don't you?'

'I suppose so,' Dolly said dubiously.

Tony laughed. 'You suppose so,' he repeated, as if she'd made a joke. 'You're a funny little sexpot, aren't you?'

'Yes,' she agreed.

'Right then, let's find you a taxi, just like we planned,' he said.

'All right,' she agreed.

'There is just one more thing,' Tony told her.

'What?'

'I must admit that I'm a little hurt you've never thanked me for rescuing you.'

'Thank you, Tony,' Dolly said meekly.

ELEVEN

I t was a few minutes before the sun was due to rise, and the uniformed sergeant was sitting in the passenger seat of one of the patrol cars.

'The feller we're about to drop in on used to be a very important figure in this town, you know,' he told the driver.

'Did he?' asked the other man, though he was not really interested, and was instead mentally debating the important question of whether the overtime he would be earning was worth dragging himself from his bed at this ungodly hour.

'A very important figure,' the sergeant repeated. He glanced down the street that lay in front of them – at the decaying terraced houses and gardens filled with old prams and rotting fridges. 'And now he's living in Balaclava Terrace. How are the mighty fallen, eh?'

'That's right,' the driver agreed, as he calculated whether the overtime payment would be large enough to buy him the graphite fishing rod that he'd had his eye on for some time.

A bird – it might have been a sparrow – chirped on one of the roofs, and the sergeant switched on the car's interior light and checked his watch.

'Six twenty-seven,' he announced. 'Time to move,'

The driver turned the ignition key, flicked his back lights on and off – as a signal to the van parked behind them – and pulled away from the kerb.

'Get your foot down, lad – we don't want to give the bugger any warning we're coming,' the sergeant said.

The driver pressed down hard on the accelerator, and the patrol car shot forward.

'Seventy, sixty-nine, sixty-eight, sixty-seven . . .' the sergeant said, counting down the numbers of the houses they were now whizzing past. 'Fifty-three, fifty-one, forty-nine . . . That's it. Slam the anchors on, lad.'

The driver hit the brake, and the car skidded to a halt. Behind him, the driver of the van was carrying out a similar manoeuvre.

The sergeant leapt out of the car, rushed up to the short path of number forty-five, and hammered on the door.

'Police!' he shouted. 'Open up! Do it now – or we'll break the bloody door down.'

The residents of Balaclava Street were not the only ones to suffer a rude awakening that early morning. Those who lived in New Bridge Street, East Street, Elm Avenue and India Mills Road were similarly awoken by a sudden banging on the door and a demand from the police that they be admitted.

The disturbance did not last for long. By six thirty-two, when the last hurriedly dressed man on DI Beresford's list was led hand-cuffed to the waiting patrol car, it was all over, and those who had heard the knock on the door with some trepidation – but had not subsequently been arrested themselves – could return to their beds and their uneasy sleep.

Dolly Turner lived far enough away from any of the dawn raids to have avoided being woken up by them, but she was awake anyway. Dolly had hardly slept at all the previous night, but instead had tossed and turned – and worried.

She knew that Tony was right when he'd said that if they reported what had happened to the police, he'd probably end up in serious trouble. And she was looking forward to going to a posh restaurant in Accrington, though at least part of her suspected that if she hadn't been attacked, the question of the restaurant would never have come up at all.

But . . . but . . .

But she *had* been attacked!

She could have been killed!

And surely, *whatever* Tony said, the police would have to be told, or she'd be in trouble as well!

She heard the sound of shuffling feet in the corridor outside, then a cough, then the sound of her dad urinating into the toilet bowl.

Her dad!

She hadn't even thought about him as she'd mentally struggled over what to do next. But if the police found out about Tony, her dad would find out about Tony. And if her dad found out . . .

It simply wasn't fair that you should have problems like this to deal with when you were only fourteen years old, she told herself.

It simply wasn't fair at all.

Paniatowski examined herself in the mirror over the basin in the women's toilets. Her eyes were bloodshot, but that was only to be expected after having spent half the night studying criminal records. There were lines etched into her face, too, and not all of them – she strongly suspected – were due to exhaustion.

'Louisa was right, you're starting to show your age, Monika,' she said to the image in the mirror, and she was so tired that she could almost have sworn that image nodded back in agreement.

She turned on the tap, cupped her hands under it, and splashed some water on her face.

'Better,' she said when she looked into the mirror again, 'but not *that* much better.'

'You want to be careful, boss,' said a voice from the doorway. 'If people hear you talking to yourself, they'll start thinking that you're as far round the twist as the rest of the DCIs.'

Paniatowski turned to look at Meadows, who appeared as fresh as if she'd had a good night's sleep.

'Did you come down here *just* to take the piss, Sergeant?' she asked. 'Or was there some other purpose to your visit?'

Meadows grinned. 'I came to tell you the suspects have arrived, boss,' she said.

'All five of them?'

'Yes.'

Paniatowski looked into the mirror again, and studied her reflection's eyes. They were still red, but now that the adrenalin had started pumping through her, all signs of tiredness were gone.

'Then let's get started,' she said.

Most of the prison officers in the canteen were sitting in groups of two or three, but there was one – a sandy-haired man in his late twenties – who was alone, and it was to his table that Baxter carried his breakfast tray.

The officer looked up, and there was a slightly worried expression on his face. 'I wasn't on duty on any of the occasions that Jeremy Templar was attacked, so there's really nothing I can tell you,' he said.

Jeremy Templar, Baxter noted. Not just "Templar" or Prisoner Some-Number-or-Other, but *Jeremy* Templar. Now that was interesting.

'What makes you think I've come across here to ask you questions?' he said aloud.

'Haven't you?' the officer asked.

'No, the only reason I'm here is to have my breakfast, and I thought I might as well share a table with a fellow "ginger", unless, of course, my fellow "ginger" objects to that. *Do* you object?'

The officer shrugged. 'Not really.'

It was about as warm an invitation as he was likely to get, Baxter thought, placing his tray on the table and sitting down.

'So what's your name, son – and how long have you been in the prison service?' he asked, as he sliced off a piece of sausage and dipped it in the deep-yellow yolk of one of his fried eggs.

'I thought you said you wouldn't be asking any questions,' the officer replied suspiciously.

'This isn't questioning, son,' Baxter said, good-naturedly. 'If you want to see how I *question* people, you should sit in on one of the interrogations. All I'm doing at the moment is making a little light conversation, but, of course, if you'd rather I just shut up . . .'

The officer flushed slightly.

'I'm sorry,' he said, 'I must have sounded rather rude.'

'Think no more of it,' Baxter said magnanimously.

'My name's Tim Robson, and I've been working here for about three years,' the other man told him.

'And do you like it?' Baxter asked, cutting the corner of a piece of sliced bread.

'I wouldn't say I exactly *like* it,' Robson answered, 'but it's a necessary job that's not as easy as it looks, so there's a certain satisfaction to be gained from doing it well.'

'It certainly *is* necessary,' Baxter agreed, and then, deciding to test the water, he added provocatively, 'The longer we keep this scum off the streets, the better it is for everybody. Don't you agree?'

'There are certainly some prisoners in here who shouldn't be released for a long, long time,' Robson said carefully.

Baxter nodded. He just about had the lad's number now, he decided. Robson was something of a vague, polite liberal. Within the prison context, he was probably slightly uncomfortable about both his liberality and his good manners, and thus would always do his best to keep out of any discussions in which his true self might be revealed. All of which meant that if he was going to say anything useful, he needed to be steered into it.

'Most of the officers in this prison think I'm here to pin the blame for Templar's suicide on them, but that's not the case at all,' Baxter said. 'In fact, the longer I'm here, the more convinced I am that, working under these conditions, there wasn't much at all they could do to protect him.'

'No, I don't think there was much they could do,' Robson agreed.

'That's not to say that I don't get the distinct feeling that any of them lost much sleep over what happened to the man,' Baxter continued. 'I'd even go far as to guess that most of them consider that whatever punishment he took from the other inmates was well deserved.' He paused for a significant moment. 'I expect that's how you feel yourself, isn't it?'

'And how do *you* feel?' Robson asked, evasively.

'As far as I'm concerned, the only punishment that any man should be subjected to is to serve out the sentence handed down to him by the judge,' Baxter replied.

Robson nodded, but said nothing.

'Of course, it would be unreasonable to expect the ordinary, decent prisoners, who are forced to rub shoulders with the dirty pervert every day, to have the same attitude as I do,' Baxter continued.

'But what if he wasn't a filthy pervert at all?' Robson asked.

Now he hadn't been expecting *that*, Baxter thought.

'Are you telling me that Templar didn't do it?' he asked.

'I can't say, with any degree of certainty, that he *was* innocent, but I believe that he was,' Robson replied.

'You talked to him, did you?'

'No, we're not supposed to have conversations with the prisoners about anything – and especially about the crimes they've been convicted of.'

'So where does this belief in his innocence come from?'

Robson looked embarrassed. 'This will sound stupid.'

'No, it won't,' Baxter assured him.

'It comes from having observed his wife on visiting days,' Robson said in a rush – almost as if he believed that expressing the thought quickly would somehow make it sound less idiotic.

'Go on,' Baxter encouraged.

'There are some women who decide not to stick by their husbands when they've been sent to prison, but they're in a small minority,' Robson said. 'A lot of the prisoners' wives don't actually approve of what their men did to end up in jail – but they still come to see them religiously, every visiting day, and give them what comfort they can.'

'And a great comfort it must *be* to them,' said Baxter, who still had no idea where the other man was heading.

'The one exception to that rule is in the case of the sex offenders,' Robson told him. '*Their* wives are so disgusted by what they've done that they never visit. But Mrs Templar came every single visiting day. And we looked forward to it almost as much as he did, because she was a very attractive woman, and all the officers fancied her.'

Baxter sighed. The problem of talking to young men with an idealistic streak, he thought, was that they invariably got things wrong.

'It's not as straightforward as that, son,' he said. 'A man can have a beautiful wife and still fancy little girls – or little boys, for that matter. I've seen it happen scores of times myself.'

'I'm not a simpleton, you know,' Robson said, and now there was a hint of real anger in his voice. 'In fact, I'm very far from the naive fool that you seem to take me for!'

'Sorry, lad, I never meant to suggest . . .' Baxter began.

'It's my fault,' Robson interrupted, calming down a little. 'I should never have talked about Mrs Templar's looks, because her looks weren't what was important about her.'

'Then what *was* important?'

'Her sensitivity and her intelligence were what mattered. If he'd been guilty, she'd have known – and she'd never have come to see him like she did.'

'Maybe she'd simply forgiven him,' Baxter said, speaking tentatively, so as not to upset Robson again.

The officer shook his head firmly. 'If she'd just forgiven him, you'd have been able to tell.'

'You think so?'

'I *know* so. There was pity in her eyes – yes – but it wasn't pity for a man who had fallen short of the standards she expected of him, it was pity for a man who should never have been in the awful situation he now found himself in.'

An innocent man in Templar's position would be just as likely as a guilty man to take his own life, Baxter thought. Perhaps even more likely to, because he would see no point in continuing to live in a world in which right and wrong had been turned upside down.

He reminded himself that as a special investigator, his only task was to determine whether or not Templar's death could have been prevented – and that the man's guilt or innocence was well beyond his remit. But if Templar *had* been innocent, then it seemed to Baxter more important than ever that the report he wrote reached the right conclusions.

'Who would I go to if I wanted some fingers breaking?' he asked.

'I beg your pardon!' Robson said, shocked. '*Do* you want to have someone's fingers broken?'

'Of course not,' Baxter replied. 'But I would like to know who's in control on the other side of the bars.'

Robson glanced guiltily around him, as if to check that none of the other officers were listening.

'The man you're looking for is called Lennie Greene,' he said in a whisper.

According to his record sheet, Harold William Swain was fifty-four years old, and though his body looked a lot older than that, there was still a hint in his eyes of the much younger man's obsession that had driven him to lose everything he must once have valued.

Paniatowski and Beresford sat down opposite him, and Paniatowski said, 'Sorry to have dragged you in here so early in the morning, Mr Swain.'

'No, you're not,' Swain replied. 'You're not sorry at all. And I didn't do it, you know.'

'Didn't do what?' Paniatowski asked.

'I didn't kill that young girl in the Corporation Park. I've never killed anybody.'

'That's surely more by luck than judgement,' Paniatowski pointed out. 'You gave the girl who you raped such a thorough and vicious beating that she certainly *could have* died.'

'I couldn't help myself. I'm not a violent man, but I was in the grip of a force beyond my control – a force I didn't even understand back then.'

'Do you understand that force now?'

Swain nodded. 'Yes, I believe I do.'

'Then why don't you explain it to me?'

'The girl didn't make me happy,' Swain said simply.

'And that was your reason for half killing her, was it?'

'Yes, that was my reason. It wasn't a good reason – but it was reason enough, at the time. I felt she'd betrayed me, you see.'

'How could she have betrayed you? You didn't even know her!'

'It didn't matter that we were strangers to one another. She was still *supposed* to make me happy.'

'Who told you that?'

'Nobody. It was just something I knew, deep inside me. She was supposed to quench the terrible yearning that had been burning me up. And she didn't. All she did was cry and scream. So I punished her – though I now know that the person who I really wanted to punish was myself.'

'I'm sure it would be a great consolation to her to know that,' Paniatowski said sarcastically.

'Don't think I haven't tried to explain it to her,' Swain said passionately. 'When they finally let me out of prison, the very first thing I did was to find out where she lived, and beg her to forgive me. She wouldn't listen. She called the police instead, and they warned me that if I didn't want to go back to gaol, I'd better keep away from her.'

'You can hardly blame either the girl herself, or the police, for that,' Paniatowski said.

'No,' Swain admitted. 'I can't.'

'So tell me, Mr Swain, do you still feel the same urges?'

'Yes, I do, but I'm getting treatment for them.'

'Is it working?'

'I think so. The urges are still there, but they're nowhere near as strong as they used to be.'

'So on Saturday, when you were in the park . . .'

'I was not in the park when that poor girl was killed.'

'How do you know *when exactly* she was killed? There was nothing about her time of death in the papers.'

'I don't know when she died, but that doesn't matter, because I wasn't in the park at all. I was attending a weekend residential course in Preston, to help deal with my problem.'

Swain had never been her prime suspect, Paniatowski thought, but she still couldn't help the sinking feeling she had when he mentioned an alibi which she was sure would check out.

'Why didn't you tell me you were on this residential course earlier?' she demanded.

'My wife – my ex-wife – won't speak to me,' Swain said. 'When we pass in the street, she looks right through me. All my old friends give me the cold shoulder. Even the landlord of the disgusting little bedsit in which I now exist can barely bring himself to collect the rent from me, because he doesn't want to touch the same envelope that I have.'

'Get to the point,' Paniatowski snapped.

'None of them – not my wife, not my friends, not even my landlord – want to hear me say how sorry I am for what happened,' Swain told her. 'And if I had given you my alibi for Saturday at the start of this interview, you wouldn't have wanted to hear it either. But I didn't do that, so you had to listen – and I feel just a *little* better for having told you.'

TWELVE

Paniatowski and Beresford were sitting in the police canteen, chain smoking and drinking industrial strength tea from large brown mugs.

'Well, that was a complete waste of three hours of our valuable time,' Beresford said.

Yes, it had been, Paniatowski agreed silently. Of the five men who had been taken into custody that morning, they'd already questioned four. Two of them had alibis for the whole of Saturday afternoon. One had a partial alibi that made it highly unlikely he would have had time to commit the murder. And the fourth, who had no alibi at all, was such a wreck that he would have struggled to tie his own shoelaces, let alone strangle a girl.

'But we always knew they were long shots, didn't we?' Beresford asked. 'Bill Horrocks has been our prime suspect from the moment young Crane pointed us in the direction of lesbian-bashing.'

'It's still only a theory that Jill was killed because she was a lesbian,' Paniatowski said cautiously.

'It's a theory that fits all the facts we have like a glove,' Beresford said. 'We know Jill was a lesbian, don't we?'

'Yes.'

'We also know that Bill Horrocks *hates* lesbians – and, in the past, has been prepared to do more than just talk about it.'

'That's true.'

'And we know he was in the Corporation Park on Saturday. It's game, set and match. He did it – I'm sure he did it.'

Paniatowski had been almost sure herself a few hours earlier, but the closer they got to the interview with Horrocks, the more she could feel her confidence ebbing away.

The problem was, she thought, there was far too much riding on it. She had assured the chief constable that she was the best person to handle the case – had promised him that she would get a result. But if Jack Crane's theory was wrong – if there had been another motive behind the murder – then they were no further on with the investigation than they had been when she'd made that promise to

Baxter in the car park of the Drum and Monkey. And even worse, she had no idea where to start looking next.

'Let's get it done and dusted, shall we?' Beresford suggested, standing up. 'Then we can all go to the Drum for a marathon piss up.'

'Wait a minute,' Paniatowski said, reaching up and touching his arm. 'I think I'll use Kate in this interview.'

'Well, you're the boss, and you must do what you think best,' Beresford said, trying not to look hurt. 'Is there any particular reason that you want to use Sergeant Meadows?'

'Yes, there is,' Paniatowski replied. 'Horrocks is a big man, and so are you – and if you're in the interview room, it'll be like waving a red rag at a bull. He'll spend his whole time trying to prove he's so much more masculine than you are, and I don't want that.'

'Then what do you want?'

'I want him to focus on the thing that happened between him and his wife – and what that should tell him about himself – because if anything's going to break him, it will be that.'

'You're right,' Beresford said. 'Good thinking.'

Yes, it was, Paniatowski agreed, but that wasn't the only reason she wanted to keep Beresford out of it. The simple fact was that she was desperate for the interview to go well – and she was terrified that her inspector's cocksureness would screw the whole thing up.

William Horrocks was a large man in his early forties, with hands more than wide enough – and more than strong enough – to have easily choked the life out of little Jill Harris.

'And how are you on this fine morning, Bill?' Paniatowski asked, as she and Meadows sat down opposite him.

'I'm not called Bill any more,' Horrocks told her. 'My name is William now.'

'But you used to be known as Bill, didn't you?'

'I was a different man, back then.'

'It's true – he was,' Paniatowski told Meadows. 'Back then, when he was a builder's labourer, he was a very different man indeed. It's all in his record – charged with being drunk and disorderly, charged with disturbing the peace, charged with common assault . . . That's right, isn't it, William?'

'I don't drink no more,' Horrocks said.

'That's true as well,' Paniatowski agreed. 'He's hooked on quite a different drug now, aren't you, William?'

Kate Meadows began silently counting up to ten as she waited for Horrocks to respond, and when she had reached that number – and he still had not spoken – she said, 'So just what drug *is* William hooked on now, boss?'

'Religion,' Paniatowski said. 'You surely must have seen him preaching in the Corporation Park.'

'No, I don't think I have.'

'It's quite a sight. He gets himself worked up into a right old lather.' Paniatowski paused. 'But I have to admit, I'm not quite sure which church you belong to, William.'

'I don't belong to none of them,' Horrocks said. 'They're all in league with the Devil.'

'How do you know that?'

Horrocks crossed his arms over his chest. 'I'm not saying no more,' he told Paniatowski firmly.

'Well, we certainly can't force you to speak if you don't want to, so we'll just talk to each other,' Paniatowski said. 'Do you know when William first got this so-called religious calling of his, Sergeant?'

'No, boss, I don't.'

'It came to him, funnily enough, around about the time that his wife decided to leave him.'

'She did not *leave* me,' Horrocks growled. 'I cast her out – for she had been defiled!'

'I stand corrected. Thank you for that,' Paniatowski said. 'Forget what I just told you, Sergeant – she didn't leave him, he cast her out. But isn't it true, Bill, that as this "casting out" was going on, your Thelma had already packed her bags, because she was planning to move in with her lover?'

'Satan – in his most diabolical form – had her in his grasp,' Horrocks said. 'He held her in his slimy fingers.'

'For Satan, you should read a woman called Lucia Evans,' Paniatowski told her sergeant.

'Lucia Evans?' Meadows repeated, in mock-surprise. 'I thought you said Bill's wife was moving in with her lover.'

'And so she was,' Paniatowski agreed. 'Lucia Evans *was* that lover.'

'Good grief – how shocking,' Meadows said.

'William doesn't blame himself for any of what happened, of course. As he sees it, he was a totally innocent party. And the amusing thing is that I don't think he blames his wife, either. In fact, I believe that he thinks – deep down – that she's just as innocent as he is.'

'Even though she left him?'

'Now, Sergeant, you know she didn't leave him – she allowed herself to be "cast out".'

'Sorry, boss.' Meadows said. 'Still, it's strange that he doesn't blame his wife for any of it, isn't it?'

'No, it isn't strange at all,' Paniatowski disagreed. 'William thinks that way because he has no choice *but* to think that way.'

'No choice? What do you mean?'

'Put yourself in his shoes for a minute. Imagine you're a big strong builder's labourer, just like Bill used to be. You work hard on the building site, carrying hods of bricks up ladders all day, and you go to the pub at night to sink a few pints with your mates. Are you with me so far?'

'Yes, boss.'

'So you're in the pub, and closing time comes around. That's when you stand up and say something like, "Well, I'd better be going, lads – the wife's waiting for me at home, and I know for a fact that she'll have been gasping for a good rattling all day." And you're sure, as you leave the pub, that all the others are looking at you enviously, because you're a *real* man, and though they'd like to be just like you, they know they never can be.'

'Sounds like a nice feeling to have,' Meadows said.

'As intoxicating as the beer – maybe even more so,' Paniatowski agreed. 'And then your wife – who you claim has been gasping for a good rattling all day – leaves you for a *woman*! There's only two ways to explain that, aren't there?'

'The first one being that you're not as attractive – and not half as good at giving her a rattling – as you thought you were,' Meadows suggested.

'Exactly,' Paniatowski agreed. 'And that's clearly not acceptable to any self-respecting man. So you turn to the other explanation. The other woman used underhand tactics to trick your wife into leaving you, in which case, the lover is the only villain of the piece.'

It's probably only a short step from thinking one lesbian is evil to thinking that all lesbians are evil – and that they're the Devil's agents,' Meadows said.

'And that's exactly what William *does* think, and why he founded his one-man church, which I suppose – since he refuses to give it a title himself – I'll have to call the Church of God the Lesbian Basher. And you *did* bash some lesbians, didn't you, William?'

'I smote the foul Beelzebub in whatever nether regions he dwelt,' Horrocks replied.

'Or to be a little more accurate, you smote a woman called Shirley Maxwell when she was standing on the Boulevard one Saturday afternoon,' Paniatowski said dryly.

'She was tempting other innocent souls to join her in her abomination,' Horrocks said.

'Yes, she certainly *was* handing out leaflets advocating equal rights for female homosexuals,' Paniatowski agreed. 'You served three years in Strangeways Prison for that attack, didn't you, William?'

'It was God's way of testing me,' Horrocks told her. 'I bore the suffering, and I emerged a stronger man.'

'You bore your suffering and emerged a stronger man,' Paniatowski said, with a mixture of scorn and disbelief. 'That's not what the governor of Strangeways told me on the phone, just half an hour ago. He says that for the first three months of your sentence, you stayed huddled in a corner, sitting in your own shit. He says that they had you on suicide watch *three times*!'

'You . . . you don't know hard it is for a man used to the open air to be locked in a cage like a rat,' Horrocks said. 'You can't imagine it.'

'But *you* can – very easily,' Paniatowski countered. 'You've only got to close your eyes and you're back in that cage.' She turned to Meadows. 'And that's why, since he got back to Whitebridge, he's been very, very careful.'

'Careful?' Meadows repeated. 'What do you mean?'

'There have been a number of attacks on lesbians since William was released, but most of them have taken place at night, when there were no witnesses around to see them. And after every attack, you've been pulled in for questioning, haven't you, William?'

'You know I have.'

'But they've never been able to pin any of those vicious assaults on you, have they?'

'Almighty God protects me as I go about His work.'

'In other words, you *did* attack those women – but God's letting you get away with it!'

'I didn't say that.'

'Maybe not directly – but you *as good as* said it.'

'No, I didn't.'

She was giving this interview all that she had, Paniatowski thought – and it wasn't working.

She took a deep breath, and marshalled whatever strength she had left to draw on.

'I'm willing to bet that recently you've started to question whether you've been doing Almighty God's work *well enough*,' she said.

'I don't know what you mean by that.'

'Then let me put it another way – one you might find easier to understand. The Lord demands that you smite the guilty with the flaming sword of vengeance, doesn't he?'

'Yes.'

'But you've been doing no more than give them a little tap with a toffee hammer.' Paniatowski lit up a cigarette. 'Are you with me yet?'

'No.'

'One Saturday afternoon – probably two or three weeks ago – you were in the park, spouting out your venom as usual, when you happened to notice two young girls. And it was immediately plain to you that they were more than just friends – they were lovers. You do remember them, don't you?'

'No.'

'Of course you do. You saw them, but you were too cowardly – too afraid of going back to Strangeways – to do anything about it. Now that's right, isn't it?'

'No.'

There were no witnesses, and if he kept denying it, she had nothing, Paniatowski told herself miserably.

And then a thought that she'd been keeping locked away in the back of her mind escaped, and galloped into the forefront – and that thought was that maybe he was denying it because he *hadn't done it*!

'Let's move on to *last* Saturday,' she suggested. 'You were standing in your usual place, but the park was emptying, and even you are not crazy enough to carry on preaching when there's nobody there to ignore you. So you were just about to call it a day when you suddenly saw one of the girls again – and this time she was alone. Isn't that what happened?'

'No.'

'And it not only enraged you that she was there at all, but that she was wearing a crimson top – like some kind of whore.'

'The top was yellow,' Horrocks said.

'Thank God!' Paniatowski gasped silently.

'What was that you said?' she asked.

'Nothing.'

'You said the top she was wearing was yellow.'

'No, I didn't.'

'It's down on tape, Bill,' Paniatowski said, pointing to the recorder.

'No, it isn't.'

'Recording suspended at twelve oh seven p.m.,' Paniatowski said.

She stopped the tape, wound it back a little, and pressed down the replay button.

'*And it not only enraged you that she was there at all, but that she was wearing a crimson top – like some kind of whore,*' said a voice which was a little tinny, but clearly her own.

'*The top was yellow,*' said a second voice, which equally clearly belonged to Horrocks.

'Well?' she asked, when she'd restarted the recording.

'I didn't see her last Saturday,' Horrocks said. 'She was wearing that top the other time I saw her – with the other girl.'

'I thought you said you *hadn't* seen her with the other girl.'

'I did see them – I just forgot.'

'I know for a fact that, until last Saturday, she never wore that top unless she was out with her aunt,' Paniatowski said. 'Now where was I? Oh yes. You saw the girl in the yellow top all by herself, and you asked God what to do. And God replied that this time you should show her no mercy. This time, you shouldn't just beat her up – you should kill her! And so you did, didn't you?'

'No.'

'Really?'

'No.'

'Didn't you even *want* to kill her?'

'Yes.'

'But you didn't do it?'

'No.'

'So God gave you a direct command – kill this demon, this spawn of Satan – and you disobeyed Him! You're a real coward, aren't you, Bill. You're worse than any of the sinners who'll end up burning in the pits of hell for all eternity.'

Horrocks' lip trembled, and for a moment it looked almost as if he would burst into tears.

'It's not like that,' he said weakly.

'It's *exactly* like that,' Paniatowski countered. 'If you didn't obey the Lord's command, then you *are* a coward and a sinner. There's simply no other way of looking at it.'

Horrocks lowered his head. 'I did it,' he mumbled.

'You did what?' Paniatowski asked. 'Spell it out clearly for me, William.'

'I saw the girl in the yellow top in the park,' Horrocks said. 'I knew why she was there. When she went into the bushes, I followed her.'

'And then what did you do?'

'I grabbed hold of her throat, and I strangled her.'

THIRTEEN

Things were slowly starting to take a turn for the better, George Baxter thought, as he walked along the corridor towards his afternoon appointment with the governor. True, his wife was still refusing to speak to him after spotting his car in Whitebridge. And true, he was still groping in the dark as far as this particular investigation went. But at least the other big concern had been cleaned up – at least Monika Paniatowski had come through on her promise and made an arrest in the Jill Harris case.

He found the governor sitting at his desk. He was not alone, but then, since he'd had forewarning of this meeting, it was only to be expected that he'd have invited his pet Rottweiler along.

'You don't have any objection to Chief Officer Jeffries sitting in on this conversation, do you?' the governor asked.

'No objection at all,' Baxter replied. 'Even if he wasn't here, I expect you'd tell him everything I'd said the moment I'd gone.'

'Err . . . yes, I like to keep my staff informed,' the governor said awkwardly. 'You told my secretary that you had a request you wanted to make, didn't you?'

'Not exactly,' Baxter countered. 'I told her that I had something I needed you to arrange for me.'

'Isn't that the same thing?' the governor asked.

'No,' Baxter replied. 'The former means you have a choice in the matter, the latter means you don't.'

'You're sounding rather belligerent today,' the governor said.

'Excellent,' Baxter said. 'That's just the tone I was aiming at. And before you ask *why* I'm sounding belligerent, I'll tell you – it's because I'm tired of being buggered about.'

'My staff have been most cooperative,' the governor protested. 'They've given you everything that you've asked for.'

'That's true of the kitchen staff, certainly,' Baxter agreed. 'If I ask for an egg, they give me an egg. If I ask for a sausage, there it is on my plate right away. But the prison officers are another matter. They give me what they want me to see – and no more.'

Wilton sighed. 'Well, I suppose we'll just have to agree to

disagree on that,' he said. 'What is it in particular than you want this afternoon?'

'I want you to arrange for me to see one of the inmates.'

'Ah, perhaps you wish to see life from the prisoners' perspective,' the governor guessed. 'Well, I'm sure that Chief Officer Jeffries can select an inmate who is both intelligent enough and articulate enough to . . .'

'I want to see Lennie Greene,' Baxter said.

'Lennie Greene?' the governor repeated.

He turned to his chief officer for some guidance. He seemed to do that a great deal.

'Leonard Arthur Greene is serving a long sentence for – among other things – blinding a police officer, and he's probably the most dangerous man in this prison,' Jeffries said.

'Are you sure that's true?' Baxter asked, sounding slightly puzzled. 'Don't get me wrong, I'm not doubting that he was very dangerous man when he was on the outside, but I've looked at his record . . .'

'You've looked at his record?' Jeffries asked, flushing. 'Who the bloody hell gave you permission to do that?'

'Nobody gave me permission,' Baxter replied. 'I asked your records officer for the file, and he immediately handed it over to me. You see, he, at least, seems to have grasped one simple fact that has quite eluded you, Mr Jeffries – and that fact is that I don't *need* permission.'

It was the turn of the chief officer to turn to the governor for support, but Wilton only shrugged.

'I'm afraid Mr Baxter's quite right, Mr Jeffries,' he said weakly. 'Under the terms of his Home Office remit, he is granted access to anything he considers pertinent.'

'As I was saying, I've looked at his record, and it seems he's never been in trouble while he's been serving his time in Dunston,' Baxter continued. 'In fact, he could be said to have an exemplary record.'

Jeffries shook his head at Baxter's naivety.

'You really have no idea how prisons work, do you?' he asked contemptuously. 'Of course Greene has an exemplary record. Of course he hasn't put a foot wrong while he's been here. That's because he gets some other lag to do his dirty work for him.'

'So if he wanted Jeremy Templar beaten up, for example, he'd get another prisoner to do it?' Baxter asked.

'Yes,' Jeffries admitted. 'And if you want my opinion, it's more than likely that he *was* behind the attacks.'

'Then it's strange you never mentioned it before,' Baxter said.

'I didn't see any *point* in mentioning it before,' Jeffries countered. 'If Greene is behind the attacks, he's not going to admit it to you, is he? Besides, we can't force him to even *talk* to you, and I'd be more than surprised if he agrees to.'

'He'll agree,' Baxter said confidently, 'and the reason he'll agree is because I've got something that he wants.'

'You really think you can bribe a prison kingpin like Greene with an ounce or two of snout?' Jeffries asked, the contempt in his voice thicker than ever.

'No, I don't,' Baxter replied. 'But, as I've said, I've read his file – and I know I can offer him something he'll value much more than tobacco.'

'I thought you couldn't show any more ignorance of how things work than you already have, but you've exceeded yourself this time,' Jeffries said. 'There *is* nothing a prisoner values more than snout. It's just like money behind bars – it's what greases the wheels.'

'I'm well aware of that,' Baxter said.

'And in prison terms, Greene's already a millionaire, so just what is it that you think you can offer him that he can't get for himself?'

'I can offer him knowledge,' Baxter said.

As Jack Crane made his way towards Liz Duffy's flat, he was reflecting on the lunchtime victory celebration that the team had held in the Drum and Monkey. It should, on the experience of previous such celebrations, have been a monumental – and boisterous – piss up. All the components had certainly been in place – the murderer had been charged, the case was closed – yet somehow it had never hit quite the right note, and when the boss had suggested, quite early, that they call it a day, the rest of the team had agreed immediately.

Maybe the problem was that the case had been too straightforward, he thought. A girl had been killed, an obvious suspect had presented himself to them, and a confession had been extracted. There'd been none of the twists and turns they'd had to untangle in some of their other investigations – and that meant there was little scope for congratulating themselves on just how clever they'd been when it was all over. In fact, they had all been left with the vague suspicion that even PC Plod could have cracked this particular case.

He was almost at Liz Duffy's garden flat when the butterflies started in his stomach.

Nerves?

No, it couldn't be!

He must have eaten something that was upsetting him.

Yet the closer he got to the door, the more furiously the butterflies flapped their wings.

This was ridiculous, he thought. He was a grown man – a grown *policeman*, who'd just been involved in an unpleasant murder investigation – and he didn't get an attack of nerves at the mere thought of visiting a woman. The callow youth that he'd been during his first few weeks at Oxford – a boy who'd only recently said goodbye to adolescent pimples – might have stood on a girl's doorstep, a bunch of flowers in his hand, and wondered how he could avoid the biological urge to dash straight to the toilet the moment he was admitted, but the Jack Crane that he was now had left all that far behind him.

He looked down at his hand, and was almost surprised to see it clutching a bunch of red roses. He considered his stomach, and decided it would be demanding a visit to the loo quite soon.

'Ridiculous!' he said aloud.

He took a deep breath, and knocked firmly on the door.

When Liz answered, he took a second breath. She was wearing a kaftan like the ones she had worn when they were at college together – it may even have been one of those old kaftans – and she seemed to him to be absolutely beautiful.

'You look like you've seen a ghost,' she said.

And he had, he thought – and not just the ghost of a person, but the ghost of a life.

'Anyway, I'm glad you could make it after all,' Liz said. She looked down at his hand. 'You've brought me flowers!'

'Yes,' Crane said, glancing at the hand himself, and noticing that his knuckles were almost white.

Liz laughed. 'Well, you'd better give them to me before you choke the life out of them,' she said.

So she'd noticed the white knuckles too, Crane thought. Well, she *was* a doctor.

He held out the flowers stiffly, and she took them from him, turned around, and walked down the hall.

'Don't just stand there in the doorway – come inside,' she said, over her shoulder.

He followed her into the living room.

'I'll just put these in water,' Liz said, heading for the kitchen.

With some relief, Crane noted that his stomach seemed to have settled down. He looked around him, and his eyes immediately rested on the two framed posters on the wall, one the iconic Che Guevara photograph, another advertising the Magdalen College May Ball.

Liz returned, holding a cut-glass vase in which she had artistic-ally arranged the roses. She saw him looking at the posters, and laughed self-consciously.

'I know it's foolish of me to keep those old mementos, but they were happy times,' she said.

She was right, he agreed silently. They'd been happy times, and – despite the fact that they'd all considered themselves to be sophis-ticated free spirits – they had been strangely innocent times, too.

'What do you think of the fireplace?' Liz asked expectantly.

Drawn fully into the world of the posters, he hadn't even noticed it, but now – since it seemed important to her – he gave it his full attention.

It was a large fireplace for such a relatively modest flat, and it was tiled in pink granite. A thick – and obviously expensive – rug – had been laid in front of it, and three small logs blazed merrily in the grate.

'It's very nice,' he said.

'It was what really sold this place to me,' Liz told him. 'I love an open fire – they're so romantic.'

'And do you light it *every* night?' he asked.

She laughed. 'Of course not. Who has the time? Most nights, I rely on the boring old central heating. But I do like it for special occasions.'

'And is *this* a special occasion?' Crane asked, before he could stop himself.

'Yes, it's . . .' Liz began – and then seemed unsure of how to continue. 'It's . . . it's bound to be special occasion when two old friends meet up after so long apart, isn't it?'

'Yes, it is,' Crane agreed, grateful that at least one of them seemed capable of keeping things on the right track.

*   *   *

It was a quiet night in the Prince Albert Bar of the Royal Victoria Hotel, and that was just as well, thought Harry, the head barman, because when there was trouble, you didn't *want* a lot of people around.

Not that there had been any actual trouble yet, admittedly, but Harry had been in the business long enough to see it coming, and knew that the blonde woman who had been sitting at the far end of the bar for over an hour was a ticking bomb.

As he polished a half-pint glass, he found himself wondering just what her problem was.

Her marriage, probably, he decided.

Most of the people who created difficulties in the Prince Albert had marriage problems – the women because they thought their husbands were playing away from home, and the men because they thought their wives suspected that that was exactly what they *were* doing.

'Harry!' the woman called, rather too loudly.

With a sigh, the barman made his way reluctantly over to where she was sitting. 'Yes, madam?'

'I'd like another G and T.'

'Are you sure?' the barman asked. 'You've had four already.'

And they weren't your first drinks of the day either, he added mentally.

The woman swayed slightly on her stool. 'What was that?'

'I asked you if you were sure you wanted another one.'

The woman rested her elbows heavily on the bar – perhaps to show how displeased she was, perhaps only to ensure her stability.

'Here's how it works,' she said, slurring slightly. 'I'm the customer, and you're the barman. I tell you what it is that I want, and you go and get it for me. Understood?'

'Understood,' Harry replied.

It was difficult to know whether or not he was doing the right thing, he thought, as he held the glass hesitantly under the optic. On the one hand, he didn't want to piss off the wife of a man of some local importance, but on the other hand, he didn't want to piss off the man himself, by sending his wife home drunk. Then he remembered that the man in question was out of town at that moment, and – with a shrug – pushed the glass upwards and let gravity do the rest.

It was as he was using the tongs to pick up a slice of lemon that the woman said, 'Are you married, Harry?'

He sighed for a second time, and wondered why these dreary discussions *always* had to follow the same well-trodden route.

'Yes, I am married, as a matter of fact,' he said, using the tongs to extract some ice from the bucket.

'Do you ever find yourself wondering if your wife married you on the rebound?' the woman asked.

'Not really,' the barman said.

And it was true. He knew exactly why his wife had married him, and as she walked down the aisle – her stomach already bulging under her wedding dress – so did everybody else in the church.

'It's a mistake to start a marriage with doubts,' the woman said miserably. 'You think they'll go away in time, but the longer you're married – the more you have the chance to compare yourself to the other woman – the worse they get. And I'll tell you another thing—'

'I really do have to get back to work, madam,' Harry interrupted her.

'Of course you do,' the woman said. 'I'm not really being fair, am I, heaping all my troubles on you?' She paused and took a sip of her drink. Then, finding she no longer seemed to have the urge for it, pushed it to one side. 'I'm sorry I was rude to you earlier. That wasn't fair, either.'

'That's all right, madam,' Harry said.

The woman dismounted – awkwardly but carefully – from her stool. 'I think I'll go home now,' she said.

'Have you got your car with you?' the barman asked.

The woman seemed confused by the question. 'Here? In the bar?'

'Out on the street.'

The woman thought about it. 'Yes, I have.'

'It might be wiser to leave it here, and take a taxi home,' Harry counselled.

'I'll be all right,' the woman said.

'It wouldn't be good for a lady in your condition to be stopped by the police,' Harry argued.

'In my *condition*!' the woman said, getting angry again. 'Are you suggesting I'm drunk?'

Yes, I bloody am, the barman thought. You're as pissed as a rat.

'No, I'm not suggesting that at all, madam,' he said aloud. 'But you have drunk more than the legal limit, and, given your husband's position, it could be rather embarrassing all round if you were pulled over.'

The woman nodded woozily. 'You're right,' she agreed. 'Do you think *you* could call me a taxi, Harry?'

'It'd be my pleasure,' the barman said.

'You've been very kind and very patient, and I really do want to thank you for that,' the woman said.

'Think nothing of it, Mrs Baxter,' Harry said, reaching for the phone.

Liz had produced a bottle of Bordeaux wine and a few nibbles, and they sat on the rug in front of the fire, reminiscing.

They talked mostly about their first year at Oxford – about bicycle rides along the river; debates in the Union which had made them both feel angry and passionate; evenings of theatre in St John's College grounds, where they had eaten strawberries and cream, and drunk Pimm's No. I Cup.

He missed it much more than he had ever imagined he would, Crane realized. He didn't regret his new life – far from it – but he did sometimes wish he could talk to his colleagues (who were fast becoming his closest friends) in the same way as he was talking to Liz now. Perhaps, he thought, the ideal was not to live one life, but two – Superman in the daytime, and Clark Kent at night.

'There were times in the first year when I thought we'd be together forever,' Liz said fondly. 'Why did we ever break up?'

She had to be a little drunk to even ask that question, Crane thought. Or perhaps she was just so intoxicated by memories of that first year that she had temporarily forgotten how it ended.

'Why *did* we break up?' she repeated.

'You tell me,' Crane said. 'You were the one who made the decision.'

'Yes, I was, wasn't I?' Liz agreed, suddenly sounding more sober.

'Then, a couple of months later, Simon came along,' Crane said.

And Simon was everything I wasn't, he thought – rich, cosmopolitan, self-assured . . .

'Yes, and then Simon came along,' Liz repeated.

Crane was not sure what to say next, and found his eyes searching the living room, as if hoping something he saw would provide him with the answer.

'He's not hiding in that cupboard, waiting to jump out and surprise me, is he?' he heard himself say.

And he thought, 'You total idiot, Jack! You completely tasteless bloody buffoon!'

'Is that a rather clumsy way of asking me if Simon and I are still together?' Liz asked softly.

'Yes, I suppose it is,' Crane admitted, shamefacedly.

'We're not. He left me.'

'When?'

'Oh, some time after we all came down from Oxford.'

'I'm sorry,' Crane said.

'That he left me? Or that you've chosen such a gauche way to acquire the information?'

'Both.'

'About the latter, I think I believe you,' Liz said. 'About the former, I'm not quite so sure.'

'I *am* sorry,' Crane protested. 'If Simon made you happy, then I wish he'd never deserted you.'

'That sounds very harsh – *deserted* me,' Liz said. 'And, in a way, I can't entirely blame him for it, because he was going through a difficult time, and there was nothing I could do to help him.'

We talked quite enough about that bastard Simon, Crane thought. Let's change the subject, shall we?

And then, something within him – some self-loathing goblin – made him say, 'You still miss him, though, don't you?'

'Yes,' Liz agreed. 'I do. I think perhaps I'll *always* miss him. But I'm no Miss Haversham. I'm not about to spend the rest of *my* life sitting around and moping over the loss. I have a good job, I have a strong purpose, and, perhaps, eventually, I'll have love, too.'

The fire continued to gently flicker, the wine sat comfortably in his stomach, and Crane leaned over and kissed Liz warmly on the lips. If she'd pulled back, he would have apologized and left immediately, but she didn't, and he sensed that she wanted this just as much as he did.

The phone rang.

Their lips were still locked together. Crane put a hand on Liz's shoulder, and the gesture said, 'Ignore it, and it will go away. Give us just another ten minutes, and we can make the *whole world* go away.'

But as the phone still screeched out its incessant demand to be answered, Crane heard his beeper start to buzz.

Liz pushed him gently away from her, and then stood up.

'I'll deal with whoever's calling me, and then you can ring police headquarters,' she told him. She lifted the receiver and said, 'Dr Duffy,' in a crisp voice which seemed to belong to quite another woman than the one she'd been moments earlier.

'I see,' she said, nodding as she spoke. 'Yes, I've got that, and I can be there in twenty minutes. She replaced the phone on its cradle, and turned to Crane. 'I think I know why you've been beeped,' she said. 'There's been a second murder.'

A *second* murder, Crane noted – not *another* murder, but a *second* one.

The butterflies had returned to his stomach – except that this time they seemed more like large moths with metal tips on their wings.

'It can't have any connection to the Jill Harris case,' he said. 'We've got her killer safely behind bars.'

'Are you sure of that?' Liz asked.

'Of course I'm sure,' Crane replied, as he did his best to ignore the rampaging moths. 'He's confessed to the killing. What made you think there *might* be a connection?'

'The victim's about the same age as Jill, and it looks like she's been strangled,' Liz told him. 'And her body was discovered in the Corporation Park.

'Well, shit!' Crane groaned.

FOURTEEN

There was a standing joke they had shared when they were up at Oxford – one of those which had been funny the first time it had been said, had quickly grown into a cliché through repetition, and finally become funny again precisely because it *was* a cliché – and as Crane parked his car next to the main gates of the corporation park, it came into his head for the first time in years.

'This is like *déjà vu* all over again,' he said to Liz Duffy.

Liz chuckled.

'Now there's a blast from the past,' she said. Then she instantly grew more serious and added, 'It's not really a laughing matter, is it?'

No, Crane agreed, it really wasn't – not when applied to a situation in which a fresh murder bore all the hallmarks of the one for which they'd already made an arrest.

Of course, the fact that Bill Horrocks had been behind bars since that morning didn't *necessarily* mean that he couldn't also have killed the second victim, he thought hopefully, as they stepped through the park gates. The corpse could have been lying there undiscovered for some time – perhaps even for days.

Then he saw the floodlights, blazing down on a spot not fifty yards from where Jill Harris had been found, and that slim hope faded and died – because if the body had been there the day before, the officers scouring the area for clues to the first murder would almost certainly have found it.

He saw Paniatowski standing at the edge of the circle of light, as rigid if she'd been carved from stone. What had happened was bad for the whole team, he thought, but as team leader, it was bloody catastrophic for her.

Hearing the footsteps approaching from behind, the chief inspector turned.

'Thank you for getting here so quickly, Dr Duffy,' she said. 'The SOCO's have already checked out the ground around the body, so you can get to work as soon as you like.'

If Paniatowski had noticed that he and Liz had arrived together, she gave no sign of it, Crane thought – but then, she had other things on her mind.

Crane looked down at the victim, who was sprawled out close to the bushes. She was wearing a short black skirt, a red top and a beige anorak, he noted. The clothes were cheap and shoddy, and did not look particularly well cared for. The girl's hair had been bleached blonde, but whoever had done the bleaching had not made a very good job of it, and an irregular wave of dark roots ran across the top of her skull. Her tights had been torn during the struggle, and visible through one of the holes was a crudely etched tattoo of a skull.

Liz Duffy bent down beside the cadaver. It seemed wrong – in the presence of death – to admire the graceful way in which the doctor moved, Crane told himself, but there was nothing he could do about it.

'The body was found by a man walking his dog,' Paniatowski told him, 'or rather, the dog found the body, and when it didn't come back, the man followed it into the bushes. We don't have any identification yet – no handbag, no library card – but I'd guess she's probably about the same age as Jill Harris.'

'So would I,' Crane said.

'And it's not really surprising there's no library card,' said Colin Beresford, who had only just arrived. 'I doubt this girl's ever thought of going into a library in her whole bloody life.'

'And now she never will,' Paniatowski said. 'We need to get her identified as soon as possible. Can I leave it to you to see that a sketch of her appears on all the late-night news programmes, Colin?'

'I'll get on it right away,' Beresford promised. He paused. 'Has the chief constable been informed?'

'Not directly, but Sergeant Meadows has rung and left a message,' Paniatowski said gloomily, 'which probably means that by morning he'll be back here, breathing down our necks. And who could blame him?'

Liz Duffy stood up, and peeled off her surgical gloves.

'There's not a great deal more I can do here, so as soon as the ambulance arrives, I'll take the body down to the morgue,' she said.

'Is there anything you can tell us now?' Paniatowski asked.

'Not much, I'm afraid. The victim hasn't been mutilated in any obvious way, and I'd say that, on first appearances, she hasn't been sexually assaulted either – but I'll have a clearer idea on that when I've cut her open. The cause of death was strangulation – as you can see for yourself.'

'Was she strangled in the same way as the previous victim?' Paniatowski asked.

'What you're really asking me is if it could have been the same killer, aren't you?

'Yes.'

'In each case, the killer had quite large hands, but a lot of men do, and if you were to ask me if DC Crane would have left a similar pattern of bruising if *he'd* choked this girl to death, then I'd have to say yes. And there's not much scope for variation in manual strangulation, so it would be almost impossible for the killer to have left his "signature" on his victim.'

'I see,' Paniatowski said despondently. 'Can you at least tell me how long she's been dead?'

'The body's still warm, so I'd say it's between two and three hours – but again, I'll have a much better idea when I've opened her up.'

Crane felt an unexpected burden of guilt suddenly descend on him. Three hours ago, Liz was just opening a bottle of Bordeaux. Two hours ago, they were having a chat about the jolly times they had had in Oxford. And at some point between those two things, this girl was having the life choked out of her.

It wasn't his fault, he told himself. He couldn't have known. Yet he could not shake the feeling that he was partly responsible – that instead of recapturing his youth, he should have been out looking for this killer.

The ambulance men had arrived, and were carefully lifting the body onto a stretcher.

'I'd appreciate it if you could get the results of the autopsy to me as quickly as possible, Liz,' Paniatowski said.

Duffy nodded. 'Understood. I'll work through the night, if that's what's necessary.'

Well, that was his cosy evening buggered, Crane thought.

What in God's name is the matter with me? he asked himself. One second I'm weighed down with guilt, and the next I seem to have lost all perspective on what's actually important.

It was meeting Liz again that had done it, he decided – meeting her again had turned his world upside down.

The ambulance men lifted the stretcher off the ground, and carried it towards the waiting ambulance. Dr Duffy followed them.

Paniatowski turned to Crane. 'I've got something I have to do right now, but it shouldn't take me more than an hour, and I'll see you all in the Drum,' she said heavily.

'Are you going to see Bill Horrocks?' Crane guessed.

'Yes, of course I'm going to see Bill Horrocks,' Paniatowski snapped waspishly. 'What *else* would you expect me to do?'

'Would you like me to come with you, boss?' Crane asked.

Paniatowski shook her head. 'No,' she said. 'This is something I have to do alone.'

Paniatowski was sitting in the interview room – awaiting what she was almost sure would be a confirmation of her failure – when the door opened and the custody sergeant ushered in William Horrocks.

Horrocks had put on years since that morning. His eyes were hollow, his gait faltering, and had there not been a chair at the table for him to sink down into, he might well have collapsed.

'You're going to prison, Bill. You do understand that, don't you?' Paniatowski asked.

Horrocks nodded – it was no more than a tiny movement of his head, but even that seemed to take him a great deal of effort.

'And it won't be like the last time you were sent there,' Paniatowski continued. 'They won't be opening the gate and letting you out after just three years. It'll be twenty years – maybe more – before you see the light of day again. Do you understand *that*?'

Horrocks nodded again.

'I need to hear you say it, William,' Paniatowski told him.

'Yes, I understand,' Horrocks croaked.

'So tell me again what you did.'

'I don't want—'

Paniatowski slammed her hand down on the table.

'Tell me!' she said.

'I saw the girl in the yellow top in the park . . .'

'What time was this?'

'About five o'clock.'

'And what did you do?'

'I followed her into the bushes, and I strangled her.'

'Did she fight back?'

'A little. But I was much too strong for her.'

'I can understand you killing her, William,' Paniatowski said. 'After all, you were only following God's instructions. But did He also tell you to smash her face in so badly that she was almost unrecognizable?'

'No, He . . .'

'Then why did you do it?'

'She . . . she was struggling. I had to do something to stop her struggling.'

'I thought you said she couldn't really fight back, because you were much too strong for her.'

'That's true.' Horrocks' brow furrowed as he searched for an answer to the apparent contradiction. 'I don't know why I did it,' he said, giving up on the task. 'I . . . I think I must have panicked.'

'I lied to you just now,' Paniatowski said. 'Her face was completely unmarked.'

'Then maybe I've remembered it wrong,' Horrocks said helplessly.

'You didn't kill her, did you?' Paniatowski demanded.

'I saw her in the park . . .' Horrocks mumbled.

'I know you saw her in the park. You wouldn't have known about the yellow top if you hadn't. *But you didn't kill her, did you?*'

'No,' Horrocks admitted. 'I didn't kill her. I wanted to. God wanted me to. But she looked so small and helpless that I just couldn't.'

'So why did you confess? Why did you condemn yourself to twenty years inside?'

'Because if I hadn't confessed, it would have been admitting to you that I was a coward.'

She'd put that idea in his head, she realized.

If you didn't obey the Lord's command, then you are a coward and a sinner, she'd said. *There's simply no other way of looking at it.*

'Why would it matter if I knew you were a coward?' she asked.

'I thought you'd tell my Thelma,' Horrocks said. 'And if she knew I was a coward, she'd never come back to me.'

FIFTEEN

There was no invisible cordon around the team's table in the Drum and Monkey that night, but there might as well have been. All the other regular drinkers were giving the table a wide berth, and few – if any – were even glancing in that direction.

'Is that because they know that if we're going to crack this case we need space,' Paniatowski wondered, noting their behaviour, 'or are they just steering clear of the lepers?'

She couldn't blame them if it was the latter. Two girls had been killed now, and while there was nothing she could have done about the first murder, she couldn't dismiss the feeling that she should have been able – somehow – to prevent the second.

'The murderer will have made mistakes when he killed Jill Harris – because murderers always do,' she said aloud. 'Now he's killed a second time . . .'

'We don't yet know it was the same man in both cases,' Sergeant Meadows interrupted.

'Yes, we do,' Paniatowski said firmly.

And so they did, for though it was still possible that there had been two killers, they all accepted – at a gut level – that Jill and the unnamed girl had been killed by the same man.

'Now he's killed a second time, and he will have made more mistakes,' Paniatowski ploughed on. 'All we have to do is discover what those mistakes were.'

It all sounded so simple when she put it like that, though none of them thought for a second that it was.

'Let's start with the obvious question,' Paniatowski said. 'Is there anything connecting the two girls? Is it at all possible that this second girl was a secret lesbian, too?'

'It's possible – but very unlikely,' Meadows said.

'And what makes you reach that conclusion?'

'The second victim didn't take enough pride in her appearance to have been a lesbian.'

'Oh, come on now,' Colin Beresford said. 'I've seen some of the lezzies parading on their Boulevard in their combat trousers and boots, and you can't tell me that . . .'

'With respect, sir,' Meadows said, in a voice which suggested a marked *lack* of respect, 'you may have *seen* them, but you haven't really *looked* at them. They sometimes do dress aggressively, and perhaps you personally don't find that particularly attractive – I imagine they'd be pretty horrified if *you* did find it attractive – but their clothes are well cared for. The girl who was found in the park tonight had no pride in anything.'

'The sergeant's right, sir,' Crane said. 'If you look at Jill Harris, with her Miss Selfridge's top, and then compare it with the way that this second girl . . .'

'All right, I get the point,' Beresford interrupted brusquely. 'And there's no need to look like that, Sergeant Meadows, because I'm a bloody good bobby, even if I do act a bit like a caveman, now and again.'

'A *bit* like a caveman?' Meadows repeated. 'Now and again?'

'That's enough, Sergeant,' Paniatowski said.

'Sorry, boss,' Meadows said, looking down at the table.

The team was under more pressure than it had ever been before – and the cracks were starting to show, Paniatowski thought.

'So we're now all agreed the second victim probably wasn't a lesbian, aren't we?' she said.

Meadows nodded, and so did Beresford.

And completely out of the blue, Jack Crane said, 'This is all my fault.'

'What's all your fault?' Paniatowski asked.

'If I hadn't suggested the lesbian connection, the investigation would have gone in an entirely different direction, and we might have arrested the real killer by now.'

'For God's sake, Crane, grow up!' Beresford said. 'You're supposed to be a police officer – act like one. You made a mistake, but we all went along with it, so stop snivelling.'

'And that's quite enough from *you*, Inspector,' Paniatowski said. She turned to Crane. 'It's not your fault,' she told him. 'If anybody's to blame, it's me, because I'm in charge, and so I have to shoulder the responsibility. But we're not here to parcel out blame anyway. Our only task is – and always has been – to catch the killer. So there'll be no more backbiting. Is that clear?' She waited for the others to nod, then she continued, 'So, if the second girl wasn't a lesbian, what *does* connect the two victims?'

'I know it sounds unlikely, but it's always possible they went to the same school, or had the same friends,' Crane suggested.

'There's no chance they went to the same school,' Meadows said. 'I've visited Fairfield High, and I can tell you that the girl who was killed tonight wouldn't have lasted a day there before she was expelled. And as far as having friends in common, do any of us seriously believe that someone who liked neat, pretty, little Jill Harris would also want to make friends with a girl who had a skull tattooed on her thigh?'

No one did.

'They might just have been murders of opportunity,' Beresford said. 'Perhaps both girls were simply unlucky enough to have been in the park at the same time as the murderer was.'

'But why would he *want* to kill them?' Paniatowski asked. 'He doesn't fit the profile of a sex offender or a psycho – so what *is* driving him?'

The phone rang behind the bar.

'It's headquarters, Chief Inspector,' the landlord called out. 'I'll switch the call through to the phone in the corridor, shall I?'

The rest of the team watched as Paniatowski crossed the room and opened the door to the corridor.

'I'm sorry, Jack, I shouldn't have been so harsh just now,' Beresford said, once the door had swung closed behind her.

'I'm sorry, too, Inspector,' Meadows said. 'You may be a caveman, but at least you're *our* caveman – and if we don't pull together on this, we'll all sink without trace.'

'Especially the boss,' Crane said.

'Yes, especially her,' Beresford agreed.

The door swung open again, and Paniatowski emerged, looking grim.

'We may have a lead on the identity of our second victim,' she said, when she reached the table. 'A woman called in, after seeing the sketch on the news. She says that the girl's name is Maggie Hudson, and that she herself is Maggie's social worker.'

'And how likely is it that a girl who has her own social worker would know Jill Harris?' Beresford asked.

'It's not likely at all,' Paniatowski said.

*   *   *

George Baxter was sitting at the desk of his office/bedroom in Dunston Prison. In front of him was a wad of photocopied timesheets which Chief Officer Jefferies had finally – and reluctantly – handed over to him.

It had puzzled him right from the start of his inquiries that not a single officer had been on duty during more than one of the attacks on Jeremy Templar – that seemed statistically unlikely, given the limited number of officers and the limited number of shifts – but now, having spent over an hour studying the timesheets, he thought he had his answer.

What he had found during his examination was a pattern – or rather, he corrected himself, a *non-pattern*. Officer Fellows, for example, had been there when Templar was attacked in the showers, because he'd been on the morning shift. He should also have been there when Templar had been assaulted in the yard, because that incident had occurred during the afternoon shift, and that week Fellows had been *on* the afternoon shift. Yet though he had worked that shift on Monday, Tuesday and Wednesday, and was back on it again on Friday, he had worked the morning shift on Thursday – the day that the attack actually took place.

It was plain what had happened. The sheets had been doctored after the event – probably when the Home Office had ordered an inquiry. It was plain, too, *why* it had been done. Jefferies was spreading the responsibility (or diluting the blame, depending on how you looked at it). And it was the natural instinct of a leader to try and protect his men – Baxter had done the same himself, on some occasions.

But the real question was – as it had been right from the start – what was he protecting them *from*? Was he attempting to prevent them from being punished for something they had had no control over? Or was he merely doing his best to mask their incompetence?

Baxter stood up, and walked over to the window. There was a three-quarters moon that night, and in the pale glow he would clearly see the high walls which ran around the prison. He could see beyond them, as well – to the road that stretched out across the dark empty moors, a thin strip of tarmac leading away from this unnatural world and back to civilization.

What motivated a man to apply for a posting in a desolate place like this, he wondered.

It was true that some of the officers had local connections – Officer Higgins, for example, could not have been born more than twenty miles from the prison, if his accent was anything to go by. But there were others – Fellows, Robson and Jefferies, to name but three – who were clearly not even native Yorkshiremen, yet had pulled up their roots and planted them afresh on this semi-barren heath.

It was a mystery, Baxter told himself – but then so much about Dunston Prison was mysterious.

Until a few hours earlier, Maggie Hudson had lived on the Pinchbeck council estate – but now, of course, she didn't live anywhere.

The estate was often referred to in town council meetings and official documents as a 'mixed' area – and what that actually meant was that while many of the residents were honest, industrious folk – who were just about getting by in life through hard work and determination – there was a sizeable minority which was drunken, lazy, dishonest and just plain vicious.

Monika Paniatowski knew all about the estate, and as she drove towards it behind the wheel of her bright red MGA, she gave an involuntary shudder.

'Is something wrong, boss?' asked Meadows, who was sitting in the passenger seat.

'No,' Paniatowski said quickly.

Nothing at all was wrong – except that she had been brought up on this estate herself, under the same roof as her sexually abusive stepfather, and each street – each lamppost – held memories of a time when killing herself had started to seem like a pretty good option.

It was getting late, and as they drove down Oak Tree Avenue – a street on which there was no evidence of oak trees – there were few lights on in the downstairs windows of the houses. Number eleven Oak Tree Avenue, however, was the exception to the rule. Here, the front room was ablaze with illumination, and despite the windows being closed, the music being played inside could be heard halfway down the street.

Paniatowski pulled up next to the house, and she and Meadows got out of the car. As they walked up the path – which was so overgrown with weeds it was almost as slippery as a skating rink – an upstairs window in the next-door house slid open, and a woman bawled out, 'Are you the bobbies?'

'Yes, we are!' Paniatowski shouted back

'Well, about time,' the woman screamed. 'I'm sick to my back teeth of complaining, and nothing being done.'

Then she slammed the window closed again.

The noise of the music – Gary Glitter's 'I'm the Leader of the Gang' – was so overpowering that Paniatowski was hammering on the door for at least a minute before anyone answered – and even then, it was only a small, dirty child, who should have been in bed hours earlier.

'Mam wants to know what the bloody hell you want at this time of night?' the little girl said, looking up at them.

'I'm called Monika,' Paniatowski said, bending down and looking into her eyes. 'What's your name, sweetheart?'

'Diane,' replied the girl, who seemed puzzled at being addressed by an adult in such a friendly manner.

'We'd like to come in, Diane,' Paniatowski said softly. 'Would that be all right?'

The girl shrugged. 'Suppose so,' she said, then turned and walked back down the litter-strewn hallway.

Baxter was still at the window, thinking about his other problem – the one in Whitebridge.

He had been far from happy at the idea of Monika Paniatowski handling *one* child-murder after her recent experience, so he was even less enthusiastic about her handling *two,* and when he had heard about the second murder, his immediate instinct had been to make another visit to Lancashire, and have a second talk with his DCI. Then, having thought it through, he decided there were a number of reasons why that would be a mistake.

As if to convince himself of the rightness of his decision, he began to count the reasons off on his thick, ginger-haired fingers.

One: to do so would be a signal to Monika – and to all the other officers in Whitebridge HQ – that he did not have confidence in a detective chief inspector he had personally promoted.

Two: by undermining Monika, he would also be undermining her effectiveness, making it less likely that she would get a result.

Three: he had an important job to do in Dunston Prison, especially if, as Officer Robson seemed to think, Jeremy Templar had not been guilty of the crime for which he been imprisoned.

And four . . .

There was no four, he tried to tell himself, but self-deception had never been his forte.

And four, he thought firmly, marking it out on his index finger: he was not prepared to sneak in and out of Whitebridge like a thief in the night, so Jo would soon learn he'd made that second visit, and his wife's recriminations would start all over again.

'You could always go and see her, too,' he said aloud.

But even if he did that, she would still be convinced that his main reason for returning to Whitebridge was to see Paniatowski. She would never be able to accept that it was *DCI Paniatowski* and not *Monika* that he had gone to talk to.

Perhaps he should have gone straight back home the moment Jo had hung up on him, he thought, but he had believed at the time – and still believed – that to have done that would only have strengthened her suspicions, because no man goes running home unless he has something to hide.

He opened the window, and breathed in the crisp, chill night air.

From somewhere in the distance, he heard a hooting sound.

An owl?

Out on the moors – where there were no barns and no trees?

Perhaps it had got lost, he thought. Or perhaps it had been caught in a particularly strong wind, and blown off course.

Both those things were entirely possible, but given that what he *didn't* know about owls was enough to fill a book, there was probably another explanation he couldn't even begin to guess at.

Whatever the case, he was certain that he and the owl shared a feeling of bewilderment at suddenly being in a totally unfamiliar environment.

'But at least the bloody owl can see in the dark,' he muttered.

He returned to the desk, took a small sip of his whisky, and wished that life wasn't always so bloody complicated.

Meadows and Paniatowski had followed little Diane into a living room which was a social worker's vision of hell. There was more garbage on the floor here, too, (including a number of aluminium trays that had once held Chinese or Indian takeaway food), and the whole place stank of sweat and urine. Two other children, even smaller than Diane, were playing lethargically on the dirty floor, while their mother – a grossly fat woman – lounged on a battered sofa.

Meadows crossed the room, and switched off the hi-fi.

'Here, what do you think you're doing?' demanded the woman – who looked so much like the dead girl that she could only have been her mother.

Paniatowski held out her warrant card. 'We're from the police, Mrs Hudson,' she said.

'I've kept telling the kids to turn the noise down, but they just won't listen to me,' Mrs Hudson said, slurring her words.

'Do you have a daughter called Maggie?' Paniatowski asked.

'What's she done?' the fat women demanded. 'Just tell me, and I'll get her dad to give her a real good belting when he gets back from the pub.'

She'd be wasting her time being sensitive with this one, Paniatowski thought, reaching into her bag and producing a picture of the dead girl in the park.

'Is this your daughter?' she asked, thrusting the photograph under Mrs Hudson's nose.

The fat woman squinted at the picture. 'She don't look right,' she said. 'What's wrong with her?'

'She's dead,' Paniatowski said bluntly. 'She was murdered, sometime this afternoon.'

'Oh God, that's terrible,' Mrs Hudson said, screwing up her face. Then she reached down for a can of lager that was lying on the floor, and took a generous swig.

'When did you last see her, Mrs Hudson?' Paniatowski asked.

'Don't know,' the fat woman confessed. She turned to Diane for help. 'Did our Maggie come home for her tea?'

'We didn't have no tea,' the little girl reminded her. 'No dinner, neither.'

'Don't you be so cheeky, or you'll be feeling the back of my hand,' her mother rebuked her. 'Was our Maggie here or not?'

'We haven't seen her since yesterday,' Diane told Paniatowski. 'She sometimes stays with her friends.'

And I certainly don't blame her for that, Paniatowski thought.

'You'll have to come down to the morgue to identify the body,' she told Mrs Hudson.

'Couldn't you wait until her dad gets back, and take him instead?' the other woman asked.

'There'll be a patrol car round in fifteen minutes to pick you up,' Paniatowski said, in disgust. 'Be ready for it when it arrives.'

'Are you sure it couldn't be her dad?' the fat woman whined. 'I've not really been very well, you see. I'm under the doctor.' Then she added, as if to clinch her case. 'I'm on seven kinds of pills.'

'If you're not ready when the patrol car arrives, I'll see to it personally that you spend a night in the cells,' Paniatowski promised.

'There's no need to go cutting up nasty like that,' Mrs Hudson replied, clearly offended.

'We'll see ourselves out,' Paniatowski said, turning towards the door.

'Just a minute!' Mrs Hudson called after her.

Paniatowski swivelled round. 'Yes?'

'Will there be any compensation?'

'I've no idea what you're talking about,' Paniatowski said coldly.

'Well, if she is dead, like you say she is, then surely there must be compensation,' the fat woman explained.

'And whose job do you think it is to compensate you for the loss of your daughter?' Paniatowski wondered.

The fat woman shrugged. 'I don't know. Maybe the council should come up with the money,' she suggested. 'And if they won't do it, then it's the government's responsibility, isn't it? I don't really care who coughs it up – as long as somebody does.'

'No, you *don't* care, do you?' Paniatowski asked angrily. 'As long as somebody pays out your blood money, you don't give a toss.'

'You can't go talking to me like that,' Mrs Hudson said. 'I've a good mind to report you.'

'And I've a good mind to kick the shit out of you – if only to give your kids a good laugh,' Paniatowski told her. She turned towards the door again. 'Fifteen minutes, remember,' she said over her shoulder. 'Be ready.'

SIXTEEN

PC Jim Clarke was young, fresh and enthusiastic, and while many of the other officers had spent their time in the locker room bitching about the fact that they'd been called in for extra duty, Clarke himself had not joined in with the moaning. The truth was that he was thrilled to be part of this early morning canvass, and the thrill only increased when he was assigned a bus stop near the park – which was no more than a quarter of a mile from where the murder had actually been committed! Thus, it was hardly surprising that as he approached the bus stop – the folder and clipboard he'd been issued with held firmly in his right hand – he should be nursing a secret hope that he would return to police headquarters with a vital piece of information that would crack the investigation wide open.

There were about a dozen people standing at the bus stop, and they were a fair cross-section of the Whitebridge bus-travelling public – men and women, boys and girls, young and old. It was a schoolboy who noticed Clarke first, and after concealing the cigarette he was smoking in the palm of his hand – because bobbies could be buggers about under-age smoking – he passed the information on to his mate. The mate told the man next to him, who informed the woman next to him, and by the time Clarke arrived at the shelter, there were twelve pairs of eyes fixed on him.

Clarke drew himself up to his full height – an impressive six feet one – and cleared his throat.

'Could I have your attention, please,' he said. 'My name is PC Clarke, and I'm here to ask you—'

'Is this about the murder?' asked a cloth-capped middle-aged man, with a cigarette dangling from the corner of his mouth.

'Of course it's about the murder, Juggins,' said the woman standing next to him. 'What else would get a bobby out of his bed at this time of day?'

Sensing he was losing control of the situation, Clarke decided to abandon the rest of his opening speech, and get to the heart of the matter.

'I have in this folder the photograph of a girl,' he said.

One of the schoolboys nudged the other in the ribs, and both sniggered.

'A photograph of a girl,' Clarke repeated, glaring at the boy. 'In a moment, I'm going to give them out. I want you to look at them very carefully. If you saw her at any time yesterday, I'd like you to tell me. Then I'll take down your name and address, and one of my colleagues will visit you later today.'

'One of your *what*?' asked the man in the cloth cap.

'Colleagues,' said the woman next to him. 'Don't you know what that means?'

'No,' the man replied. 'What *does* it mean?'

'Well,' the woman said, suddenly looking helpless, 'it's . . . err . . . it's like colleges, only different.'

'What I meant was that another police officer will call round and see you,' Clarke explained.

'Then why didn't you say that in the first place?' the man in the cloth cap wondered.

Clarke took the pictures from the folder and passed them around. Several of the women tut-tutted in a sympathetic sort of way, most of the men seemed vaguely embarrassed to find themselves in a situation in which any emotion was being expressed, and the two schoolboys merely looked disappointed.

'Poor little mite,' said a woman in headscarf and curlers. 'You used to feel safe walking round this town, but you don't any more.'

'It was different before the war,' the woman who was standing next to her contributed. 'Times were hard, but at least you didn't have to worry about being murdered in your bed.'

'The girl was murdered in the *park*,' Clarke pointing out.

'And the buses ran on time back then,' said first woman, ignoring him, and looking hopefully down the road. 'There were always plenty of buses around before the war.'

It wasn't like this in films, Clarke thought. In the films, members of the general public showed the greatest respect for the police, and were always falling over themselves to help see that justice was done. But then, he supposed, that was because most of those films weren't set in Whitebridge, the dour and grumpy capital of the north.

'Has *anybody* seen the girl?' he asked, hoping for one of those breakthroughs that always come about a third of the way through the movie.

Nobody had.

By eight thirty, reports were beginning to land on Beresford's desk, some filed by constables who had canvassed public places (like PC Clarke), some from the units that had stopped drivers on their way to work and shown them Maggie's picture, and some from officers who had disturbed householders at their breakfasts in order to put the standard questions.

There were already a fair number of positive responses, and a younger, less-experienced Beresford would have been over the moon about them. This Beresford, however, had now acquired a great deal of experience of that kind of work – and was prepared for disappointment.

'*I know I said I'd seen her, but I'd forgotten that I was in Accrington that day.*'

'*Turns out the girl I saw was the niece of Mrs Clegg from next door, who's come up for a visit.*'

'*Yes, I saw the girl, but I won't tell you who killed her until you've told me how big the reward is.*'

'*Of course I recognized her. She's my sister – and she's been missing since 1943.*'

Yes, they would get all that – and more.

All kinds of cranks – and lonely people who simply wanted some attention paid to them – would come crawling out of the woodwork, as they always did whenever there was a murder. Hundreds of police hours would be spent in chasing up the delusional or the merely confused. But it had to be done, because there was just a chance that one of those people wouldn't be delusional, and might give them the lead they now so desperately needed.

Beresford lit up a cigarette – he calculated it was his fourth one of the morning – did a couple of stretches to get his muscles working again, and then set off to brief his team.

Lennie Greene was already sitting at the table in the interview room when Baxter arrived. He was not a big man, but with his square body and bullet-shaped head, the chief constable had absolutely no doubt that he was a very *hard* one.

'It was good of you to agree to meet me,' Baxter said, as he sat down. 'The prison authorities didn't think you would.'

'The prison authorities don't know shit,' Greene replied.

'The reason you're in here is because you blinded a policeman, isn't it?' Baxter asked. 'They gave you twenty years for it.'

'That's right, they did – the justice system doesn't like it when a member of the criminal classes attacks a guardian of law and order. The only thing is, I didn't do it.'

'You didn't blind him?'

'Oh, I blinded him, all right. I hit him so hard that when he came to, he couldn't see. But I didn't attack him.'

'Tell me more,' Baxter invited.

'He was one of those coppers who not only thinks he's really hard, but always has to prove it. You know the type?'

'Yes, I know the type – and it's a type not confined to police officers,' Baxter said.

'Granted,' Greene replied. 'Anyway, we happened to be in the same club one night. He was drunk, and looking for trouble, and when he saw me – a man with something of a reputation – he couldn't resist the temptation to start pushing me around. I held off until he actually hit me, then I hit him back.'

'And blinded him?'

'No, I only gave him a little tap – just to show him how out of his depth he was. But he wouldn't learn his lesson, and he came after me with a broken bottle. That's when I *really* hit him.'

'The way you've described it, it sounds like self-defence,' Baxter said.

'And so it was – except that when it came to trial, nobody in the club seemed to be able to remember the broken bottle. I didn't blame them for that – the filth were determined to get me banged up, and they'd have crushed anybody who got in their way.'

'So you're an innocent man?'

'Of course I'm not an innocent man. I've done enough in my time to have earned half a dozen life sentences – but I didn't do that!'

'You were an important man on the outside, weren't you?'

'Within my own small community, I had a certain amount of influence, yes,' Greene agreed.

'And being in prison hasn't really changed that, because, from what I hear, on this side of the bars, you're an absolute monarch.'

Greene grinned. 'Now that's an interesting choice of words. Have you been dipping into my file?'

'I have.'

'I never had much interest in learning before I got banged up, but now I really do love history,' Greene said, in a surprisingly dreamy way.

'And you've got an O-level in it,' Baxter said.

'And I've got an O-level in it,' Greene agreed. 'You're completely wrong with that "absolute monarch" idea, you know.'

'Am I?'

'Couldn't be wronger. Take Louis XIV of France, for example – now there *was* an absolute monarch. He once said, "*L'etat, c'est moi*," – I am the state – and he was right. He could do anything he wanted to.'

'And "you are the prison" – at least as far as the other inmates are concerned,' Baxter countered.

'It's not the same,' Greene said. 'Louis XIV never had to worry that if he overstepped the line, he'd be woken up in the middle of night by three or four screws armed with truncheons – but I do. And after the beating, I'd be on the next bus out of here, en route to another prison – which wouldn't be good, because I'm too old to start building up my reputation again from scratch.' He paused. 'Where exactly is all this chit-chat leading?'

'I want to make a deal with you,' Baxter said. 'I need to know how things work in this prison – not in specific terms, but generally – and you're in a position to tell me.'

'And what do I get out of it?' Greene asked.

'You get the chance to do a long-distance learning degree in history at the Open University,' Baxter said.

A hunger – a deep yearning – appeared in Greene's eyes.

'You can fix that?' he asked, with a tremble in his voice.

Baxter nodded. 'I think so. You know how things work – I don't know anybody at the Open University, but I do know a professor at Lancaster University who owes me a favour, and I've no doubt that he's got a mate in the OU who owes him a favour . . .'

'Wheels within wheels,' Greene said.

'Wheels within wheels,' Baxter agreed. 'So, yes, I think I can swing it – but only if you give me what I need.'

'I'll try,' Greene said earnestly. 'What do you want to know?'

'You say you're nothing like the absolute monarch in this prison, so just what are you?'

'I'm a facilitator. Dunston Prison is a cooking pot, sitting on a high heat and in constant danger of boiling over. I'm the one who keeps the lid on.'

'And how do you do that?'

'I don't really want to tell you – and you don't really want to know,' Greene replied. 'Let's just say that since I've been here, not a single prison officer has been attacked.'

'And in return, the prison authorities turn a blind eye to whatever you get up to?'

Greene shrugged. 'If it wasn't me who was given a bit of leeway, it would be somebody else, because there are some jobs – like tobacco distribution – that always need to be done.'

'Do you ever have anybody beaten up?' Baxter asked.

'Next question,' Greene said.

'If you want to get on a history course, you'll have to do better than that,' Baxter told him.

'Put it this way,' Greene said, 'in any organization, there has to be some instrument for enforcing discipline. Does that answer your question?'

'I think so,' Baxter said. 'Second question – does anybody ever get beaten up *without* your permission?'

'What you mean is, did I authorize the attacks on Jeremy Templar.'

'And did you?'

'I didn't try to stop them.'

'And why was that – because he was a sex offender, and so he only got what he deserved?'

'No, it was because, as we've already established, I'm not an absolute monarch.'

'Something's not quite adding up here,' Baxter mused. 'Power's not just about deciding who gets hurt – it's also about deciding who *doesn't* get hurt. And if you don't have *that* power, then you really have no power at all.'

'What happened to Templar was nothing to do with me,' Greene said, and in his tone there was the implication that he was not prepared to debate the matter any further.

'You do know who attacked him though, don't you?'

'Would you believe me if I said I didn't?'

'No.'

'So there's no point in denying it.'

'I want to know about the attacks,' Baxter said. 'I want to know if they were so carefully planned that there was nothing that the prison officers could have done to prevent them, or if the attackers merely took advantage of a lapse in prison security. In other words, were the guards outmanoeuvred or simply incompetent?'

'So now you're asking me to snitch on my fellow lags?'

'No, not at all. I don't need to know their names, just the circumstances in which the attacks took place.'

'I can't do it,' Greene said flatly. 'It'd be a step too far.'

'Then I can't recommend you to the Open University,' Baxter said, just as flatly.

'I know,' Greene said – and there were tears in his eyes.

The police surgeon's office at the morgue had been central to so many cases that Monika Paniatowski had almost come to regard it as an extension of her own office, and looking around it at that moment – at the prints of Indian gods that had been hung by Dr Shastri, and the bag of golf clubs belonging to Dr Taylor – she reminded herself of just how important a good police doctor was to any investigation.

The newest police doctor – Liz Duffy – was sitting behind the same desk that Shastri and Taylor had occupied, and she seemed very, very tired.

'Yes, I know that I look like death warmed up,' Dr Duffy said, reading Paniatowski's expression, 'but then I do work in a morgue, so it's really quite appropriate, isn't it?' She smiled weakly. 'That's a little pathologist's humour for you, Monika.'

'Did the autopsy take all night?' Paniatowski asked.

'No – just most of it.'

'So you haven't been home at all?'

'There didn't seem much point, and anyway, I didn't know exactly when you'd be coming, and I wanted to make sure that I was here when you did.'

'That was very thoughtful of you.'

'I'm the assistant police surgeon – it's my job,' Liz Duffy said, with a tired grin. 'Would you like to hear what I've got?'

'Yes, please.'

'Maggie Hudson's death was due to strangulation, which should come as no surprise to anybody who's seen her. Last night in the park, I estimated that she'd died between two and three hours earlier, but having run some tests, I'd be inclined to say it was closer to two than to three. I hope that's of some help to you.'

'So that would put her death at around seven o'clock?'

'Yes.'

When it was already dark, Paniatowski thought – when, chances were, the park was all but deserted.

'I also found a contusion on the back of her head,' Liz Duffy said.

'Was it recent?'

'Very recent. I'd say the blow was delivered shortly before death, and my guess – and bear in mind that I'm no detective – is that since she was obviously much stronger than Jill Harris, the killer did that to ensure she didn't struggle too much.'

'Last night in the park, you told me that you couldn't say whether there was one killer or two,' Paniatowski said. 'From the way you're talking now, it seems as if you'd decided there was only one.'

'That's my gut feeling,' Liz Duffy said, 'but I'm afraid I don't have any conclusive medical evidence to back it up.'

'Was Maggie unconscious when she died?'

'She may have been – but if she wasn't, she'd certainly have been too dazed to put up much of a struggle.'

'Was there any evidence of sexual assault?'

'There was some bruising in the vaginal area, but the bruises are at least a few days old.'

An image of her stepfather, lowering himself on to her, flashed across Paniatowski's mind, and then was gone.

'Do you think that Maggie was raped?' she asked.

'It's possible,' the doctor conceded, 'but there aren't any bruises on her thighs or arms, which was what you'd expect with forcible penetration.'

'So what conclusions do you draw from that?'

'That while the sex may have been rough, it was probably also consensual. Some girls like it rough – or, at least, they *expect* it to be rough, so they don't complain when it actually is. From her own appearance – and from that of her mother, who came in last night to identify the body, but seemed more interested in talking about compensation – I suspect Maggie may have been one of those girls.'

'I think you're right,' Paniatowski agreed.

'For a girl of her age, she wasn't in great shape physically,' Liz Duffy asked. 'Her diet was poor, her teeth were beginning to rot, and she wasn't getting nearly enough exercise. She was also suffering from gonorrhoea – and had been for several weeks.'

'Would she have known she had the clap?' Paniatowski asked.

'Not necessarily. When men catch it, they usually experience pain when urinating within four to six days. In the case of women, there *may be* vaginal discharge, and having intercourse *can* become painful, but fifty per cent of women are totally asymptomatic, and have no idea they're infected.'

A possible scenario flashed through Paniatowski's mind . . . Maggie sleeps with a man, and four to six days later, it starts to hurt when he pees. He realizes what has happened and flies into a rage. When he confronts Maggie in the park . . .

But that would mean there were two killers, and even the cautious Dr Duffy now believed there was only one.

'Maggie had consumed quite a lot of alcohol in the hours preceding her death,' Liz Duffy continued. 'My guess would be that it was cheap cider.'

What did the two girls have in common? Paniatowski asked herself.

One of them had had an overprotective mother, the other a mother who didn't give a damn about her.

One had been a virgin, with lesbian tendencies. The other had been heterosexual, and sexually active.

Yet they died not only in almost exactly the same way, but also in almost exactly the same place.

'I was hoping you might have been able to find something that linked the two victims,' she said.

And then she saw the look of utter dejection that came instantly to the other woman's face, and wished she hadn't spoken at all.

'What sort of thing did you have in mind?' Liz Duffy asked, in a subdued voice.

'I don't know,' Paniatowski confessed.

'Perhaps that they shared the same rare blood group or had both got appendix scars from operations which were clearly performed by the same doctor?'

Paniatowski grinned. 'Something like that,' she said. 'Look, you shouldn't take anything I've said to heart,' she continued in a more serious tone. 'It's no reflection on you. The fact is that I'm so desperate over this case that I was hoping for a miracle – and miracles simply don't happen every day.'

'Is it really as bad as that?' Liz Duffy asked. 'Is your boss giving you a hard time?'

'Not at the moment,' Paniatowski said. 'He's in Yorkshire, investigating a prison suicide. But when he gets back, the fat will really be in the fire.'

'Oh God!' Liz gasped. She turned away, and began to pace the room. 'I didn't realize how much you were depending on me – and I've given you *nothing*!'

'As I said, I've no right to expect miracles,' Paniatowski said.

But Dr Shastri would have worked miracles, she thought.

If Shastri hadn't had the right *answers*, she would at least have asked the right *questions*, which would have set the team on the path towards finding the right answers for itself.

It wasn't Liz Duffy's fault. She was young and inexperienced, and in time she would no doubt grow into just as fine a police doctor as Dr Shastri. But given that she had two murders on her hands, Paniatowski needed someone as fine as Dr Shastri *now*!

SEVENTEEN

Meadows was prepared to concede that the traffic was fairly heavy in the centre of Whitebridge that morning, but it still didn't seem quite heavy *enough* to merit either the intensity of concentration or the caution with which DC Crane – who was behind the wheel – was treating it.

'Do you know, Jack, the way you're driving is so reminiscent of my Great-aunt Matilda that it's almost uncanny,' Meadows said.

Crane signalled to overtake a van, then thought better of it, and dropped back slightly.

'Yes, good old Aunt Matilda,' Meadows continued. 'What a character she was! You could always tell when she'd taken the Roller out for a spin because there'd be a tailback of traffic that could stretch for miles.'

Crane said nothing.

'Still, I suppose that's only to be expected when you're a ninety-one-year-old woman and as blind as a bat,' Meadows ploughed on. 'Are you ninety-one, Jack?'

'Sorry?' Crane said.

'I was just asking you if you'd ever been to Bridlington-on-sea,' Meadows said.

Crane shook his head. 'No, I haven't.'

'What's on your mind, young Jack?' Meadows asked.

'Nothing,' Crane replied.

'You might as well come clean right away,' Meadows told him, 'because you know I'm easily smart enough to guess eventually, don't you?'

'Yes, I do know that,' Crane agreed.

'Well, then?'

They reached the roundabout at the end of the High Street, and Crane took a left turn.

'Have you ever been in love, Sarge?' he asked.

'I was *married* once,' Meadows replied.

And because there was something in her tone which suggested

that that particular avenue of conversation was permanently closed, Crane said no more than, 'Fair enough.'

For a while, as they drove through the industrial wasteland that had once been the beating heart of Whitebridge, they fell silent again.

Then Meadows said, 'All right, since I was the one who insisted on knowing what you were thinking, I suppose it's only fair that I answer your question honestly. No, Jack, I've never been in love. Why do you ask? Are you?'

'I'm not sure,' Crane admitted.

'And how long have you been suffering from this period of uncertainty?' Meadows wondered.

'About twelve hours.'

'Ah, then it must be the new police doctor who you think you might have fallen for,' Meadows guessed. 'Falling in love so quickly was rather impulsive, don't you think?'

'It's not so much a case of having discovered new feelings as it is of resurrecting ones which I thought were dead and buried,' Crane explained.

'So she's an old flame, is she?'

'That's right.'

'From your university days?'

'Yes.'

'Then you'd better tell Aunt Kate all about it, hadn't you?'

'We were together for a little under a year . . .' Crane began.

'Can you be a little more precise than that?' Meadows interrupted him.

Crane grinned sheepishly. 'We were together for three hundred and twenty-seven days,' he said.

'Ah, so *she* jilted *you*.'

'How do you know that?'

'Because you're the one who's kept the score.'

'You're right, of course,' Crane agreed. 'She jilted me. And at the time, it was a bit of a relief.'

'Why was that?'

'Because I was young and foolish, I suppose. She saw us as a complete pair. She worshipped me . . .'

'You flatter yourself,' Meadows told him.

'No, I don't think I do,' Crane continued seriously. 'I could do no wrong in her eyes, and, to be honest, I was starting to find it a bit stifling.'

'So perhaps she jilted you because she thought you were about to jilt her,' Meadows suggested.

'Do you know, I've never considered that possibility,' Crane said thoughtfully, 'but now you bring it up, it sort of makes sense. Anyway, it wasn't long before I started to miss her more than I'd ever imagined I would, and I was on the point of suggesting we try again when she met Simon.'

'Who was tall, handsome, and drove a very expensive sports car?' Meadows suggested.

'Yes, you're right about all those things,' Crane agreed. 'Anyway, I made the best of a bad job, and started going out with other girls, some of whom were quite stunning.' He paused. 'And I'm not flattering myself there, either,' he added, as if to nip the expected criticism in the bud.

'No, I'm sure you're not,' Meadows agreed. 'You're not my type at all, Jack, you really aren't . . .'

'There's no need to go on about it,' Crane told her.

'. . . but even allowing for that, I don't find it particularly hard to believe you can pull beautiful girls just by clicking your fingers.'

'I've tried to put her out of my thoughts over the years, but now – totally unexpectedly – we've met again,' Crane continued. 'And Liz isn't attached any more! Simon left her – she told me that last night.'

'Wouldn't it be a bit dangerous to pick up just where you left off?' Meadows cautioned. 'Might you not soon start to feel hemmed in again?'

'I don't think so,' Crane said. 'I'm older now, and the prospect of getting together with someone who wants to make you the centre of her universe – and who you want to become the centre of yours – doesn't seem anything like as daunting as it once did.'

'Even so, it's always a mistake to rush into things,' Meadows cautioned. 'You won't rush into them, will you, Jack?'

'We're there,' Crane said, sidestepping the question.

They were indeed, Meadows thought, looking through the windscreen and seeing Wood Rise High School looming up in front of them.

The school had cold slate roofs and gables that seemed to gaze down disapprovingly at those below them. It looked more like a Victorian workhouse – which was what it once had been – than a centre of enlightenment, and it was hardly surprising that it was known locally as *Blood Eyes* High School.

'We're expected, are we?' Meadows asked, as she got out of the car.

'We are,' Crane confirmed. 'The headmaster will be waiting for us in his study.'

'What do you know about him?'

'Not a great deal. I believe he was a military policeman in the army before he retrained as a teacher.'

Meadows looked at the gaunt, austere building again. 'He must feel quite at home here, then,' she said.

Baxter was sitting at his desk when he heard an awkward cough, and he looked up to find Chief Officer Jeffries standing in the open doorway.

'Can I do something for you, Mr Jeffries?' he asked.

'I've been ordered by the governor to ask you how your interview with Lennie Greene went,' Jeffries said woodenly.

Having been in the prison for a few days, and seen for himself who actually pulled the strings, it was difficult to imagine the governor *ordering* Jeffries to do anything, Baxter thought. So if such an order had, in fact, been issued, it was only because Jeffries *wanted* it issued.

'Did you hear what I said?' Jeffries asked.

'Yes, you said you'd been ordered by the governor to ask me how my interview with Lennie Greene went.'

'And how did it go?'

'It went fine.'

'You're not being very cooperative,' Jeffries said.

'I must have learned that from someone else,' Baxter countered.

'Look, you must have realized by now that we rely on Greene to keep things in order on the other side of the bars,' Jeffries said.

But did they, Baxter wondered – or did they only *think* they did?

Was there some other prisoner secretly calling the shots – a prisoner who Greene was so afraid of that even though he desperately wanted to study with the Open University, he didn't dare to expose him? Was that what he had meant when he'd said that telling Baxter what he wanted to know would be taking a step too far?

'Are you listening to me?' Jeffries demanded angrily.

'I'm listening,' Baxter said.

'Since you talked to Greene, he's been unusually quiet. He may even have been crying. And as his state of mind has a direct effect on the running of this prison, I demand to know what went on between the two of you.'

'I'll make a deal with you,' Baxter suggested. 'You tell me why you felt it necessary to alter the timesheets, and I'll tell you what I said to Greene.'

'Why I altered the time sheets?' Jeffries repeated. 'I have no idea what you're talking about.'

Baxter picked up the timesheets that were lying on the desk. 'These are what you gave me – and they're only photocopies,' he said.

'That's right,' Jeffries agreed.

'And not even very good ones. Was that deliberate?'

'No, it wasn't deliberate,' Jeffries said. 'The prison service isn't like the police force, you know. We don't get money showered on us every time we hold our hands out.'

'Oh, for God's sake, do you think you're the only ones working under budgetary constraints?' Baxter said, exasperatedly. 'Some of my officers are driving around in patrol cars that should have been retired years ago. I'm so understaffed that I'm continually moving men from one important job when it's only half completed because I need them on another important job.'

The smile that came to Jeffries' face signalled that he thought he was just about to win the argument.

'So you're understaffed, are you?' he asked.

'That's what I said.'

'I take it that means that sometimes you have to go out on foot patrol yourself?'

'Of course not! That would be ridiculous.'

'Would it? Well, sometimes *we're* so understaffed that I personally have to work one of the shifts. Me – the Chief Officer!'

'My heart bleeds for you,' Baxter said.

'I don't want your sympathy, I just want you to appreciate the conditions we have to work under here,' Jefferies countered. 'We have to make-do-and-mend, so if the photocopies I provided you with aren't very good, it's because the machine I used wasn't very good – and if the machine I used wasn't very good, it's because we can't afford a new one.'

'If that's the case, then I'd better see the originals of the time sheets, hadn't I?' Baxter asked.

'The originals are official documents,' Jeffries told him.

'And I'm conducting an *official* inquiry,' Baxter reminded him. 'I want those time sheets on my desk by – at the latest – eight o'clock tomorrow morning.'

'And what if I can't produce them?'

Baxter shook his head. 'You still don't get it, do you?' he asked. 'If you refuse to deliver them – or come up with some pathetic excuse like they've been lost or destroyed – I'll get straight on the phone to the Home Office, and you'll be out of a job.'

'If you – or any other do-gooder bloody liberal – ever came to work here, you'd soon learn what prison was all about,' Jefferies snarled. 'And I'll tell you something for nothing – you wouldn't last a week.'

Baxter lit up his pipe and took a reflective puff. 'You may well be right,' he agreed, 'but that still doesn't alter the fact that I *will have* those reports.'

Jeffries turned on his heel, and stormed off down the corridor.

The chief officer was like a rat trapped in a corner, Baxter thought – and he wondered just what Jeffries would do next.

The headmaster of Wood Rise High School was called Coles. He was in late middle age, tall and thin. His eyes were cold, his head was almost shaven, and if he'd ever had any laughter lines, they'd probably been surgically removed.

The office was as Spartan as the man, and the chairs that he invited Meadows and Crane to sit down on seemed to have been deliberately designed for maximum discomfort.

'It must have been a great shock for you to learn that one of your pupils had been murdered,' Meadows said, 'but, I have to admit, looking at you now, it really doesn't show.'

Crane recognized this gambit of Meadows' for what it was. In training, you were told that you'd get most out of a witness by being sympathetic and giving them the impression you were on their side. And sometimes, Meadows *was* sympathetic – genuinely so. But there were other occasions – and this was clearly one of them – when she decided that she'd get better results by deliberately poking the witness with a sharp mental stick.

The headmaster winced slightly at Meadows' comment, then thought for perhaps ten seconds before he spoke.

'I am sorry that Margaret Hudson is dead – of course I am,' he intoned finally. 'As the poet says, the death of anyone, however much we may dislike them personally, diminishes us all.'

'But . . .?' Meadows prompted.

'But while I am surprised that she died *so* young, it is not surprising at all that she came to a violent end.'

'Because . . .'

'You're a police officer,' the headmaster said. 'You will have seen some unpleasant things in your time, so I assume that you don't subscribe to the view that no one is ever really guilty of anything they do – that, for example, when a group of thugs beat up an old-aged pensioner, it's only because they've had an unhappy childhood, and so they are entitled to our sympathy rather than our condemnation.'

'I'm with you so far,' Meadows said, non-committally.

'Margaret Hudson was a vicious young woman, and the people she attracted to her were also vicious,' the headmaster said. 'She was a bully. She was disruptive. And she had the morals of an alley cat.'

'That seems a bit harsh,' Meadows said, prodding again.

'Does it?' the headmaster asked. 'Perhaps you'll no longer think so when I tell you that my senior mistress caught her having sexual intercourse with a boy behind the bicycle sheds, and that there were another four boys lined up to take his place when he'd finished the filthy business.'

'Well, at least they'd formed an orderly queue,' Meadows said. 'That shows some sense of propriety.'

'It's not funny!' the headmaster said.

'No, of course it isn't,' Meadows replied, with mock contrition. 'I apologize unreservedly. Do carry on.'

'We can't prove she stole from the school office, any more than we can prove she smashed up the girls' toilets – but we know she did both things. She could poison any class, and whenever a teacher had a nervous breakdown – and there've been a few of those – she took it as a personal triumph.'

'In other words, despite what you said earlier, it's a relief that she's dead,' Meadows said.

'It's a relief that she'll no longer have such a disruptive influence on this school,' the headmaster replied.

'Was she in school yesterday?' Meadows asked.

The headmaster consulted the register, which was lying on the desk. 'She was here yesterday morning – though only because her social worker personally frogmarched her in – but she was missing at afternoon registration. So I would imagine that –' he scanned the columns of the register – 'yes, Polly Johnson and Lillian Beakes were absent, too.'

'They would be her gang,' Meadows said.

'They would be her gang,' the headmaster confirmed.

'And are they in school today?'

The headmaster scanned more of the register's columns. 'Yes, by some miracle, they are.'

It wasn't a miracle at all, Meadows thought. When you're upset, there's some comfort to be found in being in familiar places, even if they happen to be places you hate.

'I'd like to see both girls,' she said. 'When would it be convenient to speak to them?'

'Whenever you like,' the headmaster said. 'If you want to talk to them, it's no problem at all. But getting them to talk back to you – well, that's a different matter entirely.'

EIGHTEEN

The deputy headmaster's name was Hughes, and an aura of disillusioned idealism clung to him like a thick and uncomfortable overcoat. When he arrived at the conference room, he was accompanied by two girls.

'They look so much like Maggie Hudson that they could be her sisters,' Crane thought.

But after a few seconds reflection, he realized that his first impression had been wrong, and that the girls had very little in common with Maggie in terms of either figure or bone structure. One of them – Polly Johnson – had quite delicate features, and could have been rather pretty if she'd made the effort. The other – Lillian Beakes – had a quirky face which, framed differently, could at least have been charming. But these two girls didn't want to look either pretty or charming. With their rats-tail hair and permanent scowls, they wanted to look like Maggie, their leader.

'Will the parents be attending this interview?' Kate Meadows asked the deputy head.

Hughes shook his head. 'We haven't seen either set of parents since the girls were enrolled in this school. That's right, isn't it, Lil and Polly?'

'They got better things to do with their time,' replied Lillian Beakes, not even looking at him.

And Polly Johnson said nothing at all.

'Well, take a seat, girls,' Meadows said, in a jolly girl-guide leader sort of way. She waited until the girls had plopped themselves reluctantly into the seats opposite her, then turned to the deputy head, and gave him what Crane could only describe as an alluring smile. 'I don't really think it's necessary for you to stay, Mr Hughes,' she continued.

'Aren't I supposed to?' the deputy asked.

'Possibly – in theory,' Meadows said, still smiling. 'But a man like you must have many more important things to do – and if you don't tell anybody you weren't here, then I most certainly won't.'

'I'm not sure . . .' Hughes began.

'Of course, I'd be very disappointed if I didn't get the chance to talk to you later,' Meadows interrupted him. 'I'm certain there's a great deal I could learn from you. Do you think it might be possible for us to meet over a coffee – or perhaps a quick half in the nearest pub?'

Hughes pretended to be considering it. 'Yes, I think I can find the time for that,' he said finally.

'Wonderful!' Meadows gushed. 'Then I'll come and find you as soon as I've finished talking to Lil and Polly.'

'I don't want you giving the sergeant any trouble,' Hughes warned the two girls. Then, in the face of their blank indifference, he stepped into the corridor and closed the door behind him.

'When you've had a drink with him, are you going to shag him?' asked Lil challengingly.

'I might,' Meadows said airily. 'It depends how I feel at the time.' She turned to Crane. 'Why don't you take yourself off as well, Jack?'

'I really don't think that would be a good idea,' Crane said firmly.

'No, perhaps not,' Meadows agreed, 'but the least you can do is to go over into the corner, where you won't be in the way.'

The two girls were looking questioningly at each other, and were clearly wondering what made this strange bobby tick.

'Off you go then,' Meadows said, and when Crane had stood up, she reached into her handbag and pulled out a packet of cigarettes. 'Fancy a gasper, girls?'

The girls exchanged another look, as if they suspected a trick, then Lil – who was clearly the bolder of the two – reached out for a cigarette, and Polly quickly followed.

Meadows produced a lighter and lit up the cigarettes. She didn't take a cigarette for herself, because she didn't smoke.

From the corner of the room, Crane shook his head in either admiration or disgust – and he still wasn't sure which.

Meadows pushed her chair back, and put her feet on the table. 'I'm sorry your mate got murdered,' she said.

Lil sniffed slightly, and Polly said, 'She was one of the best.'

'It's my job to catch her killer,' Meadows said. 'Will you help me?'

The two girls nodded.

'So the first thing I want to know is where you all were yesterday afternoon,' Meadows continued.

'We were—' Polly began.

'We were round and about,' Lil interrupted her.

'Did you see anybody paying any special attention to you when you were "round and about"?' Meadows asked.

'Not particularly,' Lil said.

'No more than usual,' Polly added.

'No more than usual,' Crane repeated silently from his corner. He imagined that three girls like them – "out and about" when they should have been in school – would attract attention and probably concern wherever they went, and that by the time he and Meadows got back to police headquarters, there would be reports of several sightings waiting on Meadows' desk.

'Did Maggie have any enemies?' Meadows asked.

'Lots of them – everybody hates us,' Lil said fiercely.

'Except the lads,' said Polly, with a snigger.

'They only like us as long as we're giving them what they want,' Lil said, slapping her down.

'What I meant was, did anybody hate Maggie enough to want to kill her?' Meadows said.

Both girls looked blank, then Lil said, 'Nobody would risk going to prison just to kill one of us – not even our dads.'

'OK, let's go back to where you were yesterday afternoon,' Meadows suggested. She raised her hand, as if to hold back the flood of information she was expecting. 'No, don't tell me – let me guess.' She pressed the fingers of her free hand to her brow. 'Now where would three young girls, who were out for a good time, decide to go? My best guess would be the new shopping precinct out on the Preston Road.'

'No, not there,' Lil said quickly. 'We don't like it there.'

'Oh well, good try,' Meadows said, philosophically. 'Let's have another shot at it, shall we? You went to the Corporation Park.'

Polly shuddered. 'No, not there, neither.'

'Then you must have bought a couple of bottles of cheap cider – don't worry, I know all about that, and I'm not bothered – and taken it down to the river.'

'That's right,' Lil agreed. 'We bought some cider and took it down to the river.'

'Well, there we are then,' Meadows said, taking her feet off the table, and standing up. 'That's about it, girls. Thanks very much.'

'You mean we can go?' Polly asked.

'I mean you can go,' Meadows confirmed.

Seeming hardly able to believe they'd got off so lightly, the two girls stood up and headed for the door.

Meadows waited until Lil's hand was on the handle, then said, 'Hang on a minute!'

The girls turned again, the expressions on their faces saying they had always known it was a trap.

Meadows smiled at them, and held out the waste paper basket.

'I know you don't really give a toss what your teachers think, but if I was you, I still wouldn't step out into the school corridor with a burning cigarette in my hand,' she said.

The two girls returned the smile, and stubbed out their cigarettes on the inside of the basket.

'I wish my mum was like you,' Lil said.

'No, you don't,' Meadows said seriously. 'Believe me, you really wouldn't want a mother like me.'

'You couldn't be any worse than the one I've got,' Lil replied, with a tinge of sadness in her voice.

Crane waited until the girls had closed the door behind them, then said, 'You could get in trouble for giving ciggies to kids.'

'I could get into trouble for most of things I do,' Meadows said. 'You should have realized that by now. But I thought that if I got them relaxed, they might tell me what they knew.'

'And do you think they did?'

'They told me as much as they knew – which was practically nothing – but at least we've confirmed that they don't think there was anything personal behind the murder.'

'They'd know, would they?' Crane asked sceptically.

'Of course they'd know,' Meadows said. 'They're feral. They've trained themselves to spot danger. That's why they lied about where they were yesterday afternoon.'

'So you don't think they were down by the river after all?'

'Of course they weren't by the river. And I wasn't really asking them if they had been.'

'Then what were you asking them?'

'I was trying to find out if they were with Maggie when she drank the cheap cider that your old-new girlfriend found traces of her stomach. And it seems as if they were.'

'So where *did* they spend yesterday afternoon?'

'In the Preston Road Shopping Precinct, of course.'

'They said they didn't like the shopping precinct.'

'Yes, they did – and that was what tipped me off to the fact that they must have been there.'

'How can you be so sure of that?'

'Because of all the lies that they could have told, that was the real mother-lode.'

'I'm not following you,' Crane admitted.

'There's not a teenage girl in the world – whatever her background – who doesn't like a shopping centre.'

'Then why didn't they say that's where they were?'

'Probably because *while* they were there, they did something wrong, and they don't want me to find out about it.'

'So even though they knew that by lying about it they'd be sending us off on a false trail, they decided to do it anyway,' Crane said.

'Decided!' Meadows repeated, with sudden passion. 'Girls like them don't *decide* anything. They react! They think the world's a hostile place – and for them, as they are, it is – and that their survival depends not on long-term strategies but on short-term tactics.'

'You seem to know a lot about them,' Crane said, knocked off kilter by the unexpected outburst.

'I *was* them!' Meadows told him.

'How could you have been? You're from a different class entirely.'

'Misery can be very democratic,' Meadows said. She took a deep breath. 'Our work here is done,' she continued, sounding much more like the Meadows who Crane thought that he knew. 'Now let's see just what we can unearth at the shopping precinct.'

'You're not going to see the deputy head?'

'No.'

'He'll be very disappointed.'

'In case you didn't pick up on the fact earlier, his life has been full of disappointments, so one more won't make much difference. Besides, my priority at the moment is saving the boss.'

It was as Jo Baxter was pouring the tonic into her glass that she noticed how much her hand was shaking.

And that was bad, she told herself.

No, it was worse than bad – it was bloody tragic!

She looked up at the clock.

It was only half-past twelve, for God's sake!

What was she doing, already on her third drink of the day, at only half-past twelve?

And how long had it been going on?

She placed the tonic bottle carefully on the table, and walked over to the armchair.

'Pull yourself together, Jo – drinking's not the answer,' she said aloud, and noticed how slurred the words sounded.

No, drinking wasn't the answer, she thought, as she sank heavily into the chair. But then what was?

She loved George. He was her life.

And perhaps that was the problem.

Perhaps if she'd been more independent – like Monika Paniatowski – she might have been able to handle everything so much better.

You couldn't build your life around just one person. She saw that clearly now. You had to have something you could call your own – something that defined you as unique.

She would develop new interests, she promised herself. She would do something to add extra dimensions to her personality. Perhaps if she did that, George would come to see that he'd been lucky to find her, rather than unlucky to lose Monika. And even if he didn't see it, it wouldn't be quite as devastating as it might otherwise have been, because she would have something to fall back on – something to cushion her against the disappointment.

She would start her new life immediately, she thought. No, not immediately, because you can't start a new life when you're drunk.

Very well, then, she would start her new life first thing the next day.

But in the meantime, it would be a pity to waste the gin and tonic she'd just poured for herself.

The Preston Road Shopping Precinct was a three-storey construction of shimmering glass and vividly painted concrete, and was located on the outskirts of Whitebridge, next to the road that led – unsurprisingly – to Preston. It proclaimed the town's attempt to cast off its old industrial image, and embrace a bright new future, though to Meadows – standing in the middle of the central piazza – it seemed more like a monument to glitzy bad taste.

'Shouldn't we go back to headquarters, and see if any sightings have been reported?' asked Crane, who was standing by her side.

'We could do that,' Meadows agreed, 'but I don't really think it's necessary.' She looked around her. 'Put yourself in the shoes of Maggie and her gang, Jack. Where's the first place you'd go?'

'I don't know,' Crane admitted.

Meadows surveyed the shops around the piazza.

'There!' Meadows said, pointing to a boutique in the far corner.

'You think so?' Crane asked dubiously. 'It's looks a bit cheap and flashy to me.'

'It's certainly not somewhere you'd think of buying a dress for your new girlfriend—' Meadows began.

'I'm sorry I ever mentioned it now,' Crane interrupted her. 'What have you got against Liz?'

'Nothing,' Meadows replied. 'She seems a perfectly nice woman, and she'll probably turn out to be a very good police surgeon.'

'But . . .' Crane said.

'But I don't think she's good for you.'

'Why not?'

'Because I think she's about to rob you of your independence.'

'And what if I don't want my independence?'

'Then you're a bigger fool than I took you for.'

'You almost sound as if you're jealous,' Crane said.

'Don't be absurd,' Meadows said dismissively. 'You and I are too different to ever become an item – and anyway, you're no more than a boy.' She paused. 'Sorry, Jack, this is getting far too personal.'

'Yes, it is,' Crane agreed.

'Then let's start again,' Meadows suggested. 'That boutique over there is certainly not somewhere that Dr Duffy would consider shopping, but girls like Maggie consider it a wonderland. It's the very crudity – the obviousness of it – that draws them in.'

'If you say so,' Crane said flatly.

'I *do* say so,' Meadows asserted, 'and I'll prove it to you.'

She strode across to the boutique, with Crane following in her wake.

There was only one assistant on duty – a woman in her late twenties – and her eyes lit up with a commission-earning smile when she saw Meadows.

'Now yours is a figure we can really work with,' she gushed. 'It's the figure these clothes were made for!' Crane grinned at Meadows' obvious discomfort, but the grin quickly faded when the assistant added, 'And I'm sure your young man will be enchanted.'

When Meadows produced her warrant card, the assistant's enthusiasm notably dimmed.

'This is about the girl, is it?' she asked.

Meadows nodded, and smiled complacently in Crane's direction.

'I rang the police station first thing this morning, to say I'd seen her yesterday,' the assistant continued. 'And a uniformed bobby's already been round to take my statement.'

'Would you mind going over it again?' Meadows asked.

The assistant shrugged. 'Suppose not.'

'When did the girl come into the shop?'

'Into the boutique!'

'Into the boutique,' Meadows corrected herself.

'Must have been about half-past three.'

'And was she alone?'

'No, she had two other kids with her – they all looked a bit rough, and I think they'd been drinking.'

'I'm surprised you let them in,' Meadows said.

'I probably shouldn't have,' the assistant agreed, 'but the manageress was out on one of her many breaks, and I didn't want a scene.'

'Did they buy anything?'

The assistant laughed. 'You've got to be joking.'

'So what did they do?'

'They went over to the bargain bin,' the assistant said, pointing to a large cardboard bin in the corner. 'They all stood in front of it, so I couldn't see what they were doing, and that's when I decided that however unpleasant it might turn out to be, I'd have to throw them out.'

Meadows walked over to the bargain bin, and looked down at the mishmash of things it contained

'Did they steal anything?' she asked.

'Hard to say,' the assistant admitted. 'They certainly looked as if that was what they were intending to do, but to be honest with you, anything chucked in there has already been taken out of invoice. If it was left to me, I wouldn't bother with having the bin at all, but Mrs Bowles, the manageress, says that even if we only get fifty pee for something, it's better than just chucking it away.'

Meadows took hold of the bin and lifted it off the ground.

'Here, what are you doing?' the assistant demanded.

Meadows upended the bin, and the 'bargains' it had contained – shoes and tops, spangled tights and cheap handbags – all cascaded onto the floor.

'Do you notice anything missing?' she asked.

'No, like I said, it's only old junk and . . .'

'Look closely,' Meadows said, in a not-to-be-denied voice.

'There were two of them wigs there yesterday, and now there's only one,' the assistant said.

Meadows picked the wig up off the floor. It was made of nylon, and was bright purple.

'They call them "fun" wigs,' the assistant explained. 'They were all the rage last year – for about three weeks.'

Meadows shook the wig, and put it on her head.

'You look quite different with that on,' Crane said.

'I think that's rather the idea,' Meadows told him. She turned back to the assistant. 'You're certain there were two of them here yesterday – before the girls came in?'

The assistant thought about it.

'Yes, I am,' she said finally. 'I noticed them while I was stuffing the spangly tights in the bin, and I remember thinking that while we might sell some of the other rubbish, we wouldn't even be able to *give* them away.'

'Stick one of these wigs under your jumper, and nobody would notice it was even there,' Meadows said to Jack Crane. 'I'd like to buy this wig,' she told the assistant.

'It wouldn't suit you, you know,' the assistant cautioned.

'I'd like it anyway,' Meadows replied. 'How much do you want for it? Shall we say – a pound?'

'You can have it for nothing.'

'Better to pay,' Meadows said firmly, handing a pound note over, 'and if you want to regard it as a fair reward for information received, that's perfectly all right with me.'

'You what?'

'If you want to put it in your handbag, instead of the till, nobody will be any the wiser,' Meadows said over her shoulder, as she headed for the door.

'So where do we go now?' Crane asked, once they were outside the boutique.

'We go to the nearest stationer's shop,' Meadows told him.

'I can't see Maggie Hudson going to a stationer's,' Crane said.

'She won't have done,' Meadows agreed. 'But I need to – because I want to buy some coloured pencils.'

NINETEEN

Paniatowski studied the mother and daughter who were sitting across the desk from her.

The mother – Mrs Turner – was in her late thirties, and had the look about her of a woman who was both firmly convinced of her own rightness on all matters, and energetic enough to grind down everyone else until they agreed with her. She was wearing a sensible coat and – possibly because she was in a police station – a hat with a feather in it.

The daughter – Dolly – was thirteen or fourteen, and bore the long-suffering expression of an only child who was desperate to break away from the cage in which her domineering mother had imprisoned her for so long. She was wearing a sensible coat, too, and despite the fact that it was quite warm in Paniatowski's office, had a scarf tightly wrapped around her neck.

'The desk sergeant said you might have some information which could be pertinent to my investigation,' Paniatowski said.

'For the last two days, this one's been looking as miserable as I-don't-know-what,' Mrs Turner began. 'Well, I didn't say anything – because I'm not the kind of mother who likes to interfere – but when I caught her sobbing her heart out, I insisted on knowing the reason. And it turns out that's what's been upsetting her was something that happened to a friend of hers. It appears that this girl was walking through the park and—'

'Perhaps it would be better if you let Dolly tell the story,' Paniatowski interrupted.

'Oh, all right, if you insist,' Mrs Turner said, in a huff. She folded her arms across her chest. 'Well, tell the lady what you told me, our Dolly.'

'This . . . this friend of mine was attacked when she was walking through the park,' Dolly said, hesitantly.

'Of course, the first thing that I said was that the girl should come in and report it herself,' Mrs Turner said, 'but our Dolly – who's always been a stubborn one – won't even tell me her name.'

I'm sure she won't – because it's a name you won't want to hear, Paniatowski thought.

'When did this attack take place?' she asked the girl.

'It was the night before last.'

'So it was one night *after* Jill Harris was killed, and one night *before* Maggie Hudson was killed.'

'Yes.'

'Do you know what time this attack occurred at?'

'Just after half-past eight.'

'You're sure that was the time?'

'Yes, the clock on the cathedral had just struck.'

'So it had already been dark for quite a while?'

'I suppose so.'

'What exactly was this friend of yours doing in the park, on the night after a murder?'

'I don't know.'

'Wasn't she frightened to be there?'

'No, because she had her . . . she had her . . .' Dolly began.

Then she clamped her mouth tightly shut.

'Had her what?' Paniatowski asked.

Dolly struggled for an answer. 'She had her whistle with her,' she said finally. 'She knew that if anybody attacked her, she could blow her whistle.'

'And did she?'

'Did she what?'

'Did she blow her whistle?'

Dolly looked down at the table. 'No – she screamed, instead.'

'Tell me exactly what happened during the attack.'

'She . . . she was walking towards the gate. The man crept up behind her. She didn't even know he was there until he grabbed her round the throat, and started to choke. It was terrible. I . . . I . . . couldn't breathe.'

'*You* couldn't breathe?' interrupted her mother, who had only just realized what Paniatowski had known almost from the first moment the woman and girl had walked into the room.

'I meant her,' Dolly said quickly. '*She* couldn't breathe!'

'Take that scarf off,' her mother ordered her.

'I've got a sore throat, mum.'

'Take it off – right now!'

Slowly and reluctantly, Dolly unwrapped the scarf. The marks around her throat had started to fade, but they were undoubtedly bruises.

'You told me you were at Jackie Earnshaw's house the other night,' her mother said.

'I . . . I was,' Dolly said feebly. 'I was taking a short cut home, back through the park.'

'The park's not a short cut,' her mother said, showing signs of hysteria. 'It's right out of your way.'

'You need to calm down, Mrs Turner,' Paniatowski said.

'And you don't even *own* a whistle,' the mother said.

'Do you want to find out what happened to Dolly or not?' Paniatowski asked urgently. 'Do you want to know what *damage* was done? Because if you *do* want to know, you'd better just shut up and listen.'

'It's all very well for you,' Mrs Turner began. 'You're not—'

'Now!' Paniatowski said firmly.

For a moment, it looked as if the mother would continue to argue, then she lowered her head, and began to sob softly to herself.

'How did you get away, Dolly?' Paniatowski asked softly.

'I . . . I kicked him,' the girl said. 'I think I must have hurt him, because he fell over.'

'And then you ran away?'

'Yes.'

She was lying, Paniatowski thought.

'Or was it him who ran away?' she asked, taking a stab in the dark.

'Yes, it was him,' Dolly admitted.

'And what do you think made him do that?' Paniatowski prodded.

'He . . . he heard somebody coming.'

'*Somebody*?'

Dolly glanced nervously at her mother, who seemed to have gone into shock, then mouthed the words, 'My boyfriend.'

'You can't keep it a secret any longer, you know,' Paniatowski said, kindly but firmly. 'Is he a big lad – this boyfriend of yours?'

'Yes . . . no . . . I don't know.'

'Because he must have been quite big, to frighten your attacker off, don't you think?'

'Yes, he's . . . he's quite big.'

'I'll need his name,' Paniatowski said.

'But why? He didn't have anything to do with it.'

'He might have seen something that you didn't – something that could help us catch the man who attacked you.'

Dolly started to cry. 'He didn't. He didn't see *anything*. He *told* me he didn't see anything. And I daren't give you his name.'

'Why not?'

'I just can't! That's all!'

'It really is important,' Paniatowski cajoled.

'Tell her his name!' said Mrs Turner, suddenly coming back to life. 'Tell her the bloody bastard's name!'

Paniatowski sighed. Another minute or two, and the girl might well have given her the name, but the mother's intervention had closed off all possibility of that. She *would* reveal the name in the end, of course – but it might take days.

Meadows and Crane were back in the central piazza.

'My guess is that the next thing Maggie did after leaving the shop – pardon me, after leaving the *boutique* – was to go to the ladies toilets on the second floor,' Meadows said.

'And why would she have done that?' Crane wondered.

'Because it's the nearest thing to a Bat-cave she'd have been able to find,' Meadows said.

'A Bat-cave?'

'In the daytime, Bruce Wayne is like any other mild-mannered millionaire, but at night he descends into the Bat-cave and re-emerges as a superhero,' Meadows said, in a pseudo-Hollywood accent. 'In Maggie's case, she would have gone to the toilets, put on the wig, and admired herself in the mirror.'

'And stepped out of the ladies' loo as a superhero?'

'In her own terms, yes.'

'And then she'd start looking around for bank robbers to arrest, and fair maidens to pull out of the path of approaching trains?' Crane asked.

'I'm being serious,' Meadows told him. 'Putting on the disguise would have empowered her. She'd have become a completely new person, much freer from restraint.'

And you'd know all about that, wouldn't you? Crane thought. Because when you go out on your fetishist dates, you're not DS Kate Meadows any more – you're Zelda, a dark force of the night.

But wisely, all he said aloud was, 'So even with the wig on, Maggie wouldn't start thinking about leaping over tall buildings?'

'No, she wouldn't have the imagination to come up with anything original,' Meadows said, perhaps a little sadly. 'She'd be more likely to follow her normal pattern of behaviour – but with less concern about the risks involved.'

'She'd do some more shoplifting,' Crane said.

'Exactly – she'd go straight from the Bat-cave to Aladdin's cave.'

'To *where*?' Crane asked.

'To Woolworths,' Meadows said.

The Woolworths manager studied the photograph of Maggie Hudson for a few moments, then said, 'She looks vaguely familiar, but if I thought I'd seen her yesterday, I would – like any other law-abiding citizen – have contacted the police the moment the appeal for information appeared on the television news.'

Meadows reached into her handbag and produced a second photograph – one which was identical to the first, save for the fact that she'd drawn a purple wig on it.

'How about her?' she asked.

'Good God!' the manager said. 'It's the same girl, isn't it?'

'Yes, it is,' Meadows agreed.

'It's so obvious when you have the two pictures side by side, but without the second to compare to the first . . .'

'Nobody's blaming you,' Meadows said soothingly. 'It's a mistake most people would have made. Do you now think that she might have been here yesterday, after all?'

'She *was* here,' the manager said, positively. 'And she had two other girls with her.'

'Could you describe them?' Crane asked.

The manager frowned. 'They all looked rather slutty, though one of them could have been quite pretty,' he said finally.

That would be Polly, Crane thought.

'They tried their hand at a spot of shoplifting, did they?' Kate Meadows asked.

'They did indeed,' the manager confirmed, 'though it wasn't actually the girl in the wig who stole – it was the pretty one.'

'Tell us exactly what happened.'

'The pretty girl went over to the stationery counter, and started stuffing pens into the sleeve of her cardigan – though why any of those girls would want a pen is quite beyond me.'

'They *didn't* want them,' Meadows said. 'They wanted to *steal* them – which is not the same thing at all.'

'I expect you're right. At any rate, the store detective – who was standing by the bras and knickers at the time – saw what was going on, and strode quickly towards the pretty girl. And that's when the other girl – the one in the wig – stepped in the way and blocked his passage.' The manager suddenly reddened. 'Actually, she did more than just obstruct him. What happened next was really rather unpleasant.'

'What *did* happen next?'

'She . . . well, she . . . it was all rather crude, and I'd rather not talk about it in the presence of a lady.'

Meadows made an elaborate show of looking around her. 'No ladies here, as far as I can see,' she pronounced.

'Rather than have me describe it, wouldn't it be easier to just look at the tape?' the manager asked, growing more embarrassed by the second.

'The tape?' Meadows repeated.

'Oh, of course, you wouldn't know about it,' the manager said, visibly relieved to be changing the subject. 'I'm talking about the tape from the closed-circuit television camera.'

'I'm still not with you,' Meadows admitted.

'It's a German invention – they used it to monitor the launch of their V-2 rockets during the war,' said the manager – and from the new tone that had entered his voice, it was clear that he was merely repeating a lecture he had heard at some company booster conference. 'Yes, it was the Germans who developed it, but it was the Americans – naturally – who saw its fuller potential. The New York Police Department installed some of these cameras in Times Square last year, in an effort to cut down on crime, and one of the directors in our head office – which is also in New York – thought they might help us reduce shoplifting.'

'So all Woolworths stores have these cameras installed, do they?' Crane asked.

The manager laughed at his obvious naivety. 'Certainly not! That would be a huge undertaking. But it was decided to run a number of pilot schemes in selected Woolworths stores. We were chosen to be one of those stores, which was, of course a great honour, but – when you think about it – hardly surprising. Woolworths UK has always been an innovator, you know. It was in the Liverpool

Woolworths that the first lunch counter was introduced, and now all the Woolworths in America have one, so you could say that we—'

'So you've got this encounter with Maggie Hudson on recording tape?' Meadows interrupted.

'Well, yes,' said the manager, a little miffed at being cut off mid-flow. 'It's a rather expensive process, so I don't suppose we'll carry on recording *everything* once the pilot scheme is completed, but for the moment at least, head office is interested in seeing just how it is working out, and—'

'We'd like to see the tape,' Meadows said.

And she was thinking, There's just a possibility that the killer could be on it! There's just the remotest possibility that this is where he made the decision to kill Maggie!

'If you come back in the morning, I'll arrange for our store detective – a very sound chap called Sam Houghton – to show it to you,' the manager said.

'Maybe I didn't make myself quite clear,' Meadows replied. 'I'd like to see it *now*.'

'I'm afraid that's not possible,' the manager said frostily. 'It's Sam Houghton's day off.'

'And will he be at home?'

'I shouldn't think so. He's a very keen walker, and he's probably in the middle of the Yorkshire Dales at this very moment.'

It had been a mistake to interrupt the man in the middle of his party piece, Meadows thought. She should have listened quietly, the expression on her face saying there was nothing in the whole world that she found more fascinating than the minutiae of retail marketing.

'Oh dear,' she said, in a softer, more alluring voice, 'that is rather inconvenient.'

'Well, I'm afraid there's nothing we can do about it,' the manager said, unyielding.

'Couldn't *you* show us the tape?' Meadows asked sweetly. 'I know you're a very *busy* man, but it would be *such* a help to us.'

The charm was working, and the manager looked as if he would be willing to do a series of backward somersaults if she asked him to – but he still regretfully shook his head.

'It's very complicated equipment,' he said. 'Sam went on a week's course to learn how to use it, and he's the only person in the whole store who even knows how to switch it on.'

TWENTY

It had only just gone dark, but already the thin ribbon of road that connected Dunston Prison with Dunston village was covered in a thin sheen of frost that twinkled in the glare of George Baxter's headlights.

He was far from the first person to have felt the need to escape from the prison, he thought as he drove along, but unlike most of the others who nurtured the desire, he actually could.

When he was leaving instructions with the switchboard operator to transfer all calls from Whitebridge to the village pub, he had noted the secret smile – so slight it was a bare twitch at the corners of the operator's mouth – and had known exactly what it meant. Nobody in the prison liked him – not even the ones with nothing to fear – and no doubt they felt a sense of collective victory in having succeeded in driving him out, albeit temporarily.

Well, they were wrong, he thought, as he pulled on to the pub car park. He wasn't running away at all – he was merely recharging his batteries – and after an hour or two in the pub, a couple of pints and perhaps a little conversation with some 'normal' people, he would return to the prison with fresh resolve.

The Red Lion, it turned out, was the kind of parochial village pub that seemed to think that because it had three different flavours of crisps on sale, it was in the food-catering business – the kind of pub that believed that its darts champion was world class, and its domino players performed with far more skill than the so-called grand masters in the much inferior game of chess. Still, for all that, there was a log fire blazing away in the bar, and the locals – if not exactly effusive – were friendly enough.

By the time he was halfway down his first pint of John Smith's Best Bitter, Baxter was starting to relax, and as he took the first sip of his second pint, the process was almost complete.

Then a voice in his head said, 'You should ring Jo tonight, you know,' and he felt his neck muscles tighten.

He wondered where his marriage was heading, whether it was

already damaged beyond repair, and if it *was* irreparably damaged, whether it was his fault.

He loved Jo. He really did. True, he did not love her *as much* as he had once loved Monika Paniatowski, but you can't rewrite the past, so there was really not much he could do about that.

Perhaps the best solution to Jo's problem with Monika was for him to resign from his post, he thought.

Perhaps, when all was said and done, he had no choice but to leave the job he had wanted all his adult life, and move away with Jo to some other part of the country, where Monika might no longer be a ghostly presence in their bed.

It would be hard – very hard – to do that, but it was the *right* thing to do.

He drained his second pint, wished the few people in the bar a good evening, and stepped out into the cold Yorkshire air.

It was then that he saw the man and the girl – and knew there was trouble ahead.

The two were standing by his car, waiting for him. The man was stocky, and about forty years old. The girl was perhaps sixteen – and careworn.

'I'm Arthur Williams, and this is my daughter Susan – and we want to talk to you,' the man said, in a Midlands accent.

'I'm listening,' Baxter replied.

'You've no right to be doing what you're doing up at that prison,' Williams said.

'And what exactly is it that you think I'm doing at the prison?' Baxter wondered.

'You're trying to blame the officers who work there for Jeremy Templar's suicide,' the other man told him. 'You're trying to ruin the lives of some good men, just because that filthy louse topped himself.'

'You know these "good men" personally, do you?' Baxter asked.

'Of course I don't know them personally – we live in Birmingham, and have done all our lives. But even if they *weren't* good men – even if they were the scum of the earth – they can't be anything like as bad as he was.' Williams turned to the girl. 'Tell him,' he said.

The girl hunched up her shoulders. 'I don't want to, Dad,' she whimpered. 'Please don't make me.'

'It has to be said,' Williams replied firmly. 'Tell him!'

'You shouldn't be putting the poor girl through any of this,' Baxter told the other man.

'You're half right,' Williams said. 'I *shouldn't* have to put her through it! But I *do* have to – and that's your fault.'

'If I wasn't carrying out the inquiry at the prison, someone else would be,' Baxter pointed out.

But Williams was there to talk, not to listen.

'Jeremy Templar took my little daughter into the woods . . .' he began.

'It . . . it wasn't exactly the woods, Dad,' the girl said.

'If I have to tell him, rather than the person who should be doing it, then at least have the decency to let *me* tell it my own way,' her father said harshly.

The girl bowed her head. 'Sorry, Dad.'

'He raped her,' Williams said. 'And then he sodomized her with the neck of a bottle. And she's not the only one he did it to – she's just the only one who saw his face.'

It suddenly occurred to Baxter that he was in the presence of the only real witness in the case against Jeremy Templar, and that talking to her might be a way of testing Prison Officer Tim Robson's belief that the verdict had been unsound.

'Would you like to get in my car for a minute, love,' Baxter said softly to the girl. 'I think we should have a little chat.'

'If she's getting in your car, then I'm getting in the car as well,' Susan's father said.

'No, you're not,' Baxter told him.

'You might be a big shot in Lancashire, but you're nothing to me, so don't think you can order me about,' Williams said.

'I never sought out this meeting – but if we're going to have it, we're playing it by my rules,' Baxter said. 'And if you're not happy with that, I'll just get into the car on my own – and drive away.'

Williams hesitated, then said, 'Once you've talked to Susan, will you listen to what I've got to say?'

'Yes,' Baxter agreed, heavily. 'Give us five minutes alone, and I'll be willing to hear you out.'

'All right then,' Williams agreed.

Baxter opened the passenger door for the girl, then walked around the car and got into the driver's seat. Even if he learned nothing from their talk, it would at least give the poor girl five minutes' relief from her relentless father, he thought.

Susan sat rigid – hardly breathing – and Baxter could tell that she was reliving the attack in all its terrible detail.

'You can relax, Susan,' he said soothingly. 'I'm not going to ask any questions about what the man did to you.'

The girl took a deep breath. 'Thank you.'

'But I would like to ask you about something else, if that's all right. *Is it* all right?'

'I suppose so.'

'Your dad said that the man who attacked you had also attacked some other girls, but you were the only one who'd seen his face. Have I got that right?'

'Yes.'

'Why didn't the other girls see his face?'

'He always wore a ski mask. The newspapers all called him the Ski Mask Rapist.'

'But he wasn't wearing one when he attacked you?'

'He was wearing one, but . . .'

'Go on.'

'While he was doing it to me, I . . . I lost consciousness, and when I came round again, he was standing up and taking off his mask.'

'He didn't know that you'd come round?'

'No.'

'But if you could see his face, then he could see yours. Surely he would have noticed that you were conscious again.'

'I was looking up at him, but he was looking over the bushes. I think he was making sure there was nobody else around when he made his escape.'

'What did he do with the mask?'

'He rolled it up and put it in his pocket. Then he walked away.'

It was a clear, careful narrative, Baxter thought, but he had had been in the police long enough to know that someone who desperately wanted Templar convicted could have primed Susan with the whole story, without her even realizing what was happening.

'And you're sure the man who attacked you was Jeremy Templar?' he asked.

'Yes.'

'You recognized him the moment you saw him in the police identity parade – without anybody prompting you to pick him out?'

'I recognized him while I was lying on the ground,' Susan said.

'What do you mean?'

'He lived near us. We used to meet at golf club socials. I even danced with him a couple of times. He seemed such a nice man, back then.'

Templar's wife had not believed in his guilt, Prison Officer Tim Robson had not believed in his guilt, but after talking to Susan Williams for five minutes, Baxter was as sure as he could ever be of anything that Templar had done it.

'Listen to me, Susan,' he said softly. 'Are there ever any times when you think that what happened to you was partly your own fault – that if you hadn't danced with Jeremy Templar in the golf club, or been wherever you were when he grabbed you, it would never have happened?'

'There are a few,' the girl admitted.

'*None* of it was your fault,' Baxter said fiercely. 'You must tell yourself that every morning, as soon as you wake up. And even if you can't quite convince yourself at first, it's worth persisting, because there'll come a day when you *will* believe it – and that's when the pain will start to go away.'

'Thank you,' the girl said.

Baxter reached into his pocket.

'Here's my business card,' he said. 'If you ever need to talk to anybody, just give me a ring at the number on it, and I'll drop whatever I'm doing immediately, and be there for you. All right?'

'All right,' the girl agreed.

'But if I was you, I wouldn't tell your dad I've given you the card,' Baxter cautioned.

'I wasn't going to,' Susan replied.

Baxter patted her on the shoulder. 'Good girl. Now, you wouldn't mind staying in the car while I have a few words with your dad, would you?'

'No,' the girl said.

Baxter got out of the car, walked a few yards clear of it, and then turned around.

Susan's father joined him. 'Well, has she told you all you need to know?' he demanded.

'More than enough,' Baxter said.

'So now maybe you'll stop persecuting those poor prison officers, and let matters rest as they are,' Williams said.

'You're too angry,' Baxter told him.

'Wouldn't you be angry – if it had happened to your daughter?'

'Of course I would – but however angry I was, I wouldn't let her see it.'

'So I'm supposed to be pretend to feel all right about the fact my daughter was raped, am I?'

'You're supposed to be concentrating on your primary concern, which is Susan. It might have made you feel better if, instead of him simply being banged up, Templar had been roasted to death over a slow fire – but it wouldn't have done her a lot of good. She needs love and reassurance, not rage.'

'Are you trying to tell me how to look after my family?' Williams asked, furiously.

'Yes. What else do you expect me to do, when I see you making such a bad job of it?' Baxter wondered.

'I've a good mind to give you a damn good thrashing, and hang the consequences,' Williams said, bunching up his hands into fists.

'Is that really what your Susan needs to witness at this moment?' Baxter asked.

The anger started to drain out of Williams, and his fists unclenched.

'What we've said to you has made no difference at all, has it?' he asked plaintively. 'You're still determined to ruin the life of a good man over what happened to a piece of shit who didn't deserve *anybody's* sympathy.'

'I have a job to do, whether I like it or not,' Baxter said.

'So you're only obeying orders, are you?' Williams screamed. 'You're no different to the bloody Nazis, Mr Baxter.'

It was then that he decided to take a swing at the chief constable, but he was no fighter, and Baxter caught the arm and held it in an iron grip.

'You should try and calm down a little before you talk to your daughter again,' Baxter said. 'She deserves better than this.'

'Let go of my arm,' Williams said.

'I will, in a moment,' Baxter promised. 'And when I do, you'll have two choices. The first is that you get back in your car and take your daughter home. The second is to throw another punch at me, and if you do that, I'll knock you down and then have you arrested. Do you understand that?'

'Yes,' Williams said, through clenched teeth.

'Are you sure?'

'Yes, I'm sure, you bloody bastard.'

Baxter released the other man's arm and stepped clear. Williams turned sharply on his heel, strode furiously back to Baxter's Jaguar, and collected his daughter.

Watching them drive away, Baxter wondered if his own words of advice might eventually sink into Williams' brain and start to have a positive effect.

Probably not, he decided. Williams would continue to look back at the past, rather than forward to the future, and though his rage might be muted by time, it would always be there.

He lit up his pipe, and took a few puffs.

It had been a distressing evening, he thought, but it had also been an informative one.

He had learned – with little room for doubt – that Templar was guilty of the crime for which he'd been imprisoned – and probably of others that he'd never been charged with.

But he'd also learned something else – that a man who lived in Birmingham had known he would be in the Red Lion pub at precisely the time he was there, had known what car he would be driving, and had been able to recognize him without them ever having met.

How any of that was possible was a very interesting question indeed – and he thought he already had the answer.

They had arranged to meet in the Drum and Monkey at eight o'clock. Nobody had actually called it a *crisis meeting*, but they all knew that was exactly what it was.

Paniatowski and Meadows were there at eight on the dot. Beresford, who had been breathing fresh fire into the team of detective constables he was sending out on the evening's round of door-to-door inquiries, arrived ten minutes late, and immediately apologized.

'And where's young Jack Crane?' the inspector asked, as he sat down.

'He'll be here shortly,' Meadows said.

'Shortly?' Beresford said, expecting some kind of explanation.

'Shortly,' Meadows agreed, offering none.

'I've been looking over the records of all the cases involving serial killers to see if I can find a pattern that matches ours – and there isn't one,' Paniatowski said. 'It's true that some killers like to leave all their victims in similar locations – there was a case in

Northumberland where the murderer always dumped the bodies at bus stops – but the key word there is *similar*.'

'Yet here we have a murderer who leaves both his victims – and if Dolly hadn't escaped, it would have been three – in almost the same spot,' Kate Meadows said.

'Exactly,' Paniatowski agreed. 'He must know that always using the park makes it much more likely that he'll be caught, so he can't be doing it simply on a whim.'

'Are you saying that he must be driven by some compulsion to use the park – however dangerous he knows that is?' Beresford asked.

'Yes.'

'Maybe he uses the park because he *does* want to get caught,' Meadows suggested. 'Some murderers do. They can't stop themselves killing, and they hope that somebody else will.'

Paniatowski shook her head.

'I've been looking at some of those cases, too. When a killer has a desire to be stopped – even if it's an unconscious one – he leaves clues as to his identity. Our killer hasn't done that. In fact, he's been very, very careful – which is why we have absolutely no leads on him.'

'Perhaps the reason he had to use the park is because it has some special significance for him,' Beresford suggested.

'Like what?' Paniatowski asked.

Beresford shrugged. 'I don't really know. Maybe he was assaulted in the park himself. Maybe, when he was a little lad, some pervert got hold of him there, and he's never recovered from the experience.'

'But unless that pervert was a woman – and I think we're all agreed that's highly unlikely – he would have no reason for killing young girls,' Meadows pointed out.

'And he doesn't get angry, which is what he would be if he'd had a life-changing experience when he was a kid,' Paniatowski said. 'There's no bruising, apart from what's necessary to get the job done, and no mutilation of any kind.'

'And there's nothing to tie his two victims – plus his potential victim – together, apart from their age,' Meadows said. 'Jill was a nice middle-class girl, Maggie came from a home that you wouldn't wish on your worst enemy . . .'

'And Dolly falls somewhere between the two,' Paniatowski supplied.

'Do you think Dolly was having it off with this boyfriend of hers just before she was attacked?' Beresford asked.

'Yes, I do,' Paniatowski replied. 'And I strongly suspect that the boyfriend is much older than she is.'

'So the common thread that's running through all three cases is sex,' Beresford said.

'With the greatest respect, sir, you might as well say that the common thread running through them is that all the victims had two arms and two legs,' Meadows said. 'Yes, they were all involved in sex in some way or another, but Jill was having a mildly lesbian affair, Dolly – as far as we know – was having a monogamous heterosexual relationship, and Maggie would pretty much open her legs for any boy who showed an interest.'

But there *had* to be a common thread, Paniatowski thought – there just had to be.

This killer was playing by a strict set of rules he'd set himself, and those rules included selecting victims in their early teens, doing no more than was strictly necessary to extinguish their lives, and leaving their bodies in the park.

He was disciplined.

He was motivated.

And she had no more idea of what was driving him now than she'd had when the first body had been discovered.

In the morning, she would inform George Baxter of the attack on Dolly. Then, the chief constable – who already thought she was too influenced by what had happened to Louisa – would take her off the case, and though she believed that no other chief inspector could have done more than she had, she knew she would feel that she had failed Jill, Maggie and Dolly.

TWENTY-ONE

The tight knot had begun to form in the pit of Jack Crane's stomach the second he had made the momentous decision, and as he approached the place where he was about to enact that decision, it grew ever tighter.

It was hardly surprising that he was nervous, he thought – what man *wouldn't* feel nervous when he was about to do something that would change the entire course of his life?

He rang Liz Duffy's doorbell. He had no flowers in his hands this time – the only gift that he was bringing to Liz was his feelings.

As he heard her footstep coming down the hallway, he searched his brain for the little speech he had so carefully constructed earlier, and could find no trace of it.

But that didn't matter, he told himself, because you didn't need to be clever and balanced when you were speaking from the heart.

The door opened, and Liz was looking up at him.

In his imagination, he had pictured an expression of delighted surprise on her face – delight when she realized that what they both knew *had to* happen was going to happen, surprise that it was happening *so soon*.

The reality was not like that at all – Liz looked startled rather than delighted, and more troubled than surprised.

'I wasn't expecting you,' she said, and as she spoke she looked past him into the street, as if she believed that he had not come alone, but had brought along an army of friends with him to argue his case.

'Half an hour ago, even I didn't know I'd be here,' he said, slightly less sure of himself now, 'but then I realized that we really needed to talk as soon as possible.'

Liz frowned. 'Talk? What about?'

What about!

Didn't she know? Couldn't she tell?

'About *us*, of course,' he said. 'Could I come inside?'

Liz hesitated for a second or two, then she said, 'Yes, I suppose you better had.'

There was no fire blazing away in the grate that night, but there were two open suitcases on the sofa.

'Are you taking a trip?' Crane asked.

'Yes,' Liz replied, woodenly.

Now he understood what was going on, he thought. Now the worried expression on her face and the deadness in her voice were starting to make sense.

It was very simple really. The sudden reawakening of their feelings for each other had, for a while, sent his head spinning – but it had plainly *terrified* Liz.

And her terror was more than understandable. She had been badly hurt once, and she did not want to have to live through the same pain again. So she was running away, like a frightened rabbit, and only when she felt strong enough to resist her natural impulses would she return.

'There's no need to be scared,' he said reassuringly. 'There's no need to go away – even for a while. I love you, and I think you love me. We can make it work this time, Liz. I know we can. And I promise, here and now, that I'll never, ever let you down.'

He was half expecting her to rush across the room and throw her arms around him, but instead she remained rooted to the spot.

'You don't seem to understand,' she said. 'I'm not packing my bags because I'm going away for a *while* – I'm leaving Whitebridge for good.'

'But you can't!' Crane gasped. 'You've got your practice to consider. And your work as a police doctor.'

'I resigned from the practice this afternoon.'

'But surely you can't go just like that – they'll have wanted you to work out some kind of notice, while they find a replacement.'

'They did want me to work out my notice – but I told them I wouldn't. And as for my work as the assistant police surgeon, my letter of resignation is already in the post.'

This was turning out so differently from the way he'd thought it would that Crane was having difficulty convincing himself any of it was real.

'It'll be a black mark against you,' he argued. 'You'll never get a decent job again.'

'I don't care.'

'You'll be throwing away everything you've ever worked for.'

'It doesn't matter.'

A sudden wave of guilt swept over Crane.

'It's because I came on too strong, isn't it?' he asked. 'That was foolish of me, I know, but when I realized what I'd let slip out of my grasp once before . . .'

'It has absolutely nothing to do with you,' Liz said.

Were there ever crueller words in the English language than those, Crane wondered, as he reeled with the shock.

It has absolutely nothing to do with you.

'So what is it to do with?' he asked, as anger swept through him, burning away the guilt.

'I've been speaking to Simon,' Liz said.

'Simon!' Crane repeated, almost choking on the name.

'He wants me to leave. He thinks it's for the best.'

'After all he's done to you, why are you even listening to him?' Crane demanded.

'He never meant to hurt me. It wasn't his fault.'

'And will you be running straight back into his arms when you leave here?'

'That's really none of your business.'

'Stay,' Crane begged her. 'Just for a month – or even a week – until you've had time to consider things properly.'

'I've already considered them.'

'If someone has to go, let it be me,' Crane pleaded. 'I know you can be happy here, and if I'm in the way of that happiness, I'll resign from the force and go somewhere else.'

'I've already told you once that it's absolutely nothing to do with you,' Liz said, as if she hadn't even noticed the sacrifices he was willing to make. She glanced at the open suitcases. 'Listen, I've still got a lot of packing to do, and I think it's best that you leave now.'

And what would have been the point in staying, he asked himself, as he stepped through the front door and heard that door close firmly behind him. Liz had spoken to Simon, he had told her what he wanted her to do, and now nothing would change her mind.

As he walked along the lonely street, he tried to convince himself that – this time – Simon would make her happy.

But he knew, deep within himself, that Simon wouldn't, because – even if you ignored the way he had treated Liz – he was still a nasty piece of work.

He was surprised that this thought had even entered his head, but now that it was there, it refused to go away.

Simon's a nasty piece of work . . . Simon's a nasty piece of work . . . Simon's a nasty piece of work . . .

It was true, and thinking back to their time in Oxford together, he could produce countless examples of Simon's nastiness to support his case.

So why had he never seen Simon in quite that light before?

It was partly that the man had used his obvious charm to paper over the cracks in his personality.

But I've done some of that papering-over for him, Crane thought. I've mentally edited out what Simon did and Simon said, because Liz so obviously loved him, and I wanted him to be the kind of man who'd take care of her.

He should not have left Liz's flat when she asked him to, he told himself. He should have stayed and tried to talk her out of throwing her life away.

He was a failure and a coward. The dashing knight could have saved the fair damsel from the dragon, but instead had pretended that the dragon wasn't a dragon at all.

Crane glanced down at his watch. It was almost nine o'clock, nearly half an hour after the time he had promised Sergeant Meadows that he would be at the Drum and Monkey. He should go there now, because the team was in trouble, and he was a part of that team.

He had reached the corner of the street. If he turned left, he would be in the Drum and Monkey in ten minutes.

He turned right.

He would certainly go to a pub, he had decided – but it wouldn't be the one where Paniatowski, Meadows and Beresford were waiting for him.

The theory that had begun to germinate in George Baxter's mind in the car park of the Red Lion had almost come to full bloom by the time he reached Dunston Prison, and all that was left to do was to see how well that theory stood up when tested against the facts.

He began the test with a phone call to the governor of Winson Green Prison in Birmingham. He had only one question to put to the man – but it was a vital one, and the governor's answer would make clear whether he had a solid foundation stone on which to build his case, or was merely left holding a handful of dust.

The foundations were solid, the governor's answer confirmed, and Baxter breathed a sigh of relief.

His second call was to Wally Small, an old friend of his, who was a reporter at the Birmingham Evening Post.

'Of course I remember the Ski Mask Rapist case,' Small said, once they'd finished exchanging pleasantries, and got down to business. 'It was really big news round here.'

'And do you also remember the principal witness for the prosecution?' Baxter asked.

'I do. She was a girl called Jane Williams, wasn't she?'

'Susan Williams,' Baxter corrected him.

'That's right, *Susan* Williams.'

'You didn't happen to do a story on the family, did you?'

'I did not,' Small said. 'For her own protection, the girl was never named in open court, and my editor made it perfectly plain that the family was off-limits as far as we were concerned.'

That was disappointing, but not entirely unexpected, and Baxter had already thought out another course he could follow.

'I don't suppose you remember where the Williams family lived, do you?' he asked.

'As a matter of fact, I do remember that. They're from Edgbaston, just like me.'

'And how many parish churches are there in Edgbaston?'

Small chuckled. 'Being an ungodly journalist, I'm not entirely sure, but I should imagine there are three or four. Why, for heaven's sake, would you want to know that?'

'Let's just say I've suddenly developed an interest in ecclesiastical architecture,' Baxter said. 'Now be a good chap, and look up the telephone numbers of the vicarages.'

The explanation for Jeremy Templar's suicide lay far beyond the narrow confines of Dunston Prison, Baxter thought as he waited for the reporter to return, but if he was ever to prove that, he would have to find links that stretched across both time and space.

There were, in fact, five parish churches in Edgbaston, and after Small had given him the numbers, the two men promised that they really would make an effort to get together soon, and the reporter hung up.

The vicar of St Augustine's was unable to give Baxter the information he needed, as were the vicars of St George's, St Wilfred's and St Bartholomew's. It was only on his fifth call – to St Luke's – that he hit pay dirt.

'I can't say I actually remember that particular christening – I've conducted so many, you know – but since the family are regular members of my congregation, I assume I must have officiated at it,' the vicar said.

'And do you have copies of the baptism certificates?' Baxter asked.

'Oh yes, indeed,' the vicar said. 'My wife is a stickler for that kind of detail, and makes sure they're all properly filed.'

'Where do you keep them? Are they in the church?'

'No, they're in a filing cabinet in my study. As a matter of fact, I'm looking towards it right now.'

'I need one detail from that certificate,' Baxter said. 'Do you think you could give it to me?'

'I don't see why not,' the vicar replied. 'What particular detail are you interested in?

Baxter told him.

The vicar promised to be right back, but it was five minutes before he came on the line again.

'I'm awfully sorry to have kept you waiting,' he said. 'I'm really not very good with paperwork. I expect my wife would have found what you wanted in a moment, but she's out at a meeting of the Women's Institute.'

'But you have found it now?' Baxter asked, reining in his impatience.

'I have – and you were quite right about the name. How on earth did you know?'

'A lucky guess,' Baxter said.

And so it was – though it was a guess that fitted so perfectly all the facts he had already acquired that he would have been surprised if he'd been wrong.

'I'd like to copy down all the details on that certificate, if you don't mind,' he said.

'I don't mind at all,' the vicar assured him.

Jack Crane only left the Green Dragon at closing time. By then, he had lost count of how many pints of best bitter with whisky chasers he had consumed, and when the cold night air hit him, he realized that he was drunker than he had ever been before.

As he walked back towards his bedsit, he made a conscious effort to try and stop weaving in wide arcs from one side of the pavement to other, but with only limited success.

Yes, he was drunk, he told himself. He was drunk, and Liz – beautiful, wonderful Liz – was leaving Whitebridge for ever.

He wondered why it was that shits like Simon had all the luck that was going in life, and then he turned a corner and wondered what it was he had just been wondering about.

Walking suddenly seemed to be a terrible effort, especially since the ground refused to stay still, and the night sky was slowly and sickeningly revolving around his head.

He stumbled into a lamppost, and heard a loud clang reverberating around his brain as his head made contact with the dull grey metal.

He clutched the lamppost for support, and tried to work out what his next move should be.

If a policeman came along now, he could well find himself – DC Jack Crane, rising young star of the Whitebridge police force – being arrested for being drunk and disorderly. That wouldn't look good on his record, but he somehow couldn't bring himself to care. Nor did he care that in the morning he would have to face the anger of DCI Paniatowski, a woman whose good opinion he had – until that night – valued as a precious jewel.

His stomach issued a warning of what was soon to come. He relinquished his grip on the lamppost, and sank to his knees.

As the bile rose, and he began to vomit into the road, it occurred to him that perhaps he didn't want to be a policeman any more.

There was no darkness like the darkness of the moors, Jo Baxter thought, as she sat in her stationary car on the edge of the moorland road.

Yes, the moors were fringed with towns, and if you looked towards the far horizon, you would see a pinkish glow.

But out here, in the very centre of it all, there was just a blackness which was as dense as treacle, as mysterious as the womb.

Perhaps she should have had children, she thought.

Perhaps if she'd had children, everything would have been different.

But it was too late to have kids now – her doctor had confirmed that at her last visit.

So there she sat, a woman entering early menopause, married to a man who would rather have been married to someone else.

She looked into the darkness again, and found it comforting. She wondered if death was like that, not a glowing tunnel leading to a new life, not haloes and everlasting bliss, but something much better – a reassuring nothingness.

She switched on the engine and pulled away. Her headlights picked out the thin strip of road that led to the next town, where, no doubt, there were hundreds of people just as miserable as she was.

Slowly but surely, she increased the pressure on the accelerator pedal, so that soon the car was racing along.

The headlights began to annoy her. By cutting their way through the darkness like that, they were denying her the mystery – the lack of *anything* – that she so craved.

She switched off the headlights and increased the pressure on the accelerator.

That was better!

She did not see the bend in the road, or perhaps she had just not been looking for it.

The car left the asphalt surface. It plunged down a sharp slope, skidding on the heather, bouncing over the large stones.

She felt totally indifferent to what was happening to her, yet her instincts kicked in anyway, and made her pull on the steering wheel and stab down on the brake pedal.

But it was already too late to take remedial action. Before it had ever reached the bottom of the slope, the car flipped over, and then – because it still had momentum – it flipped back again.

By the time it finally came to a juddering halt, it had completed three and a half somersaults.

TWENTY-TWO

I t was still only seven thirty in the morning, a time at which – for most of those on the outside – the alarm clock would only just have begun its persistent weekday harassment.

In Dunston Prison, however, the day was already well under way. The first batch of prisoners had emptied out their slops at just after seven, the second batch were now making their way carefully down the iron stairs with their buckets. The dining room was open for business, and prisoners wearing chefs' hats were ladling nutritious but unappetizing porridge into tin bowls which other prisoners held out before them. It was a Thursday, but it could just as easily have been a Monday or a Friday, because that was the thing about prison – every day was just like the one that had preceded it, and would be exactly the same as the one that followed it.

Baxter was sitting at his desk, thinking about the interview he'd had with Lennie Greene – and reflecting on just how wrong he'd got it.

When he'd asked Greene if he'd personally authorized the attacks on Templar, Greene had simply replied, 'I didn't try to stop them.'

When he'd pointed out that power was not just about deciding who got beaten up, but also who *didn't* – and that if Greene didn't have the latter power, then he had no real power at all – Greene had just said, 'What happened to Templar was nothing to do with me.'

And when he wanted more details of the attacks – and threatened to withdraw his offer of the precious Open University course if he didn't get the answer – Greene had said, almost in tears, 'I can't do it. It'd be a step too far.'

So he'd come away from that interview with the firm belief that Greene was no more than a figurehead, and that there was another prisoner behind him who was secretly pulling the strings.

Wrong! Wrong, wrong, wrong!

Greene was the king rat, all right, but as he had pointed out himself, he was not an absolute monarch.

Baxter looked at his watch. It was now seven fifty-nine, and the previous day he had ordered Chief Officer Jeffries to bring him the originals of the time sheets by eight o'clock at the latest.

At eight on the dot, Jeffries opened the door without knocking, and marched into the centre of the room. He had nothing in his hands.

'I can't give you the time sheets that you wanted,' he said. 'They've gone missing.'

'I'm not in the least surprised to hear you say that,' Baxter replied. 'You've no doubt calculated that while you'll be disciplined for losing the time sheets, that's nothing like as bad as what would happen to you if you actually handed them over to me.'

'I don't know what you mean,' Jeffries said.

'Of course you do,' Baxter countered. 'But it doesn't really matter that you haven't brought them. Now that I know what I'm looking for, I also know how to find it – and all the time sheets would have done is save me a little time.'

'Is that right?' Baxter asked, with a sneer.

But the arrogance in his voice stood in marked contrast to the worried look that was gradually enveloping his face.

'I've had the whole thing wrong for most of the time I've been in this prison,' Baxter said. 'I freely admit that. But I've finally got it right.' He paused. 'Would you like me to tell you what I used to think, and what I think now?'

'I don't care, one way or the other,' Jeffries said.

But he did care – he wanted desperately to know just what it was that Baxter knew!

'I used to think that you had a number of officers working for you who were so piss-poor at their jobs that they had no idea of how to protect Jeremy Templar from the prisoners who wanted to hurt him. I used to think that when an inquiry was ordered, you saw it as your first duty to protect your men, and so you altered the time sheets to make it seem as if those piss-poor officers had not been working on more than one shift during which there'd been an attack. And the other thing I used to think was that while your actions were misguided, they were at least understandable.'

'It's a chief officer's primary responsibility to take care of his men,' Jeffries said.

'It's a chief officer's primary responsibility to see that the job's done properly,' Baxter countered. 'But let's just assume, for the sake of argument, that you're right and I'm wrong. That raises an interesting question, doesn't it?'

Baxter reached for his pipe, tamped down the half-burned tobacco, and lit up. Then he sat back in his chair, and waited.

'What question does it raise?' Jeffries asked, after perhaps half a minute had slowly ticked by.

'If you saw it as your primary responsibility to protect your men, then why *didn't* you protect them?'

'I *did* protect them,' Jeffries said.

'So you're admitting that in order to protect them, you deliberately doctored the time sheets?' Baxter asked.

Jeffries said nothing, but it was clear from his expression that he was weighing up his options.

The chief officer recognized that the battle was lost, but he was still trying to save *something*, Baxter thought. So now he was fighting a rearguard action – giving ground, but only when he was forced to.

He had claimed to have lost the time sheets in order to avoid having it proved that he had doctored them. Now he was about to admit to having doctored them, but was still hoping that the reasons he had done it could be kept hidden.

'You know how it is,' Jefferies said, in a voice that seemed to be trying to suggest that, when all was said and done, he and Baxter were almost colleagues, and had similar problems. 'Some of the lads weren't quite up to the task, but they're getting better all the time, and I'd hate to see them lose their jobs. Yes, I did cook the books just a little, but only to shield them.'

'You hypocrite,' Baxter said harshly. 'You weren't trying to cover up for them, you were only covering up for yourself – because you were on duty every single time Templar was attacked.'

'Now that is a load of old bollocks,' Jeffries said.

'I'll go further,' Baxter told him. 'If you *hadn't* been on duty, the attacks would probably never have occurred.'

'So you're accusing *me* of being piss-poor incompetent now, are you?' Jeffries asked.

'Quite the reverse – you've been extremely competent throughout the whole sorry business.'

'Then I don't see . . .'

'Before you came here, you had a job at Winson Green Prison in Birmingham, didn't you?'

'Yes.'

'So why did you put in for a transfer?'

'No particular reason – I just felt like a change.'

'You came here for one reason, and one reason only – because this is where Jeremy Templar was being sent.'

'Why would I have done that? I'd never even laid eyes on him until I got here.'

'Last night, at the pub, I was accosted by a Mr Williams,' Baxter said. 'He told me about all the horrific things that Templar had done to his daughter. Then he suggested that I shouldn't pursue my investigation into who'd been attacking Templar too carefully. Would you care to make a comment at this point?'

'No.'

'The question is, how did he know I'd be in the pub? And the answer is – because you told him.'

'Oh, I see,' Jeffries said. 'I learn you're going to the pub, so I ring this Mr Williams in Birmingham, and by the time you've driven the five miles from here, he's driven over *a hundred* miles from Birmingham. Is that how it's supposed to have happened?'

'No,' Baxter said. 'That isn't how it happened at all. Williams and his daughter will have been staying in the area – probably at the house of a friend – awaiting their opportunity to talk to me. Tell me, Mr Jeffries, if I ask your neighbours if you've had visitors recently, what are they likely to tell me?'

'So I knew the Williams family slightly when I lived in Birmingham, and when he asked me if I could put him up for the night, I saw no objection to it,' Jeffries said, taking another step backwards. 'What's wrong with that?'

'It was more than just a slight acquaintanceship,' Baxter told him. 'Williams' daughter, Susan, was baptized at St Luke's Church on the thirteenth of September 1959. One of her godmothers was Susan Blaine, Mr Williams' sister, who she was named after. The other godmother was Jane Talbot. And her godfather was Edward Jeffries.'

'You should have known her when she was growing up,' Jeffries said, dropping all pretence and smiling fondly, despite the situation he now knew he was in. 'She was an absolutely marvellous little kid, and I learned to love her as much as if she'd been my own daughter.' The smile faded, and a mask of hatred replaced it. 'Then that animal got his hands on her!'

'And you decided that the sentence he'd been handed down wasn't harsh enough,' Baxter said. 'More than that – you decided to punish him yourself. It can't have been too difficult to get some of the prisoners to do your bidding. You had rewards and punishments aplenty to offer them.'

And even the king rat on the other side of the bars hadn't dared stand in the way, because that would have meant a late-night visit by officers carrying truncheons, and transfer to another prison the following morning.

'Put yourself in my position for a second,' Jeffries said. 'You'd have done the same.'

'No, I wouldn't,' Baxter corrected him, 'I'd have *wanted* to do the same. But I'd have stopped myself – because if we don't have the rule of law, then we don't have anything.'

'What happens now?' Jeffries asked.

'The Yorkshire Police are on the way. You probably have about half an hour before they arrest you. You might want to use that time to apologize to the other officers you've dragged into your conspiracy, and who will probably soon be arrested themselves.'

'I did what I did for poor little Susan's sake,' Jeffries said defiantly. 'Whatever happens to me now, I have no regrets, and if I had my time over again, I'd do exactly the same thing – except that this time I'd make sure Templar didn't get a chance to hang himself before I'd *really* made him suffer.'

'If, instead of coming to Dunston to wreak your revenge, you'd stayed in Birmingham and been the kind of supportive godfather that Susan needs right now, you'd have done a lot more good,' Baxter said.

Jeffries looked at Baxter as blankly as Susan's father had done, when the chief constable had said something similar to him.

'I don't see that,' he said.

'No,' Baxter agreed sadly, 'I know you don't.'

When Paniatowski and Meadows arrived at Woolworths, at eight thirty-five that morning, they found the middle-aged man, who they had arranged to meet there, pacing up and down along the pavement and glancing at his watch every few seconds.

'Sam Houghton, head of security,' he said in a clipped military tone which he couldn't quite carry off. 'I thought we'd agreed on eight thirty.'

Paniatowski could have mentioned that she'd been up half the night, going through files of previous murders and trying to establish a pattern – but when a store detective elevates himself to the position of head of security, explanations are rarely worth the bother, so she contented herself with saying, 'Sorry to have kept you waiting, Mr Houghton.'

'Well, at least you're here now,' Houghton said, in what he probably considered a magnanimous tone.

He put his key in the lock, and pushed open the main door of the big empty store.

'I almost became a bobby once myself,' Houghton said, as he led them down the shop.

'Oh yes?' Paniatowski asked neutrally. 'What stopped you?'

'Well, to be honest with you, I think I've got too much initiative – too much drive – to have ever really fitted into a stodgy organization like the police,' Houghton said. He paused. 'No offence intended.'

'None taken,' Paniatowski assured him.

They had reached the back end of the store. A nondescript door faced them, and on it was a handwritten note that said, 'Strictly No Entry to Unauthorized Personnel – this means you!'

'This is it,' Houghton said, 'the nerve centre of the store's entire security operation.'

He opened the door with a flourish, and they found themselves looking into a room that was little more than a broom cupboard, but which was cluttered with big ugly electronic machines.

'I bet you wish you had a set-up like this down at police headquarters,' Houghton said.

'We can only dream of it,' Paniatowski agreed.

They edged their way into the room, and shuffled up to the table at the far end of it.

There was only one chair, and Houghton took it.

'Sorry, ladies, but I need to sit here to be able to operate the machines,' he said.

'Understood,' Paniatowski replied.

She was not holding out great hopes that this whole exercise would lead to anything, for though she agreed with Meadows that it was always *possible* the murderer had been in the store, it did not seem like a *strong* possibility. Still, she had to admit that clutching at straws started to look like a pretty good prospect when you were drowning – and she was certainly drowning in this investigation.

There were three small television sets sitting on the table.

'Those are the monitors,' Houghton said grandly. 'There are three cameras in operation, so there have to be three monitors. I can either run them one at a time, or all three simultaneously. Which would you prefer?'

'I'm not sure,' Paniatowski admitted. 'Are the video machines anything like tape recorders?'

'There are certain similarities, though, of course, the video machines are much more complex,' Houghton said, in a superior tone.

'So it's not too difficult to rewind them?'

'No problem at all, if you know what you're doing – as I do. I can rewind them, freeze the image, anything you want.'

'Then run all the monitors together,' Paniatowski said.

Houghton clicked a few switches, and black and white images appeared all three screens.

'Monitor One is showing you the top end of the shop,' Houghton said. 'You can see me standing by the bras and knickers.'

And so she could, Paniatowski thought. It was weird to be looking down on him, but the man was clearly Sam Houghton.

'Now look at the third screen, which shows the activity at the other end of the shop, and you'll see the girls,' Houghton said.

Maggie, Polly and Lil are standing at the confectionery counter, then Maggie loses interest in the sweets, and looks around her for something more exciting. Her eyes come to rest on the stationery counter. She jabs Polly to get her attention, points at the counter, and then says something.

'There's no sound,' Paniatowski said.

'This is closed-circuit television, not the Odeon Cinema,' Houghton said, frostily,

'Go over there and grab some pens,' Maggie tells Polly. 'You can slip them up the sleeve of your cardigan.'

'What do we want pens for?' Polly asks.

Maggie has no real answer, and so she says, 'We can sell them.'

'Who'd want to buy them from us?' Polly wonders.

It's another good question, because no one they know has any use for pens – but there is something more important than logic at stake here.

'It's a test,' Maggie says. 'You've got to prove you're good enough to stay in my gang.'

'Why can't Lil do it?' Polly asks.

Why not indeed? Lil would probably be more than willing. But Maggie knows that it would be a fatal error to allow her authority to be challenged at this point.

'Either you nick some pens, or you're out of the gang right now,' she says firmly.

'It's not fair,' Polly says.

But she reluctantly heads towards the stationery counter anyway.

'You see what happened?' Sam Houghton asked. 'The girl in the wig moved further up the store. That's why she's suddenly disappeared from the end monitor and reappeared on the middle one.'

Maggie has spotted the store detective, over by the knickers, and is watching him carefully, though she occasionally turns round to look at Polly, who is clumsily stuffing pens into her sleeve.

Polly's a bloody useless thief, Maggie decides, and it'll be a miracle if the store detective doesn't catch on to what she's doing.

And no sooner has the thought crossed her mind than the store detective does catch on, and starts to make his way towards the stationery counter.

'It's an instinct you develop in this job,' Houghton told Paniatowski and Meadows. 'We see a little slag like her hovering in one place too long, and we know there's something wrong.'

'Amazing – I wish I had your powers of deduction,' Meadows said.

The store detective is heading in Polly's direction. For a moment, Maggie wonders if she should let Polly get caught as a punishment for being so pretty. Then she reminds herself that she is the leader of this gang, and that carries with it certain responsibilities.

She steps into the centre of the aisle, blocking the store detective's access. When he moves to his left, she moves to her right. When he moves back to his left, she mirrors the action.

'Get out of my way,' he says gruffly.

She has to say something to stop him, or he will be round her and collaring Polly.

'You've been watching me, haven't you, mister,' she says. 'You fancy me, don't you?'

'Don't be ridiculous,' the detective says.

'You do! You fancy me.'

'Kindly get out of my way.'

'You can cop a quick feel, if you like. I don't mind.'

'I'll do no such thing.'

The detective tries to squeeze past, but Maggie flings her arms around him, and rubs her flabby breasts up and down his chest.

'You like it, don't you!' she screams in his ear, only adding to his very obvious disorientation.

'A lot of men would have lost their cool in that situation, but I was still perfectly in control,' Houghton said.

'Yes, I can see you were,' Paniatowski agreed, flashing Meadows a warning glance.

Maggie senses the store detective is about to make another break for freedom, and, removing her left hand from his shoulder, makes a grab for his trousers with all the speed and skill she has so often demonstrated behind the school bike sheds. And to her surprise, her hand comes into contact with something hard and inflexible.

'You really do fancy me,' she says in wonder. 'Well, who would have thought that?'

The store detective has been unwilling to use his superior strength against a mere girl, but now he has had enough. He pushed her away from him with such force that she hits the opposite counter and then falls to the floor.

'Did we just see her grab your crotch?' Meadows asked, ignoring Paniatowski's second warning look.

'No, you most certainly did not,' Houghton said forcefully. 'Looking at it with untrained eyes, you might think that's what happened, but I can assure you, she never touched me.'

The store detective steps over Maggie, and makes his way hurriedly to the stationery counter, leaving the second screen and appearing on the third, but Maggie's delaying tactics have worked, and both Lil and Polly have gone. He turns around to face Maggie.

On the second screen, Maggie has already climbed to her feet, and is heading for the other exit.

'Jill, Dolly and Maggie,' Paniatowski said softly to herself.

Three young girls who have been attacked in the same park – two of them with fatal consequences – in only four days.

In all the cases of multiple killings that Paniatowski had studied, the killers had always had specific criteria by which they selected their victims – redheads, shop girls, prostitutes – and it had usually been possible to see the thread that connected them.

But what – apart from their age – connected these three girls?

Jill and Dolly did not, on the surface, appear to have a great deal in common, but neither were they all that different. Maggie, on the other hand, might almost have come from another planet.

'What *is* the link?' she asked herself.

Whatever it was, it seemed unlikely that these tapes would reveal it.

She was aware that Meadows had just spoken, but had no idea what it was she said.

'What was that, Kate?' she asked.

'A cup of coffee, boss,' the sergeant said. 'Before we run through the tapes again, I think we should go to the nearest café and have a cup of coffee to clear out the insides of our heads.'

Why not have a cup of coffee, Paniatowski thought.

And why not run through the tapes again?

After all, the recordings might not be a good lead – but they were the best lead that they had.

TWENTY-THREE

The time between throwing up next to the lamppost and waking up in his own bed was a complete blank to Crane, but he assumed that, by some miracle, he had managed to find his way back to his bedsit unaided. Now he was sitting in a corner of the police canteen, hunched over a mug of tea that he had ordered but couldn't face the thought of drinking.

He wondered why he had bothered to come to the canteen at all. Instinct, he supposed.

He wondered where he would be in a year's time – and discovered that he didn't really care.

The sound of heavy footsteps made him look up, and he saw DI Beresford glowering down at him.

'Morning, sir,' he said weakly.

Beresford sat down opposite him.

'You look like death,' the inspector said, and there was not a hint of sympathy in his voice.

'I know I do,' Crane agreed.

'And do you also know that you're in a whole lot of trouble?' Beresford asked.

'I guessed I might be,' Crane admitted.

'It's the boss's job to give you a right royal bollocking and then tell you what disciplinary action she'll be taking, and I've no doubt she'll do that as soon as she gets back from Woolworths,' Beresford continued. 'But since she's not here now, I've decided to give you a bollocking myself. Not that that will make any difference to what eventually happens to you – you've probably already kissed your career goodbye – but because it will make *me* feel better.'

'Fair enough – I deserve it,' Crane said.

'Bloody right, you deserve it,' Beresford concurred. 'Monika Paniatowski has been damn good to you, Crane. She plucked you from the ranks and made you part of her team, so that while other detective constables have been doing the grinding footwork, you've been at the very heart of the investigation.'

'I know,' Crane said.

'And do you think there's a single one of those other detective constables who wouldn't give his right arm to be in your situation?'

'No, sir.'

'To be fair to you, I have to say that you've pulled your weight up until now,' Beresford conceded. 'You've picked up on things that the rest of us might have missed a number of times. But the key words in that sentence are *up until now*. You weren't there last night – when you were really needed – and if you'd had a reasonable excuse for your absence, you'd have offered it to me by now.' Beresford lit up a cigarette. 'But you don't *have* any excuse, do you, Jack?'

'No,' Crane said. 'None at all.'

Except that my heart was broken last night, he told himself. Except that I saw all my hopes and dreams for the future shrivel up and die in Liz Duffy's living room.

'By the end of the day, the chief constable will have taken the team off the case, and given it to somebody else,' Beresford continued. 'Have you any idea how humiliating that will be for the boss? Can you even begin to imagine the harm that will do to her reputation? We'll probably be all right – given time – because we weren't in charge of the inquiry, but I doubt Monika will ever be handed a serious investigation again.'

'Maybe the chief constable *won't* take the case off her,' Jack Crane said hopefully.

'Of course he bloody will! In fact, I think the only reason he hasn't done it already is that he's too involved in this Jeremy Templar investigation. But the moment he's got that wrapped up – and knowing him, it won't be long – he'll focus his mind on Whitebridge again, and then it's a pound to a penny that—'

'What did you just say?' interrupted Crane, who seemed suddenly to come to life.

'I've just said a lot of things – and I've got more things to say,' Beresford replied.

'The name!' Crane said urgently. 'What was the name that you just mentioned?'

'Jeremy Templar,' Beresford repeated, mystified. 'The sex offender who hanged himself in Yorkshire.'

'Oh God, no – not Jeremy Templar!' Crane groaned, as a scene, long forgotten, began to play itself out in his mind.

*   *   *

It is Eights Week in Oxford – that highlight of Trinity Term when, for four hectic days, 158 boats and 1400 rowers compete for the title of Head of the River.

Crane, now in the third year of his degree, has come down to the river to watch the competition.

Quite a festive crowd has gathered on the bank of the Isis, and it includes the three young daughters of one of the dons from Crane's own college, who are wearing white lacy dresses and broad-brimmed hats, just like Edwardian ladies. Crane wanders over to tell them how splendid they look, and they show their appreciation with shy giggles.

And then Templar appears on the scene. He knows the girls too, and they seem very pleased to see him.

'I've just had a splendid idea for a competition,' he tells the oldest girl, twelve-year-old Isabel.

'What is it?' the girl asks eagerly.

'I ask you a question, if you give the right answer, I'll be your slave for the day, and I'll do anything you tell me to.'

'And what if I get it wrong?' the girl wonders.

'Ah, then you're subjected to the death of a thousand tickles,' Templar tells her.

Isabel grins. 'All right.'

'Now my question is this,' Templar says gravely. 'Which of the French philosophers is famous for saying, "I think, therefore I am"?'

'I don't know,' Isabel admits.

'Then it's the death of a thousand tickles,' Templar says, sweeping her off her feet.

Templar tickles her under her arms and along her ribs. The girl enjoys it at first, but the longer it goes on the more uncomfortable she seems to become.

'Put me down,' she says.

'Not yet – you've still another six hundred and seventy-five tickles to come,' Templar says.

'Please put me down,' the girl pleads.

And Templar does – though he clearly doesn't want to.

'How could I have seen that, and not understood?' Crane asked himself silently.

And a mocking voice from somewhere in the back of his head

replied, 'You didn't understand because you didn't *want* to understand. You were still *editing* what you saw back then.'

'Are you all right, Jack?' Beresford asked – and now there *was*
concern in his voice.

'I'm fine,' Crane said, unconvincingly.

'Only, when I mentioned that pervert's name, you sounded as if
you knew him. Have you nicked him or something?'

'No,' Crane said, burying his head in his hands. 'I haven't nicked
him – I went to university with him.'

'You've been to *university*?' Beresford said incredulously. 'Well,
that's the first I've heard of it. I don't think even the boss knows
that.'

And still the name kept bouncing around Crane's aching head.

Jeremy Templar . . . Jeremy Templar . . . Jeremy Templar.

He had been a sex offender, and now he was dead!

But he *couldn't* be dead, unless . . . unless . . .

Crane stood up. 'I have to go, sir,' he said.

'You most certainly *do not* have to go,' Beresford replied sternly.
'You have to stay here and listen to me tell you how you've let
yourself and the whole team down.'

'Sorry,' Crane said. 'I really *do* have to go.'

'Come back here and sit down again, Detective Constable Crane,'
Beresford ordered, in his best inspector's voice.

But by then Crane was already halfway to the door.

The cup of coffee had helped – though not a great deal – and now
Paniatowski and Meadows were back in the broom cupboard which
Sam Houghton called his control centre.

'Could you run through it again, Mr Houghton,' Paniatowski said,
'but this time we're only interested in what's happening on the
central monitor.'

'You know, the one where she makes a grab at your crotch,'
Meadows said. 'I mean, where she *appears* to grab at your crotch.'

'And I'd like it if you could freeze the tape every five or six
seconds,' Paniatowski added.

Houghton ran the tape back, and played the first few seconds, in
which Maggie was looking at the store detective.

Freeze.

*There are several other shoppers – mostly women – in Maggie's
immediate vicinity, but from the bland expressions on their faces,*

it's quite clear they have no idea that anything out of the ordinary is about to happen.

'Start it again, please,' Paniatowski said.

Maggie, seeing the store detective approaching, moves into the centre of the aisle. The awkward dance follows, as Houghton attempts to get past her, then Maggie throws her flabby arms around him. All the other customers in the area have stopped moving, and are now engrossed in the scene.

Freeze.

There are three shoppers close enough to the incident for Paniatowski to be able to get a clear look at their faces. One, a woman in her seventies, is obviously disgusted by what is happening. Another, a young, heavily pregnant woman, seems to find the whole thing mildly amusing. The third is a man in his thirties, and the expression on his face says that while he feels he should be offering his help to someone, he is not sure whether it should be to Maggie or Sam Houghton.

'Start it again, please.'

Maggie grabs at Houghton's crotch, the store detective pushes her away and Maggie falls down. Houghton steps over her, and disappears from the screen.

On the previous run-through, Paniatowski's eyes had automatically followed the store detective onto the third screen, but this time she kept them firmly on the middle one.

Maggie is shaken by her fall, but when the man in his thirties steps forward to help her to her feet, she brushes his offer angrily aside. The pregnant woman – who has probably been warned by her doctor that sudden jolts or falls could damage her unborn baby – has reluctantly abandoned the free entertainment. And the older woman – perhaps aware of how easily old bones crumble – has put caution above indignation, and has also gone.

But there is a new woman on the scene now – a woman in her middle-to-late twenties.

Freeze.

The expression on the new arrival's face is chilling. As she looks down at Maggie, there is a hatred blazing in her eyes which comes across even in the grainy black and white image.

'Jesus!' Paniatowski gasped.

Now she clearly saw the pattern that had been eluding her for so long. Now she understood what had prompted Maggie's murder and the attempted murder of Dolly.

And what about Jill?

What had she done to make the murderer decide that the only suitable punishment was death?

Something must have happened at the wedding reception – *after* Paniatowski had left – that had sealed her fate.

Her lesbianism had nothing to do with the murder – in fact, if the killer had *known* she was a lesbian, she would probably still be alive.

Paniatowski still did not understand why all the killings had had to take place in the park – but that was a detail, a mere tying up of loose ends.

Meadows was still looking at the screen, as if unable to tear her eyes away from the woman.

'Is that who I think it is, boss?' she asked.

'Yes,' Paniatowski replied, 'it's our killer.'

The people who lived in the villages around the edges of the moor liked their fresh bread in the morning, but most of the villages were too small to support a bakery of their own, and Tommy Dawes, who owned an ice-cream van, which was normally only used in the evenings, had seen his opportunity, and set up a bread-delivery business. The new business had its drawbacks of course – the early start, the constant criss-crossing of the moors – but then every business had its drawbacks, and the extra money it brought in was very useful.

That particular Thursday morning, Tommy had started out a little later than usual, and try as he might, he had not been able to make up the time, so it was close to half-past nine as he headed towards the last village in his route.

It was a pleasant morning, the sun was shining, and there were no other vehicles on that stretch of the moors. Feeling very relaxed, Tommy switched on the radio and began to hum along with Suzi Quatro's 'Devil Gate Drive'.

He would say later that he was not a great lover of nature, and so he had no idea why, instead of keeping his eyes on the road, he turned to look at the vast expanse of open moor. But turn he did – and what he saw made him slam on the brakes and get out of the van.

He was careful while descending the sharp slope that edged the road, but once on the flat ground, he ran as quickly as he could towards the car, which was resting on its roof. He drew level with it, and went into a crouch, so he could look inside the car.

That was when he saw the woman in the driver's seat, though he could not tell – at that point – whether she was alive or dead.

Paniatowski drove through the centre of Whitebridge at speed, her siren blaring, and it was only as she was approaching the road on which the garden flat was located that she started to slow down.

A man was standing on the pavement outside the flat. He was holding a blood-stained handkerchief to his cheek, and looking far from happy.

'Jesus, it's Jack!' Meadows said.

Paniatowski slammed on the brakes, and the two women got out of the car. Crane followed their progress with his eyes, but did not move.

'Where's Liz Duffy?' Paniatowski asked him. 'Has she gone?'

'No, she's not gone,' Crane replied. 'She's inside – handcuffed to the radiator.'

'Have you cautioned her?'

'Yes – but I'm not sure she was listening.'

Paniatowski turned to Meadows.

'Go and caution her again, Kate,' she said.

'I'm on it, boss.'

As Meadows disappeared inside the flat, Crane said apologetically, 'I should have rung you before coming here, boss, but there just wasn't time. If I'd left it any longer, she'd have been gone.'

Paniatowski nodded. 'You just did right, Jack.'

'I'm not sure I was actually intending to arrest her,' Crane continued. 'I still couldn't quite believe she'd done it, you see, even though all the evidence was pointing that way. I . . . I think I just wanted her to explain – to come up with some reasonable story that would make everything all right again.'

'Easy, Jack,' Paniatowski said soothingly. 'Just take it easy.'

'She threw herself at me the moment I walked through the door. If I didn't know better, I'd say she'd been tipped off.'

'She *had* been tipped off – inadvertently – by me,' Paniatowski said, thinking back to the conversation she'd had with Duffy in the morgue. 'Let me see your cheek, Jack.'

Crane took away the handkerchief. Four long scratches had been viciously gouged into his skin.

'Whatever were you thinking of – giving her the chance to do that?' Paniatowski wondered.

'I treated her too gently,' Crane admitted. 'I was in no doubt that she'd done it by that point – she was screaming at me that she had, and she wasn't ashamed of it – but even then, I still didn't want to use reasonable force.'

Events had been so fast that Paniatowski had not even stopped to ask herself how Crane had got there before them, but she did now.

'How long have you been here, Jack?' she asked.

'About twenty minutes.'

'That long!'

'More or less.'

Twenty minutes earlier, she hadn't even seen the woman in the film glaring down at Maggie with such obvious hatred, Paniatowski thought.

'At the time you got here, *I* didn't even know we'd be making an arrest,' she said. 'So how did *you* know?'

'Ah, well, you see, I had the advantage over you, because I was a friend of hers in the old days,' Crane said sadly. 'I knew her boyfriend, too, but I didn't know she'd eventually married him, because she never told me that. She just said he'd left her, which – in a way – I suppose he had.'

'Go on,' Paniatowski said.

'He was a handsome feller,' Crane mused. 'As a matter of fact, he looked a lot like Roger Moore did, when he was playing Simon Templar – the Saint – on television. And by one of those little quirks of fate, his name was Templar, too, so even though he'd been chris-tened Jeremy, almost everybody called him Simon.'

TWENTY-FOUR

When Paniatowski and Meadows entered Interview Room B, Liz Duffy looked up at them and smiled.

'What a pleasant surprise, ladies,' she said. 'Do take a seat.'

There was no longer any sign of the rage that Duffy had shown earlier. Now she was sitting quite calmly, with her hands clasped loosely in front of her, and but for one broken fingernail, it would have been almost impossible to believe that this woman had done so much damage to Jack Crane's cheek.

'What do we call you?' Paniatowski asked. 'Elizabeth Duffy or Elizabeth Templar?'

'Legally, I suppose, I'm Liz Templar, but professionally, I continued working under the name of Dr Duffy after I got married, so it's whichever the two of you feel more comfortable with,' Liz said accommodatingly.

'Interview with Elizabeth Templar, née Duffy begins at twelve oh seven,' Paniatowski said, switching on the recorder. 'Present in the room are DCI Monika Paniatowski and DS Katherine Meadows.'

'*Weird* DS Katherine Meadows,' Liz Duffy said. 'At least, that's what Jack Crane calls you.'

This wasn't going to be easy, Paniatowski thought – in fact, if they didn't handle it *just* right, it could end in complete disaster.

'Don't you find it ironic that geography can play such a role in the tide of human affairs?' Duffy asked taking the lead – showing, in case they had not already worked it out for themselves, that she knew she had a strong hand to play.

'I'm not sure I know what you mean by that,' Paniatowski.

'You're not sure you know what I mean? Then you really are a rather dense little chief inspector, aren't you?'

'So why don't you enlighten me?'

Liz Duffy sighed. 'Oh, all right then. I suppose it's as a good a way to pass the time as any. Are you listening carefully, so I don't have to repeat myself?'

'Yes.'

'The role of geography in human affairs,' Liz Duffy said, as if she were giving a lecture. 'The only reason I ever came to this God-forsaken industrial wasteland was because it meant I'd be physically closer to my dear husband than I'd been in Birmingham. And probably the only reason why your bumpkin of a chief constable was appointed to investigate Simon's death was that he was already conveniently just across the county border from Dunston Prison.'

That – combined with the fact that Baxter knew Yorkshire well – probably *was* why he'd been appointed, Paniatowski conceded.

'The Home Office informed me that there would be an inquiry into Simon's suicide, but, of course, they didn't bother to mention that it would be your chief constable who would be conducting it,' Liz Duffy said. 'I got that particular piece of information from you, Monika.'

Yes, she had, Paniatowski thought.

'The fact is that I'm so desperate over this case that I was hoping for a miracle – and miracles simply don't happen every day.' Paniatowski had said to Duffy in the morgue, the day before.

'Is it really as bad as that?' Duffy had asked. *'Is your boss giving you a hard time?'*

'Not at the moment. He's in Yorkshire, investigating a prison suicide. But when he gets back, the fat will really be in the fire.'

'Oh God!' Duffy had said.

And what Paniatowski thought she meant by that was, *Oh God, I'm so sorry for you, Monika!*

But that hadn't been it at all.

It had had nothing to with Paniatowski.

What Liz Duffy had really meant was, *Oh God, if it's the chief constable of Mid Lancs who's conducting the inquiry, then it's only a matter of time before Jack Crane hears Simon's name and puts two and two together!*

And then she had panicked. She had packed her bags, and when Jack Crane had visited her the previous evening, her first thought had probably been that he'd gone there to arrest her. Now, she'd calmed down. She knew the police knew *what* she'd done and *why* she'd done it, but she also knew that the case against her was based on a little circumstantial evidence and a lot of imaginative leaps – and that it would never stand up in court.

So all she had to do was sit quietly, and she would be in the clear.

'I'd like to go over your confession, if you don't mind,' Paniatowski said.

'What confession?' Liz Duffy countered.

'The one you made to DC Crane.'

'Is that what he told you – that I'd confessed?'

'Yes, and I believe him.'

'He's such a dear boy, Jack, but he's always had far too vivid an imagination.'

'So you deny it?'

'Of course I do.'

Above their heads there was a gentle pitter-pattering sound, and looking up, Paniatowski saw that rain had begun to fall on the skylight.

She needed to break Liz Duffy, she told herself, and she was not sure – even with the ammunition that Jack Crane had provided – that she could.

'Since you're not interested in confessing, I'd like to talk a little about your background,' she said. 'Do you have any objection to that?'

'You'd like me to say I *do* object, wouldn't you?' Duffy asked.

'Would I?'

'Of course, because my refusal would indicate that you'd hit a weak spot in my psyche, which you could then use to your advantage. Well, I'm sorry to disappoint you, but I have no objection at all to discussing my background, so feel free to ask whatever you want to.'

She was using her arrogance as a shield, Paniatowski thought, but then she had no choice in the matter, because if she ever lowered that shield – if she ever abandoned her belief that she was totally right and everyone else was totally wrong – she would have to face the horror of what she'd done.

'Jack Crane says that when you were at Oxford University together, he doesn't remember you once mentioning your parents,' Paniatowski said. 'Now why was that?'

Liz Duffy blinked, but said nothing.

'I never thought it would be *that* easy to find the weak spot,' Paniatowski said. 'To tell the truth, I'm a little disappointed in you.'

'I don't know whether I mentioned my father or not, but if I didn't, it was probably because he died when I was nine,' Duffy said.

'I imagine that must have been a terrible blow to you. Am I right?'

'That's really none of your business.'

'But your mother was still alive when you were studying at Oxford, wasn't she?'

'Yes.'

'So why didn't you talk about her?'

'You never went to university yourself, did you, Detective Chief Inspector Paniatowski?'

'No, I didn't.'

'Of course you didn't. Well, if you had, you know that it was considered rather "uncool" to talk about your mother,' Liz Duffy said. 'Besides,' she added, almost as an afterthought, 'there wasn't much to say.'

'So of the two, it was plainly your father who you loved the most?' Paniatowski suggested.

'I didn't say that.'

The rain was getting angrier, and pounding down on the skylight as if it thought that, with a little more effort, it could shatter the skylight and bombard those below with a lethal shower of glass.

'It would only be natural if you did love your father more than your mother,' Paniatowski said. 'When I was a little girl, I used to think of my own father as almost godlike. In my eyes, he could do no wrong.'

'Did you have to go on a course to learn how to conduct interrogations?' Liz Duffy sneered. 'If you did – and if this what they taught you – then you've got good grounds for asking for your money back.'

'He probably wouldn't have *remained* godlike to me,' Paniatowski said, ignoring the interruption. 'As I grew up, and left my innocence behind, I'd probably have started seeing all kinds of flaws in him. But that never happened, because, like you, I lost him when I was a child.'

Liz Duffy laughed. 'You have such a crude approach,' she said. 'You're doing your best to make me empathize with you, and it's simply not working. I very much doubt that your father *did* die when you were a little girl. For all I know, he's still alive.'

'My father was an officer in the Polish Cavalry,' Paniatowski said, with a sudden ferocity. 'He was a hero who died fighting the

Nazis, and I had his bones buried in Whitebridge so I could be close to them!'

The outburst had had an effect on Liz Duffy, and she looked almost ashamed of herself.

'I'm sorry,' she said, 'I never meant to . . .'

Nice one, boss, Meadows thought. Very sneaky!

But Paniatowski did not follow through on the opportunity she had created. Instead, she seemed as stricken as Duffy was.

Jesus, all that was genuine, Meadows told herself.

'Then again, perhaps you didn't love your father at all,' the sergeant said, stepping in to fill the breach. 'Perhaps the reason you didn't talk about your mother at university was that you hated her for not protecting you from him.'

'What do you mean by that?' Duffy asked, reddening.

There was a loud crash of thunder overhead, and, for a moment, the lights flickered.

'What did I mean?' Meadows asked. 'I suppose I meant that you were probably *in need of* protection. Was your father physically abusive to you? Did he visit you in your bed at night?'

'My father would never have hurt me – in any way,' Liz Duffy screamed. 'He adored me.'

'And *you* worshipped *him*,' said Paniatowski, taking control again. 'He left a gap in your life that you've been trying to fill ever since.'

Duffy unclenched her hands, crossed her arms, and clutched her shoulder-blades.

'I don't want to talk about that any more,' she said, in a much lower voice that could almost have been a whimper.

'Then what else *can* we talk about?' Paniatowski wondered. 'I suppose you could tell me about what you did to those girls – but no, that would never work, because you're far too ashamed to say anything about that.'

Liz Duffy's mood changed again, and she slammed her hands down on the table.

'I'm *not* ashamed,' she said. 'I'm not! I'm not!'

'Then why don't you tell us all about it?' Paniatowski challenged.

'All right,' Duffy agreed. 'I will.'

'I should remind you again, at this point, that you have the right to have a lawyer present,' Paniatowski said.

'Why would I need a lawyer?' Liz Duffy asked. 'It's not as if I've done anything wrong.'

George Baxter would already have left Dunston, had it not been for the telephone call from the sergeant at the local police station, who had told him that an Inspector Grimes was already on his way to the prison, and would like to speak to him.

Grimes probably had some paperwork he wanted signing – because there was *always* paperwork that needed signing – Baxter thought, as he looked out of the window at the approaching police car. Still, that shouldn't take long – probably no more than five or ten minutes.

He was not expecting anything like a hero's send-off from Dunston Prison. Ever since the police had taken Chief Officer Jeffries away, all the other prison staff had acted as if he wasn't even there. But then, that sort of thing went with the job, and he wasn't about to let it get to him.

He wondered what sort of reception would be waiting for him when he got back to Whitebridge, and suspected that it wouldn't exactly be a warm one, either. Well, he couldn't, in all conscience, complain about that.

He'd been unfair to Jo, he told himself, and that was not just a recent occurrence, either – he had been unfair to her right from the start.

He had proposed to her because he knew she had wanted him to, and because – as things had stood between them at the time – he'd been getting all the comforts of being a married man, and she'd been getting none of the status of being a married woman. It had been the logical thing to do, the civilized thing to do – but it had been so wrong.

If only Monika had wanted him . . .

'You can't go blaming Monika for your own mess,' he said aloud.

And that was quite true, but the fact remained if Monika had wanted him, he would never have courted Jo, and she would have been free to find a man without baggage – a man who could really appreciate her for the wonderful woman that she actually was.

He heard a knock on the office door, and looked up to see a uniformed inspector standing there.

Baxter smiled at the new arrival. 'Inspector Grimes?' he asked.

'That's right, sir,' the inspector said – though he did not return the smile.

'So what can I do for you?' Baxter asked. 'Is there something you want me to sign?'

Grimes shook his head. 'No, sir, it's nothing like that.' He paused for a moment, then continued, 'I'm afraid I've got some bad news for you, sir. Your wife's been in an accident.'

'I followed Jill Harris from her aunt's wedding reception to her home, because I wanted to see what she was going to do next,' Liz Duffy told Paniatowski, as the rain continued to beat against the skylight. 'I wanted to give her a second chance, you see.'

'A second chance to do what?' Paniatowski asked.

'You really are rather dense, aren't you?' asked Duffy, with a return to the arrogance she had displayed at the beginning of the interview. 'If you ask me, it's a miracle you ever became a chief inspector.' She waved her hand through the air. 'But then, I suppose, in a place like this, anyone can rise to the top.'

'A second chance to do what?' Paniatowski repeated.

'A second chance to prove to me that she was a decent girl, of course. But when she came out of the house again, she was wearing a rather tarty top – so I knew I'd been right all along.'

'You followed her to the park?'

'She should never have gone to the park,' Liz Duffy said, with sudden vehemence. 'That was a big mistake.'

'Tell me what happened in the park?'

Liz Duffy shrugged. 'What's to tell? I persuaded her to step off the path. How I did it doesn't really matter, does it?'

'No,' Paniatowski agreed, 'it doesn't really matter.'

'And once I was sure that no one could see me doing it, I strangled her. It was all very quick. She must have lost consciousness almost immediately – so, all in all, it was a much kinder death than she deserved.'

'Tell me about Dolly.'

'Who?'

'The second girl you attacked.'

'Oh, her! I went back to the park the following night.' Liz Duffy frowned. 'I don't really know why I did that.'

'Perhaps you did it to see if you'd left any clues behind,' Paniatowski suggested – though she strongly suspected that wasn't the real reason at all.

'No, it wasn't that,' Duffy said airily. 'I'm the police doctor. I

know all about clues, and I was already certain I hadn't left any.'
She paused, obviously still puzzled as to what her motivation might
have been. 'At any rate, I saw the girl – Dolly, did you say it was?'

'That's right.'

'I saw her disappear into the bushes with a man.' Another pause.
'You really ought to arrest her, you know – the man she was with
was *much* older than her.'

'I ought to arrest *Dolly*?' Paniatowski asked.

'Yes, that's what I said. Are you having trouble keeping up with
me again?'

'That second attack didn't go as planned, did it?'

'No, it didn't. The little bitch managed to kick me on the knee,
and it hurt a great deal. It was as much as I could do to escape.'

'Tell me about Maggie – the third girl.'

'Now that *really* wasn't planned at all – I was just out doing a
little innocent shopping – but the moment I saw the way she acted
with that man in Woolworths, I knew she had to die.'

'How did you detach her from her friends?'

'I didn't need to. They'd run off, and she was sitting on a bench,
all alone. I said I'd got a gentleman friend who'd like to meet her,
and if she'd come to the park, I'd give her five pounds. She jumped
at the chance.'

'You went to the park together?'

'No, I didn't want to be seen with her, so we went separately,
and met up in the bushes.'

'And this time, after your experience with Dolly, you made sure
your victim didn't have a chance to fight back?'

'That's right. I said something like, "Oh, there he is now," and
when she turned to look, I hit her over the head.'

'You killed her in the afternoon, but when I asked you for an
estimated time of death, you put it much later.'

'Yes, I did, didn't I?'

'And by establishing the time of death as much later, you were
able to use Jack Crane as your alibi.'

'You're quite correct.'

'Did you plan that in advance?' Meadows asked, with unexpected
harshness. 'Did you *always* intend to use him?'

'Not *always*, no,' replied Liz Duffy, clearly amused at having got
such a strong reaction from the sergeant. 'Always is *such* a long
time, isn't it? So let's just say that when I saw him with Monika

at the mortuary, I realized what a great opportunity I'd been presented with.'

'An opportunity to do what?' Paniatowski asked.

'To find out how the investigation was going, of course. After all, I did have a certain interest in knowing how close you were to catching the killer.'

'And you thought Jack Crane would give you that information?'

'I knew he would. As long as I could convince him I was the girl he wanted me to be, he was putty in my hands.'

'And by "the girl he wanted me to be" you meant a girl who was falling for him as he was obviously falling for you?'

'Spot on.'

'Didn't you feel guilty about using him in that way?'

'Not at all. He had his chance with me a long time ago, and he threw it away,' Liz Duffy said indifferently.

'How did he throw it away?'

'It made him uncomfortable that I cared for him so much. Then I met Simon. I didn't make *him* feel uncomfortable. He relished what I had to offer. And that's when I realized that I'd been no more than *fond* of Jack. You can only really – truly – love one man in your entire life, you know, and I love Simon.'

'You *loved* him,' Paniatowski corrected her.

'I *love* him,' Liz Duffy said passionately. 'He's still with me – and I still talk to him.'

'And does he answer?'

Duffy looked at Paniatowski almost pityingly. 'Do you think I'm some kind of lunatic? Of course he doesn't answer me! But we were so close that I know what he'd say if he *did* answer.'

'And you know he would have said you should kill Jill?'

'Yes.'

'Why would he have said it?'

'Don't you know?'

'I think so, but I'd still like you to explain it to me.'

'We used to go to a golf club in Birmingham, and sometimes – at the dinner dances – Simon would chat to a girl called Susan Williams. He didn't particularly want to chat to her, of course, but he sensed she was a lonely little girl, and he was a very kind man. As it turned out, his kindness wasn't enough for her. She wanted much more. So she tricked him into meeting her in Sutton Park.'

And that was why it had to be the park, Paniatowski thought – that was why it *always* had to be the park!

'What happened in Sutton Park?' she asked.

'Susan seduced my Simon,' Liz Duffy said. 'It was a moment of weakness on his part, I freely admit that, but he's not to blame. It would never have happened if she hadn't *made* it happen.'

Paniatowski glanced down at the notes she'd taken down when talking to Midlands Police, an hour earlier.

'There was no seduction,' she said. 'The girl was raped.'

'No, she wasn't. She only *claimed* she was raped later.

'Why would she have done that?'

'Because Simon realized his mistake almost immediately, and said he wanted nothing more to do with her. Well, she was heartbroken, wasn't she? Who wouldn't be heartbroken about being turned down by Simon? And she decided that if she couldn't have him, no one could, so she said he'd raped her.'

'For God's sake, all the evidence was there, and it was an open-and-shut case,' Paniatowski exploded. 'And when he'd finished raping her, he sodomized her with a bottle!'

'I don't think it's true that she was sodomized,' Liz Duffy said firmly.

'According to the police surgeon, there's absolutely no doubt about it. Are you doubting the word of one of your colleagues?'

Liz Duffy shifted uncomfortably in her seat.

'Well, maybe I'm wrong about her not being sodomized,' she conceded. 'But if she was,' she added, as a new thought came into her mind, 'then that only proves my point, doesn't it?'

'And what point is that?'

'That she was the kind of girl who would stoop to anything. I expect some other man did that to her – I expect she *asked* him to do it.'

'The Birmingham police found the ski mask that your husband had been wearing.'

'They planted it on him. They had to arrest someone, you see, and if that "someone" was a good-looking man who they were probably all jealous of, then so much the better.'

'It wasn't just one rape he committed – the police believe he was responsible for a string of them.'

'They *believe*! Then why didn't they charge him with more? Why did they send him to prison only for what he was supposed to have done to Susan Williams?' A single tear leaked from the corner of Liz Duffy's eye. 'I did everything I could to help him. I hired the best lawyers money could buy. It didn't do any good. I failed him.'

'So you killed Jill as some kind of warped revenge on Susan Williams?' Paniatowski asked, though she knew that wasn't the case at all.

'Of course not,' Liz Duffy said scornfully. 'I'm not so mean, petty or spiteful to have done that.'

'Then why *did* you kill her?'

'Jill was dancing with her new brother-in-law, and she started pressing up against him, and . . .'

'And . . .?'

'And that's when Simon spoke to me.'

When the phone rang on the desk in Baxter's prison office, it was Inspector Grimes who picked it up.

'Yes?' he said.

'This is the switchboard operator at Whitebridge Police Headquarters,' said the voice on the end of the line. 'Could I speak to Chief Constable George Baxter, please?'

Grimes looked across the room at the big ginger man, who was sitting on the camp bed and staring at his hands.

'I'm afraid Mr Baxter can't come to the phone at the moment,' he said. 'Can I take a message?'

'Not really,' the switchboard operator replied. 'It's this girl, you see.'

'What girl?'

'She's calling from Birmingham. She says she has Mr Baxter's business card.'

'I expect a lot of people have Mr Baxter's business card.'

'Yes, but she says he gave it to her last night. She says he told her if she felt the need to talk, she'd only to ring and he'd drop whatever he was doing and have a chat with her.'

Grimes glanced across at George Baxter again. The big ginger man was still sitting as rigid as a statue. He didn't seem to know this conversation was going on. He probably didn't even quite realize where he was.

'He can't talk now,' the inspector said. 'Tell her to ring him again in a few days.'

'Only she seems very upset,' the switchboard operator persisted.

'She's very upset!' Grimes exploded. 'How do you think *he* feels? I've just had to tell the poor bugger his wife's been killed!'

'What! Mrs Baxter? Dead! I didn't know.'

The powers-that-be had probably been keeping it quiet until Baxter himself had been informed, Grimes told himself. They often did in situations like this, and he should have thought of that before shooting his mouth off.

'Listen, don't mention it to anyone until there's been an official announcement,' he told the switchboard operator.

'I only saw her the other day. It's all a bit of a shock,' the operator said.

'Yes, I imagine it must be,' Grimes agreed.

'So I'm to tell this girl to call back in a few days, am I?'

'Yes, I think that would be best.'

'Simon spoke to you while Jill was dancing with her brother-in-law,' Paniatowski said. 'I thought you told me that Simon *didn't* speak to you.'

'You're splitting hairs,' Liz Duffy said angrily. 'But if it will make you feel any happier, let's just say that the thought which came into my head *could have been* what Simon would have said.'

'And what was it that Simon said – or could have said?'

'He said, "*Now* do you see?"'

'*Now* do you see?' Paniatowski asked, pouncing on the word. '*Now* do you see *what*?'

A look of real shame came to Liz Duffy's face.

'I'd been starting to have doubts,' she admitted.

'Doubts?'

'I was beginning to think that Simon hadn't been entirely honest with me about what had gone on in Sutton Park. That's why what happened at that wedding reception was almost like an epiphany, because suddenly I could see just what these girls were like – and how helpless the men who fall under their spell are.'

'How would killing her have helped Simon?'

'It wouldn't. He was lost. He'd given way, under the strain of all the injustice, and hanged himself in his cell. But he was the kind of wonderful caring man who would have wanted me to save others from the fate that befell him.'

'So you killed Jill to save her brother-in-law?'

'Perhaps him, or perhaps some other poor soul who would

eventually have fallen into her clutches. All I knew was that she had to be stopped before she did any real damage.'

'So it was a totally altruistic act?'

'Yes, I'm an unselfish person by nature – that's why I'm a doctor.'

'You did it for *yourself*,' Paniatowski said harshly. 'You had to believe that Jill – and all girls like her – were evil, because that meant that what Simon had claimed was true. And what was the best way to prove to yourself that you really *did* believe she was evil? Why, by killing her – because you're a doctor, and you could never bring yourself to kill someone who was innocent. But it's a circular argument – you kill them because they're guilty, and they must be guilty because you've killed them.'

'That's what we medics call "pop psychology",' Liz Duffy said, a little uneasily.

'And what you've just said is what we detectives call "self-justification",' Paniatowski countered. 'You were wondering why you went to the park again, the night after you killed Jill. Well, I'll tell you – it was because once you'd started, you couldn't stop.'

'Oh, I'd got a taste for blood, had I?'

'No, it wasn't that at all.'

'Then what was it?'

And there was at least a part of Duffy that was interested in hearing the answer, Paniatowski thought.

'You realized that if you'd killed one girl because she was guilty, then you had no excuse for letting other girls – who were equally as guilty – go on living. You saw yourself as an even-handed instrument of justice. You had to – because the alternative was far too terrible to contemplate.'

'And what alternative might that be?' Liz Duffy challenged.

'Why, that you'd willingly sacrificed your own personality – your whole sense of self-esteem – on the altar of Simon-worship, and that Simon had turned out to be no kind of god at all. That by looking for a replacement for your darling daddy – and ending up with a pervert – you'd thrown your life away. It really was much easier to keep on killing than face that truth, wasn't it?'

The thunder boomed, the lights flickered – then went off – and the sheet lightning overhead illuminated Liz Duffy's crumbling face in its ghostly yellow glow.

The power came on again, and Liz Duffy gave Paniatowski a look of pure hatred.

'I want to see a lawyer now,' she said.

'The kinds of problems that you have can't be fixed by any lawyer,' Paniatowski told. 'You need to think about what you've done and why you've done it, Liz – it's the only way you'll ever have a chance of finding peace.'

'Lawyer!' Duffy screamed. 'I demand to see a lawyer!'

EPILOGUE

Jo Baxter's funeral took place on a chill March morning. The church – St John's – was packed. Many of the people there were police officers who had not known her personally, but respected her husband, and had come to offer him their support. If Jo was in heaven – and some of those there believed that she was – then she was probably looking down on the service and reflecting bitterly that, even in death, she was not so much *Jo* Baxter as *Mrs George* Baxter.

Once the service was over, and the body laid to rest, George Baxter positioned himself by the lychgate, from where he could thank the mourners individually for putting in an appearance. He looked pretty much as he always did – big and impressive and in charge – except that though his moustache was still like a big ginger caterpillar, his shock of hair had turned quite white.

The team joined the line, which was slowly shuffling forwards. They didn't say anything to each other. Somehow, that wouldn't have seemed quite right.

They finally reached the front of the queue.

'Thank you for coming, Detective Inspector Beresford,' Baxter said, shaking Beresford's hand firmly. 'It was good of you to come, Detective Sergeant Meadows.' Shake. 'I appreciate your kindness, Detective Constable Crane.' Shake.

And then it was Paniatowski's turn.

'You did a good job with the Liz Duffy case, Detective Chief Inspector Paniatowski,' Baxter said. 'Well done.'

And though he had made eye contact with the other three, he looked through Paniatowski as if she were not there.

They filed past the chief constable and into the street.

'A drink,' Paniatowski said firmly. 'I need a drink.'

And none of the team disagreed.

The pub was just across the street from the church, and was called the Bishop's Arms. They grabbed a table near the window, and ordered a round of drinks.

'There's a rumour going round that Mrs Baxter committed suicide,' Beresford said.

'That wasn't what the coroner ruled,' Paniatowski said sharply, remembering the way that Baxter had refused to look at her.

'The rumours also say that she was doing ninety when she came off the road, and that she had enough alcohol in her to start a distillery,' Beresford said.

'For God's sake, sir, shut up!' Meadows exploded. 'The woman's dead and buried – let her rest in peace.'

'Fair enough,' Beresford said, looking a little shamefaced.

Paniatowski took a sip of her vodka, and thought about the other news she would soon have to break. Her original plan had been to inform Jack Crane, and then tell the others later, but she now decided that it might be better for Crane if he heard it while he was surrounded by his colleagues.

'Last night, Liz Duffy hanged herself in her cell,' she said.

'Oh my God,' Crane said, turning white.

Meadows put her hand on his shoulder. 'Easy, Jack,' she said softly.

'She wasn't the girl you once knew, Jack,' Paniatowski said. 'She'd turned into a completely different person.'

'But she still *could* have been the girl I knew,' Crane said. 'If only I'd tried to win her back . . . if only I'd warned her about Simon . . .'

Paniatowski's sudden rage took everyone – including herself – completely by surprise.

'Don't you *dare* blame yourself,' she shouted across the table. 'Don't you bloody dare!'

'I'm . . . I'm sorry, boss,' Crane stuttered.

'If I ever hear you talking like that again, you're off the team,' Paniatowski told him. 'If I even suspect you're *thinking* like that, you're gone.'

The people at the other tables had turned around to see what all the fuss was about.

Paniatowski stood up.

'If you'll excuse me, I think I need a breath of fresh air,' she said, and headed for the door.

'What was that all about?' Beresford asked, when she'd gone.

'I rather think she might be a little upset, sir,' Meadows said. 'And you didn't help the situation much.'

'Me? What did I do wrong?'

'You kept going on about whether or not Mrs Baxter had committed suicide. Didn't you even notice the way the chief constable avoided the boss's eyes at the lychgate?'

'I didn't, as a matter of fact, but I don't see what the one thing's got to do with the other,' Beresford said.

'No,' Meadows agreed. 'You probably don't.' She stood up. 'I think I'll grab a little fresh air myself.'

Meadows found Paniatowski in the churchyard, gazing down at a headstone that said:

Arthur Jones
1911–1961
Rest in Peace

'When I saw you coming in here, I thought you might be visiting your father's grave,' Meadows said.

'He's buried in the Catholic cemetery, along with my mother,' Paniatowski replied.

So who's this Arthur Jones?'

'He was my stepfather. He began raping me when I was eleven, and only finally stopped when I'd grown big enough and strong enough to start fighting back.'

'Oh God, I'm so sorry!' Meadows said.

'What for?' Paniatowski asked.

'When we were questioning Liz Duffy, I suggested that her father may have raped *her*.'

'Yes, you did.'

'I'd never have done it if I'd known that had happened to you. It must have brought it all back to you. It must have been terrible.'

'It *did* bring it all back to me, and it *wasn't* terrible,' Paniatowski said. 'It was exactly the right thing to say – and it got us the result we wanted.'

They stood in silence for a few moments, then Meadows said, 'Would you mind if I asked you another question, boss?'

'Not at all.'

'Why are you here, at the graveside of a man you must hate?'

'To remind myself that I *don't* hate him any longer – that I've trained myself not to hate him.'

'I see,' Meadows said.

Paniatowski smiled. 'No, you don't – not yet.'

She paused, opened her handbag, took out her cigarettes, and then, remembering where she was, returned the packet to the bag.

'I don't hate the Germans for killing my father, either,' she continued. 'I used to, but now I just accept that he was in a war, and that in wars, bad things happen. The past is gone forever, and on the journey through the rest of your life, you can't allow the dead to walk beside you and keep spewing their poison into your ears.'

'You're right, of course – but it's not always an easy lesson to learn,' Meadows said.

'No, it isn't,' Paniatowski agreed, 'but if Liz Duffy had learned it, she might have been able to look forward to a useful life and a contented old age. Instead, she ended up swinging from the ceiling of her cell. And she's not the only one who didn't learn the lesson. I've been told about another suicide this morning, and I think that – above all – is what really upset me.'

'Was it somebody you knew?' Meadows asked.

'No, we'd never even met, but I knew *of* her,' Paniatowski said sadly. 'Her name was Susan Williams. She was sixteen years old, and was once raped by a man called Templar – and last night she drowned herself in the river.'